T0288579

BEYOND
THE BOUNDARIES

BEYOND THE BOUNDARIES

*Text and Context
in African Literature*

Mineke Schipper

Ivan R. Dee, Publisher
Chicago

Library of Congress Cataloging-in-Publication Data:
Schipper, Mineke
Beyond the Boundaries : text and context in African
literature / by Mineke Schipper.
p.   cm.
Includes bibliographical references and index.
ISBN 0-929587-36-7 (alk. paper)
1. African literature—History and criticism. 2.
Literature, Comparative—African and European. 3.
Literature, Comparative—European and African. 4.
Race awareness in literature. 5. Realism in literature.
I. Title
PL8010.S37 1990
809'.8896—dc20   90-36938

To Maina wa Kinyatti (Kenya)
and Jack Mapanje (Malawi)
who are paying dearly for their
human right to freedom of expression

CONTENTS

ACKNOWLEDGEMENTS

Most chapters in this book have initially been presented as lectures at universities, conferences and seminars in Africa, Europe and the United States. Although I am the sole person responsible for what is written in this book, I wish to thank colleagues and students in many places who generously shared their views with me. I am also grateful to *Research in African Literatures* (*RAL*) and its publisher the University of Texas Press, *World Literature Written in English* (*WLWE*) and *New Literary History* (*NLH*) for permission to reprint material earlier published in those journals as indicated below. Portions of Chapter I served as an introduction to a special issue on Methods of Approach for *RAL* (vol. 16, 1, 1985, pp. 1–4). Chapter II was previously published in *WLWE* (vol. 24, 1, 1984, pp. 16–26). Earlier versions of Chapter III were read at the Universities of Kisangani, Ife and Groningen. In a first French draft, Chapter IV was prepared as part of a CNRS-Project on National Literatures, a later version was published in *RAL* (vol. 18, 3, 1987, pp. 280–293). Some parts of the material of chapter V originally appeared in French in *RAL* (vol. 10, 1, 1979, pp. 40–57). Chapter VI is a rewritten version of a paper presented at a UNESCO-PEN Conference in Dakar in 1984. Chapter VII was written for the earlier mentioned special issue of *RAL* (pp. 53–59). Chapter VIII was published in *NLH* (vol. 16, 3, 1985, pp. 559–575). Earlier versions of Chapter IX were read at the Free University of Berlin in 1987 and the University of Bayreuth in 1988. A paper presented at the ALA Conference at Cornell University in 1987 resulted in Chapter X: I especially appreciated the enthusiastic comments of first discussant Biodun Jeyifo on that occasion. My thanks for typing most of the manuscript go to Suzanne Glerum. Finally I wish to express my gratitude to the Netherlands Foundation for the Advancement of Scientific Research (NWO) and the French Centre National de la Recherche Scientifique (CNRS) for grants allowing me to participate in Seminars in Paris in 1986 and 1987 that contributed to my preparation of Chapters IV, IX and X.

I. INTRODUCTION

Comparative literature deals with the study of literature beyond the boundaries of one nation or culture or language. It also examines the relationships between literature and other areas, e.g. the arts, music, social sciences, religion, philosophy and so forth. More systematically than in the past, emphasis is now also put on literature in relation to African Studies. Theoretically, the comparative study of literature thus provides us with a wide and open field. What about the practice?

Thanks to its powerful position, the West has an enormous impact on "world literature". Western literature seems to have become normative, and literature from other cultures is in danger of being considered "deviant". In order to have their manuscripts published by Western-owned publishing houses, writers often adapt themselves to the prevailing norms. The international critical community clearly favours Western cultural values and literature. More often than not, the effect of power in the intercultural study of literature has been overlooked by comparatists whose value judgements continue to be expressed with scientific pretension. Therefore, critics should systematically ask how, why and for whom the fixed canon is a reality. Still, the idea of a world literature as an eternal canon of (mainly Western) master-pieces seems as persistent as it is fictitious.

In *Black Literature and Literary Theory*, Henry Louis Gates Jr. posed a number of relevant questions about the formal relations between Black and Western literatures:

[1]

What is the status of the black literary work of art? How do canonical texts in the black traditions relate to canonical texts of the Western traditions? As if these questions were not problematic enough, how are we to read black texts? Can the method of explication developed in Western criticism be "translated" into the black idiom? How "text-specific" is literary theory, and how "universal" are rhetorical strategies? If every black canonical text is, as I shall argue, "two-toned" or "double-voiced", how do we explicate the signifying black difference that makes black literature "black"? And what do we make of the relation between the black vernacular tradition and the black form tradition, as these inform the shape of a black text? Do we have to "invent" validly "black" critical theory and methodologies? Once fully addressed, the answers to these questions will help us to understand more broadly and convincingly the nature of the constituencies which comprise the republic of literature . . .
If Western literature has a canon, then so does Western literary criticism. If the relation of black texts to Western texts is problematic, then what relationship obtains between (Western) theories of (Western) "literature" and its "criticism" and what the critic of black literature *does* and reflects upon?[1]

Indeed, how relevant and useful are existing literary theories developed by Western scholars (formed by Western theoretical and literary traditions) for those who want to study other fields of literature, in this case African literature?

Research in the field of literature in general and of African literature in particular has expanded considerably since the 1960s. Literature is now more generally considered in the larger context of its functioning within a communication process. Many publications now study the text in its different aspects and relations to the author, the reader, and their respective social and cultural context. This is indeed quite a recent development.

[2]

For a long time, adherents of the New Criticism conceived of the task of the study of literature exclusively as the interpretation and evaluation of the individual text. Of course, critical attention focused on the text as such is of great importance, but the study of literature includes much more.

Notwithstanding all the textual interpretations that have been produced throughout the world, very little progress has yet been made toward understanding the phenomenon of literature as such and how it functions. Jonathan Culler goes so far as to state that "the most important and insidious legacy of New Criticism is the widespread and unquestioning acceptance of the notion that the critic's job is to interpret literary works".[2]

In the study of African literature, texts have often been used as historical, sociological, or anthropological documents which inform us about village life, colonization, the position of women, political or social change, and so on. Questions regarding the inherent differences between "reality" and fiction, or literature as an art form versus other sources and documents, have mostly been left open. How, if at all, does literature differ from other texts and means of communication?

In his essay "Beyond Interpretation", Culler concluded in 1981 that the principle of interpretation as the task of the critic "is so strong an unexamined postulate of American criticism that it subsumes and neutralizes the most forceful and intelligent acts of revolt" (p. 11). A number of critics in Europe had gone "beyond interpretation" a little earlier. Reacting to the positivist heritage of collecting facts about the literary work's sources and origins, Russian Formalists before the 1920s, and Czech structuralists in the 1930s started, on the basis of a large number of analyzed literary works, to make statements about what Roman Jakobson called *literarity*, the phenomenon which makes literary texts different from other texts. These scholars studied all sorts of literary devices,

[3]

such as the effect of estrangement, and the role of prescriptions and traditions.

It was much later, in 1966, that the Russian Formalists first became known in Western Europe, thanks to Tzvetan Todorov's translation of a number of their essays in *Théorie de la littérature. Textes des Formalistes russes.*

The structural story analysis as applied by Vladimir Propp to the fairy tale, too, did not become known in Europe and the United States until the 1960s. In France, Propp's theory became the basis of the structural story analysis as developed, among others, by Greimas, Bremond, Denise Paulme, and Roland Barthes. The narratological theory of Gérard Genette provided new insights into a number of aspects of the narrative text. The Russian Formalists have rightly been called the founders of new approaches in the field of literary study.

The structuralists paid a great deal of attention to the literary text as a message in the process of verbal communication. This idea has been further developed in the 1970s by semiotics (the theory of signs). Without going into details, one might say that in general the study of literature has learned from semiotic research to view literature as a particular form of the exchange of meaning between communicating individuals. The study of literature should make us understand when and why literary texts have a meaning for readers. It is clear that texts have no universal and eternal value for all the inhabitants of our globe, since they result from a large number of choices made by individual authors on the basis of their respective historical, social, and cultural contexts and their personal experiences and creativity. If an author and a reader have nothing in common, communication fails. Author and reader should share at least part of the codes of the text. Codes are the rules on the basis of which meaning can be attributed to phenomena, for instance, the rules of a genre: on the basis of prescriptions within his or her literary tradition, the author writes an epic, a novel, a dirge, or a poem of praise. The reader or auditor has, first of all, to

[4]

know the language the text is recited or written in. One is then able to establish the denotation, that is, the literal meaning of the words, but that is not enough. In a literary text, one has to take into account all sorts of connotations. Besides knowledge of the language, we need supplementary knowledge to help us detect the specific meaning of the text, which is based on connotations resulting from the text's literary traditions or the breaking of these traditions, the historical context, and so forth. Connotative codes are derived from conventions; for example, the use of masks has a particular meaning in the theatrical forms of the people who created them. The masks are part of the theatre's code, a code one has to know if one is to participate in the communication process of the masked performance. An outsider will be unable to share the deeper meaning of the performance without being given further information about the connotative code of this theatre. According to Umberto Eco,

the codes, insofar as they are accepted by a society, set up a "cultural" world which is neither actual nor possible in the ontological sense; its existence is linked to a cultural order, which is the way in which a society thinks, speaks and, while speaking, explains the "purport" of its thought through other thoughts, since it is through thinking and speaking that a society develops, expands or collapses, even when dealing with "impossible" worlds (i.e. aesthetic texts, ideological statements), a theory of codes is very much concerned with the format of such "cultural" worlds, and faces the basic problem of how to touch contents.[3]

The literary text as a sign in the semiotic sense should be conceived as a complex unity in which a denotative and a connotative system are intertwined. Connotative literary meanings result from specific devices: quotations, clichés, and historical, social, and cultural elements. It all functions in the communication process between author and addressee, if the codes are common to both.

[5]

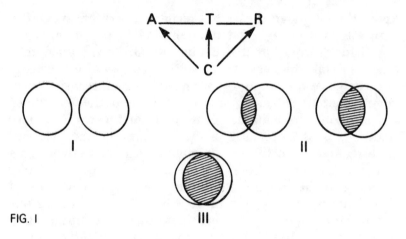

FIG. I

In a diagram the relations between author (A), reader (R), text (T) and context (C) can be rendered as impossible (I), or as a perfectly successful communication (III), with a number of varieties (II) in between (see fig. 1):

Authors as well as readers and critics are conditioned by their own context. Of course, there is an endless scale between no communication possible (I) and the largest communicative overlap in the case of the most ideal reading (III). Between authors and readers from different cultural contexts, frequently no overlap is achieved. Simply on the basis of their own conventions, critics often decide whether or not a text from outside their culture belongs to the body of "real" literature. On the other hand, authors may partially sacrifice their originality to the prevailing norm in the field of literature in order to guarantee success. Different cultural backgrounds may lead to very different interpretations of the same text. For instance, Joseph Conrad's *Heart of Darkness* has been commented upon positively by most British critics and quite negatively by an African, Chinua Achebe. It would also be quite interesting to undertake a comparative analysis of the critical comments on V. S. Naipaul from cultural backgrounds

[6]

as different as African, Caribbean, and Western. In the afore-mentioned framework of the communication process, the relations between author, text, reader, and cultural background all find their place.

The communicational approach has meant an enlargement of the field of research in comparative literature as well. Instead of transmitting fixed values from the conventional Eurocentric literary standards à la Wellek and Warren, serious scholars now make comparative studies of the very conditions and conventions responsible for the fact that texts are only perceived as literary under certain circumstances. At the same time, the personal, individual evaluation of the texts has also become an object of research. In the past the personal, evaluative judgement of African texts has often been given from a limited Western perspective, and often without the critic even being aware of his Eurocentrism.

The advantage of such new approaches and methods in comparative literature is that enough breadth of outlook is thus given to study the most divergent communication situations as they occur more and more frequently in the global field of literature, functioning in different social groups, times, and cultures. Within this broad framework, oral literature can finally receive all the literary attention it deserves.

In studying African literature, one might certainly profit from the substantial progress and the refinement of tools by literary theorists. On the other hand, these theoretical scholars continually need critical comments from the specialists in the literatures of different continents and cultures. Checking the former's theoretical results, the latter decide to accept, reject, or adapt them according to their previous and precious experience with texts from a particular cultural and social background.

Many of my ideas and insights have been the result of more than twenty years of stimulating contact with African writers and critics, countless conversations and discussions with colleagues and students in Kenya, Nigeria, Senegal, Zaïre and other countries. Thus the study of African literature

[7]

gave new dimensions to my conception of comparative literature. The latter, I believe, should take much more account of
the intercultural approach.

In this book, theory and interpretation meet. The main
purpose is to question the validity of theoretical achievements by confronting them with the main issues in African
literature research, such as literary history, oral tradition and
the writer, relations between text and reality, criticism in
its cultural context, and the political implications of literary
communication.

Chapter II on Eurocentrism discusses characteristics of
Western thought and developments in the field of the
humanities that continue to determine the study of African
literature – or its absence – at so many universities. It relates
to Chapter III in that the negritude movement is reassessed in
the wider framework of black reactions to Western economic,
political and cultural domination.

Chapter IV advocates methodological emphasis on both
the national and the international perspective in writing literary history. It also emphasizes sensitivity to the complex
interrelations between the canon and other texts as an indispensable precondition. A number of research suggestions are
made.

Chapters V and VI deal with oral tradition as a source of
inspiration for African writers. "Oral Literature and Written
Orality" draws upon a number of devices in texts that are
substantially rooted in oral culture. In other words, the effect
of "dicts" becoming "scripts" is analyzed using examples
from the works of Amos Tutuola. "Oral Tradition and African
Theatre" examines the integration and absorption of themes
and techniques from the oral performance into contemporary
plays.

In Chapter VII I apply some Western narratological findings to African first-person narrative prose forms, both factual and fictional. A number of questions and criteria are
presented with a view to demarcating the first-person genres
discussed and their possible mixtures.

Chapter VIII broaches the problematic concept of realism, which has been (mis-)used in many ways without definition. Reality and our perspective on reality are socially and culturally determined, and are relative. Then the question is whether and how the writer succeeds in making us believe that literature copies or reflects reality. Here the intentions of realistic authors, textual themes and techniques are analyzed with examples from Sembène Ousmane's *God's Bits of Wood*.

Aesthetic and ideological norms are among the ones that serve as the yardstick of the critic. These norms can be discovered in critical texts. Chapter IX argues that comments on a particular literary text are linked to the critic's cultural background and should be studied systematically and comparatively. Thus they are apt to lead to greater insight into the intercultural aspects of the literary communication process. For that purpose, a number of suggestions are presented for further research.

Chapter X tackles the subject of censorship. In colonial times, certain forms of literature were banned, from popular songs to novels and other books that might have a "bad" influence on the colonized. Since independence, a growing number of African governments do not tolerate "subversive" literature and try to suppress it with every means at their disposal. Exile, jail, torture, and many other forms of pressure have a stifling effect on freedom of expression, and reception, the *sine qua non* for the flowering of literature. Alongside the need for strong protest, systematic study is also urgently required in the field of censorship. To that end, this essay concludes with some methodological proposals designed as a starting point for more research into how the lack of freedom of expression affects African literatures and their audiences.

Those who study African literature are becoming increasingly aware of the profit that can be gained from the harvest reaped by scholars of literary theory and by specialists of other – Asian, Caribbean, Latin American, Arab, or Western – literatures. In my opinion, one should test the tools at hand and feel free to discard the ones that prove useless or have

[9]

become obsolete. In turn, our own tools, findings, and experience may be enriching for scholars of other literatures. Exchanges on all levels are stimulating and fruitful for everyone engaged in the study of literature. As an African proverb says, "The centipede's legs are strengthened by a hundred rings."

II. EUROCENTRISM AND CRITICISM: REFLECTIONS ON THE STUDY OF LITERATURE IN PAST AND PRESENT

African literatures have been and still are studied mainly by two categories of specialists: social scientists, and scholars in comparative literature. In general, the two categories have worked separately, with specialists in one discipline not knowing much of what was going on in the other. Thus, new experiences and findings leading to new ideas and new approaches did not develop in both fields at the same time: the Western discussion on cultural relativism clearly is a case in point.

The conflict between historical relativism and perspectivism in the study of literature has been a subject of discussion for many years. Historical relativism stems from historicism – an approach that sees everything in purely historical terms, unrelated to the political context, or to ethics or religion. The past was important *as* past, in the belief that it was possible to reconstruct this past exactly as it had been. The point of perspectivism, in the words of René Wellek, is "that we recognize that there is one poetry, one literature comparable in all ages". Wellek is sharply opposed to relativism which he equates with an "anarchy of values".[1] It is significant to note that this discussion took place at a relatively late stage – starting in the 1950s and gaining momentum in the 1960s and the years that followed.[2]

The term cultural relativism was used in connection with the study of literature for the first time in 1969, by Roy

BEYOND THE BOUNDARIES

Harvey Pearce in a footnote to an article in his *Historicism Once More*. The Dutch comparatist D. W. Fokkema expanded on this in his inaugural lecture in 1971 on cultural relativism and comparative literature. He defined cultural relativism in the study of literature as the approach that interprets the literary-historical phenomena of a given period within the context of a particular cultural area. This approach makes its assessment on the basis of the norms and against the background of both the period and the cultural area, and then compares with each other the various value systems that characterise the different periods and cultural areas.[3] In my opinion, to "period" and "cultural area" one must add the social group from which the particular literature has originated, and by whom it is read. The latter has often been forgotten or neglected.

Scientific research has been enriched in a number of fields as a result of western imperialism and colonialism: anthropology, as one of the first human sciences, profited enormously. Perhaps this is the reason that developments took place at such an early stage in anthropology, which only much later manifested themselves in the area of literature studies. The problem of cultural relativism can be clearly distinguished in these developments, and for this reason I now propose that we make a brief detour to anthropology. The fact that oral literature for such a long time was seen as a province of anthropology and was studied primarily by anthropologists has not always been beneficial to its literary aspects. Of course, scholars and students of literature are partly to be blamed for this.

The anthropologists went through phases of evolutionism and cultural relativism. E. B. Tylor preached evolutionism in his *Primitive Culture* (1871). His views were clearly Eurocentric: Western civilization was his norm – all non-Western peoples were "less advanced". According to Tylor they had stayed behind in an earlier stage. For him and his followers, there was a single process of evolution that encompassed all of nature and culture.

[12]

Franz Boas later opposed this in, among others, *The Mind of Primitive Man* (1911) and *Race, Language and Culture* (1940). He criticized evolutionism because it claimed to be able to reconstruct a history of culture that applied to the whole human race. Just after the turn of the century, Boas was already warning his students against projecting their own Western values and categories on the cultures they wanted to study. This brought enormous changes. The word "culture", for example, was given a plural form for the first time. People reached the conclusion that there was a nearly infinite number and variety of cultural elements.

For Tylor, the evolutionists and all who preceded them, culture had always meant "enlightenment" and "progress", resulting from rationality and creativity. After Boas, however, it began more and more to take on the opposite meaning: culture as that which binds people to tradition, to the irrational. Man is no longer seen as the creator of culture, but rather as the creation of his own culture. Familiar names from the Boas school are Ruth Benedict and Melville Herskovits: they stressed the equal value of all cultures. According to Herskovits, there is actually no one who is qualified to make judgements about aspects of another culture or about other cultures as wholes. Why?

Herskovits said that these value judgements depend on one's own cultural experience and are no more than reflections of one's own culture and its prejudices, since one assumes one's own categories to be generally valid. One is thus forced to conclude that no general judgements are possible. A culture can only be assessed by someone who is a carrier of that same culture. Unfortunately, here one is losing one's vision of the whole. In fact, what Herskovits wants is for Western scientists to overcome their ethnocentrism and take a tolerant view of all other cultures: a "peaceful coexistence" on the basis of cultural relativism, rather than ethnocentrism. Whereas ethical imperialism had led to missionarism and colonialism, ethical relativitism led to anti-missioniarism, anti-colonialism and anti-imperialism. Similar

[13]

developments also took place in such fields as sociology and history. New definitions had to be formulated and new words coined because the point of departure had changed. Pizarro, Stanley and Cook, for example, could no longer be termed "explorers", the phrase "voyage of discovery" could no longer be used.

On the surface, cultural relativism might seem very appealing, but the difficulty is the idea of "objectivity", the denial of value judgements. On the one hand, Herskovits denied that it is possible for human beings to make value-free, non-culture bound judgements; on the other hand he wanted to practise an anthropology that is objective, value-free and not bound by culture. We can see a definite contradiction here.[4] In fact, cultural relativism actually confirms ethnocentrism. The democratic idea of cultural relativism is that everyone is ethnocentric. One is preaching for the status quo, assuming an immutability of real difference between cultures, and adamantly opposed to contaminating one culture with elements from another. Emphasis comes to lie on isolation, a sort of apartheid that is, unfortunately, familiar to us from the South African context: people trapped in the strait-jacket of cultural determinism. Actually, cultural relativism is nothing more than a theoretical protest against the processes of centuries that have been Westernising the human race.

Historically, it is interesting to note how much the field of anthropology actually served colonialism. Tylor's theory, the anthropology of evolutionism, justified colonialism – "bringing civilization to the natives".[5] During the next stage, when the West thought that not too much civilization should be brought to the "natives" because it might make them troublesome, the theory of cultural relativism was very handy: it justified conservatism; existing cultures had to be respected (and inequalities perpetuated).

Nonetheless, the insight into the inevitability of ethnocentrism can be useful, not only for anthropologists, but also for scholars in other fields: value systems from various cultures should be the subject of comparative research.

[14]

Especially after the world wars, and as a result of the start of decolonization, historians also began to realize that a new approach to history and a new historiography were needed. Arnold Toynbee was one of the best known proponents of this view in Europe. In his essay "Widening Our Historical Horizon", he noted that historians can wield a great deal of political influence:

History tells us that historians, like scientists, do have an impact on society, and if the historian is a teacher, his impact is direct and immediate. Nineteenth-century historians . . . stoked up the fires of nationalism, and the consequence is that these fires are still raging today, when we have been carried by the scientists into the Atomic Age . . . The historian has a practical responsibility . . . The student and writer and teacher of history ought to strive now, with all his might, to widen his public's historical horizon; and to do this, he must begin by widening his own.[6]

Developments that have taken place in anthropology and in history indicate that a growing number of scholars have begun to take a critical look at the forms of ethnocentrism – or more properly Eurocentrism – and at the implicated value systems in their own disciplines.

What does all of this have to do with literature? Have we put evolutionist thinking behind us in our discipline as the anthropologists have? Are we, like the historians, interested in new definitions and perspectives in literature studies? What about the social relevance of our research – do we have the practical responsibility Toynbee spoke of? In anthropology and "non-Western" sociology (a Eurocentric term, by the way), the shift came because of intensive field research outside Europe at a comparatively early stage, and later, through the inevitable confrontation between Western researchers and their Asian, Latin American and African colleagues. As I mentioned before, the literature of "other"

[15]

cultures has long been considered a logical component of anthropological and sociological studies.

Why then, with a few exceptions,[7] has oral literature for so many years seldom been seen as a research topic for students of literature? Have the echoes of decolonization not quite reverberated through literary discussions? If so, what of this has been passed on to research, criticism and education? I think that the combination of analysis and qualitative evaluation that characterises so much of the Western critical tradition has played a part. But we need not be pessimistic.

The theoretical component of comparative literature study has only recently been set down in statutory terms in the *International Comparative Literature Association*. Comparative literature study is defined in this 1979 document as "the study of literary history, the theory of literature and the interpretation of texts, undertaken from an international point of view".

In this limited space, it is impossible to go more deeply into the historical developments. New approaches to literature leave ample room for the intercultural comparative study of literature, whether this involves relationships of contact (influences, for example) or of typological similarities (genre characteristics, for instance). Profiting from developments in semiotics, the study of literature has begun to liberate itself from the old approach with its inflexible Western norms and values that characterized so many researchers for so long.

Many now direct their attention to the literary communication situation and to the conventions of the production and the reception of texts that are accepted as literary under certain social, cultural and political circumstances. A distinction, as strict as possible, is now made between the reader and the researcher, between the historical reception of certain texts and one's own evaluation. Unlike New Criticism and its British variation Practical Criticism, the scientific study of literature aims neither at the transfer of literary values, nor at the creation or the defence of a literary tradition. Within

[16]

the new study of literature, the transfer of literary values and the formation of literary traditions are, on the contrary, the object of research.[8]

The developments that have led to a new vision of the scientific relevance of the field are extremely encouraging. They inevitably lead to the awareness of one's ethnocentrism, i.e. Eurocentrism as far as the study of literature is concerned. This awareness enables the researcher to adopt a critical attitude, especially an autocritical attitude and to reflect upon the social interests and the cultural, social and historical values of the group he or she belongs to. Such an attitude may help him/her to overcome his/her own ideology in studying literature.[9]

The theory, however, often bears little resemblance yet to most of the practice of research, criticism and education. Literary criticism in particular is clearly dominated by institutionalized literature and its associate value system in a given society. This leads to an attitude of exclusiveness which will make the critics refuse to look at any text which does not correspond to their established criteria.

A plea for a more inclusive attitude (more openness towards literatures from other cultures) is not out of place in such a case.

Literature has for too long been a given institution; it has been accepted for a very long time, especially in the Western world, that most of what is called world literature is necessarily Western literature. That literature is an institution is clear if one looks at the textbooks and anthologies used in schools. Pupils are exposed to these books and, in this way, an identification is created in their minds between what the book contains and what literature is or should be. Writers' names and texts or fragments of texts are included in the book because they are "literary", and they are "literary", because they are in the book. The literature textbook involves a selection, and thus presents a picture of what its editors think literature is, in terms of the value system they hold. What is passed on in history as literature – national or inter-

[17]

national – seems to be *the* heritage for the new generation, but in fact it is a heritage of which a large part has been held back and is never referred to.

An interesting study by Bernard Mouralis, *Les contre-littér-atures*, refers to this concealed part as the field of counter-literatures, which tries in many ways to attract the attention of that small, elite group who decides what may, and what may not, be counted as Literature. The counter-literatures include both oral and written works from the present and the past. Nowadays, one must also include popular magazines, comic strips, science fiction, detective stories and romances. In the Western vision of what is Literature, the vast majority of the works from other cultures also belong to this large field of counter-literatures. Nevertheless, from a historical point of view, shifts are taking place in the evaluation and assembly of a literary heritage. In his above-mentioned book, Mouralis offers a brief summary of the changes in Western Europe, particularly in France. After classicism, the supremacy of the classic heritage was disputed in France with the appearance of the *Querelle des Anciens et des Modernes*. The cultural horizon was expanded through acquaintance with other ancient civilizations (e.g. Egypt and the Middle East) or modern ones like Persia, China, and America. After this, more attention was also given in the West to the literature from other European countries and to one's own "folk literature".

In the nineteenth century, new literatures in European languages such as English, Spanish, Portuguese were disco-vered in other parts of the world. These became further and further removed from the exclusive European influence. Thanks to anthropological research, twentieth-century West-erners came into contact with the oral literature of Africa, the Americas and Oceania. Recently, there is also a large supply of literatures that stem from colonial, semi-colonial and post-colonial societies and sharply opposes Western cultural domi-nation. One must add to this that the immigration of large groups of people with other cultures, and their permanent

[18]

settlement in the Western world, is certainly influencing or will influence the literature and culture of this part of the world.[10]

In a number of ways, the counter-literature mechanism, as it has been described by Bernard Mouralis, can be compared with the polysystem theory of Even-Zohar. This theory (which is not only applicable to the study of literature) sees the sign-governed human patterns of communication (culture, language, literature, society) as systems of a heterogeneous, open structure:

> It is, therefore, very rarely a uni-system but is, necessarily, a polysystem – a multiple system, a system of various systems which intersect with each other and partly overlap, using concurrently different options, yet functioning as one structured whole whose members are interdependent . . .
> The heterogeneic structure of culture in society can, of course, be reduced to the culture of the ruling classes only, but this would not be fruitful beyond the attempt to construct homogeneic models to account for the principal mechanism governing a cultural system when time factor and adjacent systems' pressures are eliminated.[11]

He gives the example of a community possessing two literary options, two "literatures", because the society is bilingual, which has been the case, or still is, in many countries:

> For students of literature, to overcome such cases by confining themselves to only one of these, ignoring the other, is naturally very "convenient" (or rather more "comfortable") than dealing with them both. Actually, this is common practice in literary studies; how inadequate the results are cannot be exaggerated.[12]

Of course, this is not only true for literatures in different languages in one country, but also for the literatures of differ-

[19]

ent social groups in the same country, and for different litera- tures on the international and the intercultural level as far as they influence each other in different ways within the "polysystem". One cannot consider one literature as a separ- ate phenomenon neglecting all the positive and negative relationships it has with other adjacent literatures. In the Western world, scholars have too often only considered and studied as literature the so-called "masterpieces". Even- Zohar argues from a semiotic point of view against inflexible elitism, the equation of literary criticism with literary research and against writing the history of literature using only the writers of the masterpieces – who mostly represent only the culture of those who write this history of literature.[13]

Only scant traces of the trends and developments that have been summarized here can be recognized in the literary heritage that is passed on in the schools in literature edu- cation. What criteria are being used? Criteria of an aesthetic and/or ethical nature? How is literature defined? With respect to the concept of literature, perhaps only one thing can be said with certainty – that people never seem to agree on how it should be defined. The formal criteria for what is to be considered as literature have shifted and been revised so many times in the course of Western history alone, that it is impossible to see them as anything but arbitrary. The intercultural study of literature makes the recognition of this arbitrariness all the more necessary.

It is for this reason that every encouragement should be given to the above view that study and evaluation should be separated from each other as much as possible in comparative literature. The continued use of inflexible standards of "qual- ity" as in Wellek's works is inconsistent with this approach. Such an inflexible basis for study, in which Western literary values are seen as universal, has been sharply criticized in recent years outside Europe – and largely justifiably so. Until the 1960s, Western encyclopedia articles and textbooks on world literature were limited primarily to the description of Western literary works.

[20]

Such criticism from outside one's cultural context can be very enlightening; after all, anthropology benefited from Western anthropologists being confronted by the critical questions of scholars with other cultural backgrounds. Likewise, historians from Latin America, Asia and Africa have pointed to the one-sided, expansionist perspective from which Westerners tend(ed) to write history. Theological research has been given new impulses by the theologians of Liberation from Latin America and by the black theology of North America and Africa. To what extent can the same be said of the study of literature? I think that in our field the confrontations have been fairly recent. The transfer of Western literary values to other cultural contexts has been a fact of life for a very long time. In the eyes of researchers from these cultures, this may have had some advantages, but it has also been damaging. Many discussions on this subject have been taking place since the sixties and seventies, particularly in countries that have experienced Western colonialism. However, these discussions have hardly penetrated the walls of European schools and universities. Do Western scholars know, for example, that more than once the question has been asked outside Europe whether a Westerner is at all capable of studying other literatures? Perhaps they just shrug their shoulders at what seems such an impertinent question, but maybe it is pertinent after all to ask what is behind that question. For example, in an article entitled "Comparatism and separatism in African literature", Isidore Okpewho from Nigeria explains how there came to be two camps among African scholars of comparative literature. Besides those who urge using the same broad definition mentioned here, there are others who see no merit in this sort of comparatism, since Western students of literature in the past have made it plain that they saw no merit in African literature when doing their comparative research. The same narrow vision that has plagued Western research is thus adopted as a reaction by those who feel they have been sold short by this attitude. And then there is the fact that in cases where Westerners did give

[21]

attention to other literatures, they approached them from a very Eurocentric point of view. Okpewho is absolutely right when he notes that:

> the political undercurrents of comparatism do indeed deserve some emphasis, especially in the light of the painful political history of Africa. The colonial and other foreign presences among us did so much savagery to our cultural values that it is no surprise to find some of our scholars looking inward for a rediscovery of our violated essences. But we can also take what seems to me a deeper view of domination and argue that it is essentially an effort toward dehumanization.[14]

Nonetheless, Okpewho makes a plea for intercultural literature research, even though he readily admits that this research is still hampered by the historical relations based on inequality that have stood in the way of intersubjectivity, and still stand in the way because of Eurocentrism and Afrocentrism as a reaction to it. I have taken part in many such discussions myself, and in fact organized a seminar on exactly this subject for the Afrika-Studiecentrum in Leiden in 1976. The seminar examined the question of whether the same methods can be used for studying literatures from different cultures. Scholars from Africa, America and Europe came together for this discussion. Some of them quite correctly dismissed summarily any Western publications that tried, using Western criteria of quality, to indicate how far African literature has now advanced along the evolutionary line between prehistory and Western modernity. The unanimous conclusion reached was that methods themselves need not be culture-bound, providing the respective scholars are aware of the limitations that are imposed by their own historical and cultural situations.[15]

Historical research on how texts from other cultures have been received by Western readers and critics, and the other way round, would certainly produce enlightening results.

There is an interesting study by Gérard Leclerc on colonization and decolonization in anthropological research, entitled
Anthropologie et colonialisme. In the field of history, Roy Preiswerk and Dominique Perrot published *Ethnocentrisme et
histoire*. Mouralis' above-mentioned book *Les contre-littératures*
places Western literature in a broader perspective.[16] There are
indications of a changing approach in the human sciences.
As far as the study of literature is concerned, some critical
questions may be useful:

First, how do we define for ourselves the term "world
literature"? Does our definition contain any traces of cultural
evolutionism? Research in the field of national literature
requires fitting them into a larger whole to illustrate the
relationships between the literature in question and other
literatures within the same or other cultures. Such exploration also allows us to gain a better insight into our own
literature and culture.

Second, the choice of what is to be seen as literature, and
the question of who does the choosing is very significant.
Historical textbooks and encyclopedias reveal the world view
of the group from which they originate. It would be interesting to confront such a literary choice with a selection from
what has been explicitly left out – works from the "counter-
literatures". This would sharpen our insight into the problem
of value judgements.

Third, with respect to the writing of literary history, the
question is where should one choose to begin. In the West
it has not been at all unusual to begin literary history at the
point at which the West began to play a role, or first came into
contact with the area under consideration. For the history of
literature, this has often meant leaving out oral literature
altogether. The criteria for assessing quality are often heavily
influenced by evolutionism for Western critics.

There are abundant examples of which I will give two.
Robert Cornevin has theatre in Africa "come into existence"
after the coming of the Europeans to Africa. His book on the
subject, *Le théâtre en Afrique noire et à Madagascar*, is dedicated

[23]

to a colonial Frenchman, whom he calls "the father of the African stage".[17] Like the Chadwicks in the forties and C. M. Bowra in the sixties, Ruth Finnegan, in 1970, also based her definition of an epic on the written versions of the *Iliad* and the *Odyssey* that have reached us through the pen of Homer. The Nigerian Okpewho, himself a classicist, raised some questions about this after having carefully studied a number of the oral epics of Africa. He reproached Finnegan:

for setting Homer up as the yardstick of definition of the epic and for dismissing as inadequate all "primitive" heroic narratives which do not mimic the classic devices of Homer (or at least such of them as the written culture has passed on to us). I have indeed made the Homeric corpus the major counterpoint of my examination of various African texts and have consequently reached conclusions which raise questions about the validity of the fashionable premise concerning the art of Homer.[18]

The interesting thing about African epics is that they are still passed on orally and can thus yield important data about the oral transmission of the epic in general. For a long time, no Western researchers had ever considered this possibility as far as the study of Homer was concerned. The African epics were ignored or neglected.

Fourth, widely varying views are held on what "literary" means. Naturally, the notion that "literary" always means the same everywhere in the world and can thus be pinned down in a universal definition has or has had most followers in Eurocentric circles. Note that the term "universal" in this context turns out to be a synonym (or euphemism?) for "Western". The new approach to comparative study of literature leaves ample room for studying the highly various communication situations that occur in literature as it functions in different groups, eras and cultures.

Writers in the Third World are more and more aware of the dangers of Eurocentrism in world culture and they have

[24]

often reacted against it. One may think, for example, of a brilliant essay by the Cuban writer Alejo Carpentier, who speaks of the necessarily Baroque style of Latin American literature. According to Carpentier, everyone has heard of the chestnut or walnut tree, but how many people know about the ceiba or the papaya tree? Thanks to Western literature, the Latin American knows about the pine tree in the snow, even though he has never seen one, because he has read descriptions in literary texts. However, "the mother of the trees", the ceiba, has yet to be described, and the same is true for the papaya: these American trees exist and therefore have to be introduced into fiction writing. According to Carpentier, this is not easy, because they do not have the good fortune of being called "pine tree" or "birch" and "the French King Saint-Louis never languished in their shadows, nor did Pushkin ever dedicate a poem to them." That is why the ceiba and the papaya have to be talked about. Carpentier emphasizes that Latin American novelists must name everything that affects, surrounds and determines them, in order to place it within the universal vocabulary. This means, in his opinion, abandoning such techniques in vogue in the West, as those of the French *nouveau roman*, for example. In Latin America, "one must opt for Baroque style out of the necessity to give things names".[19]

This is happening not only in Latin America, but also in Africa, where it springs from the same awareness. New perspectives on the world lead to new texts, and new perspectives on literature need a new kind of criticism. Things are being described, named or renamed that had never before been put into written words, or had been described with (deliberate?) inaccuracy. Many oral "texts", transmitted for centuries exclusively in the oral form, are now being transcribed in the written form. On the basis of so much new material and data, it is inevitable that, at the level of research, a number of concepts and views must also be redefined or modified. The comparative study of criticism from different cultures will certainly be quite enlightening, because a differ-

[25]

ent cultural background may lead to completely different interpretations of a text. We'll return to this matter in Chapter IX.

The main question I wanted to ask in this chapter was how Western is the study of literature, how Eurocentric is literary research? This question is of course improper, because science, even human science, must in principle (as we teach our students) meet requirements of well-groundedness, systematics and accessibility. If this is so, the combination of "Western" and "science" is thus theoretically a contradiction in terms. In practice – partly because we know too little about the many existing literatures in our world, and partly because we unconsciously let ourselves be influenced too much by our own value systems – we make judgements that are indeed demonstrably ethnocentric and not as well-grounded, systematic or objective as our discipline demands of us.

Let us therefore conclude this chapter with a variation on Toynbee:

The scholar, critic, student or teacher of literature ought to strive now with all his or her might to widen his or her public's literary horizon; and to do this he or she must begin by widening his or her own.[20]

III. MIGRATION OF AN AFROCENTRIC MOVEMENT: FROM NEGRITUDE TO BLACK CONSCIOUSNESS

At the risk of being classified as one of "those passionate whites who consciously want to be correct this time, to avoid the errors of colonization", in the words of Ezekiel Mphahlele in his *African Image*,[1] I shall attempt to put forward some ideas on the subject of negritude and its development as a literary movement.

Let me note first of all that it is impossible to put all African literature under one heading, as many theoreticians and defenders of negritude have tried to do in the past. This tendency has not only evoked protests on the part of writers and critics within the English-speaking camp, but also among the French-speaking: think of Mphahlele, Soyinka, Franklin or Adotevi, to name only a few. Sometimes advocates of negritude have become opponents and vice versa, but the texts of the writers do not change. It is these writings that serve as our starting point as we examine this complex subject. Black American, Antillian and African writers have been inspired by common themes, the themes of negritude. This "message de la race noire" as Thomas Melone, one of the faithful defenders of negritude, defined it, has travelled from America to the Antilles, from the Antilles to Europe and to the nations of Africa. The themes were broached by the writers of West Africa before being utilized in Central Africa. The Zaïrians, for example, were unaware of the concept of negritude. As a matter of fact, they wrote very little at all

[27]

before the independence of their country, due to the policy of isolation the Belgians maintained in their colony. In the 1960s negritude has flourished in Zaïre,[2] and from the beginning of the 1970s onwards it appears to have found supporters among the victims of *apartheid*, in South Africa.

It seems unnecessary to note here the changes negritude aimed to bring about in the cultural or literary field. The history of the movement has been dealt with by Lilyan Kesteloot, Janheinz Jahn, René Depestre, Marcien Towa and others.[3] We thus know the origins of the movement, the Negro Renaissance in the United States and the literary activities in the Antilles, which preceded the birth of the term "negritude" in the 1930s in Paris. In an article entitled *Parallelism and Divergencies Between "Negritude" and "Indigenism"*, Professor Coulthard advanced the view that the "gradual build-up to negritude and the final elaboration of the concept of negritude took place largely in the West Indies".[4] However, the Netherlands Antilles and Surinam did not play any role in this. Judging from their literary production, the writers of these countries are only now discovering the roots of their "negritude".

Before examining the texts more closely, I should like to pose another question: how does one define a literary movement? In his book *The Theory of the Avant-Garde*, Poggioli devotes a whole chapter to this problem. He is of the opinion that the term *school* has become obsolete since the days of Romanticism, and artists themselves prefer to speak of their belonging to a *movement*. In general, the term *movement* designates a group of writers who write more or less in the same "esprit", but this "esprit" is, by definition, a breeding place for differences. Within the framework of their movement, writers publish "manifesto-like" magazines that are generally short-lived. Again, according to Poggioli, the movement always has ideological and psychological bases and it aspires to success, that is to say, to the confirmation of its spirit within the cultural field. In most cases, a movement consti-

[28]

tutes a reaction: to tradition, to an authority, to the public or to all of them at the same time.[5]

The features mentioned above are also evident in negritude, from the divergent meanings, via the published manifestos, the most famous of which are *Légitime Défense* and *L'étudiant noir*, to the ideological bases and the reactions to the Western cultural establishment. This would seem to justify the use of the term movement.

And what about the term negritude? In the history of literature, it sometimes happens that a movement doesn't receive its name until long after its disappearance. Just take the names Renaissance or Baroque, which weren't attributed to these respective periods until several centuries later. It can also happen that a movement's name is attributed to it by the participating artists themselves. If so, it generally proves that these artists work consciously, and this type of consciousness can deeply influence their works. This undoubtedly applies to certain artists of the Romantic movement who made use of the term, but also to certain writers of the negritude movement such as Césaire, Senghor, Damas and others who were influenced by the manifestos and theories of the movement. On the other hand, quite a few writers wrote in the same manner without consciously belonging to the movement, without using the term negritude, and even before the term came into existence. The literary texts show that, at a given moment, black writers created a new literature in different countries and even different continents, in different languages and at different moments in history.

On rereading certain passages on Romanticism in the *Concepts of Criticism* by René Wellek, one is struck by certain analogies between this European movement and negritude. First of all, both travelled from one country to another. Then, the two movements were defined in several ways, receiving at one point a global meaning comprising cultural and political aspects, and at another point a strictly literary meaning. There is a third feature worth comparing. Wellek notes that not a single English poet ever viewed himself as a Romantic

[29]

poet.[6] Isn't that perhaps also the case with many African poets writing in the English language who never wanted to accept negritude? In his article *Thèmes de la poésie africaine d'expression anglaise*, J. P. Clark discovers in the works of his fellow English-language poets the love of negritude themes like "Africa lost and reconquered". He remarks that "as far as our English-speaking poets are concerned, as poorly assimilated as they may be, the British sophistication must have rubbed off on them, because although they do not have any label and do not belong to any particular school or any famous movement, they nevertheless glorify the name of Africa and frequently use African themes".[7]

What Wellek said with regard to Romanticism, also appears to have a bearing upon negritude. Apparently the introduction of a term and its history cannot determine its usefulness to the literary historian, for in that case he would be compelled to resort to criteria that, giving due consideration to the literary movements themselves, could not be validated. So Wellek draws the conclusion that "the great changes happened independently of the introduction of these terms, either before or after them and only rarely approximately at the same time".[8] It would be interesting to compare these two movements in detail, all the more so since various African critics have alluded to Romantic aspects characterizing negritude. However, here we have to confine ourselves to the themes and texts of negritude. The common themes are especially found in poetry, which is, according to Samuel Allen, no coincidence. If negritude can be said to have given birth to poetry more than to novels, it is because novelists have to take reality, plot, setting and characterization into account:

The novelist is constrained to a certain degree of reasonableness. The poet has probably a greater chance to penetrate at once without apology and without a setting of the worldly stage to the deepest levels of his creative concern.[9]

[30]

In their poetry, black consciousness poets undertake a search for their own values, which then also represent the values and identities of the Blacks, the common history of oppressed peoples in their struggle for freedom. The themes in these poems reveal an effort on the part of the poets to define their brothers and sisters as people who differ from whites. In relation to the white world, they adopt a negative attitude, so to speak. The themes put this beyond any doubt, particularly the themes dealing with *suffering, revolt, triumph* or the idealization of Africa and black people in general, and the interracial *dialogue* that seems to mark the final phase of the movement.

Suffering

Sartre analysed the phenomenon of black suffering in his famous essay *Orphée Noir*, where he referred to the Passion (with a capital P) of the race:

Le Noir conscient de soi se représente à ses propres yeux comme l'homme qui a pris sur soi toute la douleur humaine et qui souffre pour tous, même pour le Blanc".[10]
(The conscious Black represents himself in his own conceit as a man who has accepted all the burdens of mankind and who suffers for all, even for the Whites).

This "Passion of the whole race" has inspired many poets. The past is evoked, history is analyzed, evil is diagnozed: the suffering of the black man is an inevitable outcome of the savagery of the white man. This had to be said sooner or later.

In Aimé Césaire's *Et les chiens se taisaient*, the author seems obsessed by the vision of the cruelties committed by the white man. The atrocities become concrete: the sea, the sun, the sky, the wind, the clouds, the whole natural world,

[31]

everything constitutes a horrendous picture of the sufferings of the black brothers, the groans of the victims are imprinted on:

... Le nuage a la tête du vieux nègre que j'ai vu rouer vif sur une place, le ciel bas est un étouffoir, le vent roule des fardeaux et des sanglots de peau suante, le vent se contamine de fouets et de futailles et les pendus peuplent le ciel d'acéras et il y a des dogues de poil sanglant et des oreilles ... des oreilles ... des barques faites d'oreilles coupées qui glissent sur le couchant ... Une rumeur de chaines de carcans monte de la mer ... un gargouillement de noyés, de la panse verte de la mer ... un claquement de feu, un claquement de fouet, des cris d'assassinés ... la mer brûle.[11]

(The cloud's head is the head of the old black man whom I have seen cudgeled at a market place, the low sky is a charcoal-box, the wind rolls burdens and sobs of sweating skin, the wind contaminates itself with whips and casks, and hanged men people the mapled sky and there are mastiffs with bloodstained hair, and ears ... ears ... barges made of cut ears gliding on the setting sun ... A rumour of iron collar chains ascends from the sea ... a gurgling of drowned people from the green paunch of the sea ... a cracking of fire, a cracking of whips, shouts of the assassinated ... the sea is burning).

The suffering described here is both physical and psychological: not only are there allusions to the slave trade and exploitation, but to alienation caused by the destruction of the original cultures and societies and to the imposition of a foreign economy and culture as well. This situation is engraved in the memories of the sons and daughters of slaves and of the formerly colonized peoples, and it is the common reality of Apartheid victims in South Africa to this very day. This reality inspired James Matthews to publish, with Gladys Thomas, the collection of poems called *Cry Rage* (Johannes-

burg, 1972), exposing among other things the scandalous
Pretoria policy of moving "superfluous" persons like
widows, children and the aged to remote "resettlement
areas" like Limehill and Dimbaza:

> The people of Limehill and Dimbaza
> Like those of Sada and Ilinge
> are harvesting crops of crosses
> the only fruit the land will bear
> with the fields of their villages
> fertilized by the bodies of children
> and bones of the ancient ones
>
> Cinderella resettlement areas, government gifts,
> are graveyards they stumble through
> as hunger roosts on their shoulder
> waiting for them to fill the earth
> . . .
>
> Mute evidence of white man's morality
> are the legions of walking death
> the people of Limehill and Dimbaza
> and those of Sada and Ilinge.[12]

Shortly after its publication, *Cry Rage* was banned by the
Government. According to Nadine Gordimer, it was the first
volume of poetry published in South Africa to be banned.[13]

   The two passages from the work of Césaire and Matthews
were chosen from dozens of poems in French, English, Portuguese or Dutch dealing with the suffering and exploitation
of blacks at the hands of whites. Matthews' poem illustrates
that the theme treated by Césaire about thirty years earlier
is very much alive and highly topical within the harsh context
of South Africa in the 1970s and 80s.

Revolt

To the poet who sings of suffering, revolt is never far off; he protests the injustice done to his brothers and sisters. The words of the poet are his weapon in the struggle for freedom, a weapon often forged from words in a European language. Take for example David Diop's writings, encouraging Africans to refuse to accept their miserable position.

Défi à la force

Toi qui plies toi qui pleures
Toi qui meurs un jour comme ça sans savoir pourquoi
Toi qui luttes qui veilles pour le repos de l'Autre
Toi qui ne regardes plus avec le rire dans les yeux
Toi mon frère au visage de peur et d'angoisse
    Relève toi et crie: NON![14]

(You who comply you who cry
You who die just like that not knowing why
You who struggle, waking just for the rest of the Other
You with no laughter left in your eyes
You, my brother, face full of fear and fright
    Get up and shout: NO!)

Poems that breathe the same spirit are quoted by Pol Ndu in an article entitled *Negritude and the New Breed* on current black American poetry: "The poems of the battle-criers are action-charged, ringing with blood, fire and avalanche of some global doomsday . . . The poets, as it were, are impatient. For them the offensive is on . . . " And the author refers to the poem *Black Art* by Leroi Jones:

We want "poems that kill".
We want a Black poem. And a
Black world
Let the world be a Black Poem
And let All Black People Speak This Poem

[34]

Silently
or Loud.[15]

The world and the poem ought to be black because the revolt
is directed against the white domination that has conditioned
it. If the Antagonist did not exist, the revolt would have
been superfluous and these poetic themes non-existent. In
negritude poetry, "white civilization" is under attack on all
fronts. In his poetic work, Césaire successively condemns it
as the faculty of reason, culture, technology, ideologies and
Christianity.[16]

The Idealization of Africa

The idealization of ancestral Africa, the old Africa that did
not have the misfortune of knowing the whites, is a recurrent
theme in negritude poetry. Just think of Senghor's poems
alluding to the "Kingdom of Childhood". In the English-
speaking world, there are also Odes to Africa. In his article
referred to above, J. P. Clark notes that this theme was utilized in West Africa prior to its introduction into East and
Central Africa. Well-known examples are *African Heaven* by
the Ghanaian Kobina Parkes, or, more recently, *Sounds of a
Cowhide Drum* by the South African Oswald Mtshali. This is
also a favorite theme of the Zaîrian poets of the sixties such
as Kadima-Nzuji.[17]

It is not only Africa that is idealized but also the Africans
and the black people in general. Bernard Dadié expresses his
gratitude to his God for having made him black, because
"white is a colour for special occasions". This is really a
romantic vision of a distinctive Africa, the symbol of purity
in sharp contrast to a corrupted and destructive Europe. It
is also the *black is beautiful* cry of triumph Léon Damas
expressed in his poem *Black Label*:

[35]

Jamais le Blanc sera nègre
car la beauté est nègre
et nègre la sagesse
car l'endurance est nègre
et nègre le courage
car la patience est nègre
et nègre l'ironie
car le charme est nègre
et nègre la magie
car l'amour est nègre
et nègre le déhanchement
car la danse est nègre
et nègre le rythme
car l'art est nègre
et nègre le mouvement
car le rire est nègre
car la joie est nègre
car la paix est nègre
car la vie est nègre
T'EN SOUVIENT-IL?[18]

(Never whites will be black
Because beauty is black
And black is wisdom
Because endurance is black
And black is courage
Because patience is black
And black is irony
Because charm is black
And black is magic
Because love is black
And black the waddling gait
Because dancing is black
And black is rhythm
Because art is black
And black is movement
Because laughing is black

Because joy is black
Because peace is black
Because life is black
DO YOU REMEMBER?)

Dialogue

The three themes mentioned above, suffering, revolt and the idealization of Africa, do not include dialogue; they represent three phases in which the poet defines his position in relation to the "Others" who have never been historically interested in dialogue. The negritude poets often proclaim they wish to make the world more human, and Senghor has said that "the black poem is not a monologue but a dialogue".[19]

However, this dialogue is not unconditional: prejudices must first be swept away and the same rights made available to both the groups involved. These conditions are not always formulated in negritude poetry. Senghor is often regarded in Europe as the reconciliator between blacks and whites. His literary work is much less aggressive than that of such writers as Césaire or David Diop. Senghor explains this by referring to his "harmony with African nature". Does this explain why he could write his poem *Prayer for Peace* as far back as 1945?

Au pied de mon Afrique crucifiée depuis quatre cents ans
et pourtant respirante
Laisse-moi Te dire Seigneur, sa prière de paix et de
pardon
Seigneur Dieu, pardonne à l'Europe blanche![20]

(At the foot of my Africa crucified for four hundred years
and still breathing
Let me say to you Lord, its prayer of peace and pardon.
Lord God, forgive white Europe!)

This overall and gracious pardon on the part of the father of

[37]

negritude did not find favour with all Africans. Marcien Towa
of the Cameroons reproached Senghor for being so peaceful
that he was prepared to forgive Europe its crimes even
though Europe itself did not desire this African pardon, nor
did it seem to have stopped committing new crimes.[21] Other
poets drew a distinction between those in power, who could
consequently be held responsible for the injustices committed
against people of colour, and those in the Western world
who were also victims, namely the peasants and workers. In
his poem *Pour Saluer le Tiers Monde*, Césaire envisages how
Africa is the first to reach out a hand to the "wretched" of
the other continents:

> c'est une main tuméfiée
> une-blessée-main-ouverte
> tendue,
> brunes, jaunes, blanches,
> à toutes mains, à toutes les mains blessées
> du monde.[22]

> (It is a tumefied hand
> A-wounded-open-hand
> extended to,
> brown, yellow, white,
> to all the hands, to all the wounded hands
> of the world.)

Jacques Roumain of Haïti does not forgive the guilty ones.
In his *Nouveau sermon nègre*, this poet compares the suffering
of the black man to the suffering of Christ. But whereas Jesus
asks his Father to forgive his enemies who know not what
they do, Roumain cries out: "We will not forgive them, for
they know what they do".[23] However, his solidarity is not
restricted to his black brothers, as is evident from the last
lines of his poem *Bois d'ébène* (Ebony):

Comme la contradiction des traits
se résout dans l'harmonie du visage

nous proclamons l'unité de la souffrance
et de la révolte
de tous les peuples sur toute la surface de notre terre
et nous brassons le mortier des temps fraternels
dans la poussière des idoles.[24]

(Just like the contradiction of features
Resolves in the face's harmony
We proclaim the unity of suffering
And of revolt
Of all the peoples on the surface of our earth
And we brew the mortar of fraternal times
In the dust of the idols).

With class consciousness, negritude loses its *raison d'être*: a different kind of solidarity is created that no longer requires the accentuation of the colour of a man's skin or his belonging to a particular "race". "The Negro has been created by the white man", Fanon once said. And negritude has been a reaction to this state of affairs, though, in a sense, it has also prolonged the latter since the writers defined themselves "according to the colour of the other group", as Sembène Ousmane put it in the Foreword to his *The Money Order*.[25]

After this brief outline of themes and their migration, it might be useful to examine the current discussion on negritude between its advocates and their opponents. The negritude found in poetic themes constitutes, according to Adotevi, the negritude of the first hour, "ce coup de pistolet au beau milieu du concert, lorsque l'Afrique, l'Amérique et les Antilles, tous les nègres du monde, se retrouvent hors de l'humanité du Blanc, pour affirmer leur humanité". (This pistol shot in the middle of the concert, when Africa, America and the Caribbean, all the Blacks in the world, found each other back outside white humanity, to assert their own humanity). This termination of silence, he says, is the real negritude, the one that still isn't perverted, "celle qui a permis de faire connaître l'Afrique gràce aux thèmes hurlés

de nos poètes" (the one that enabled us to make Africa
known thanks to the howled themes of our poets). To him,
these themes are "the birth certificate of a new African literature". After formulating these positive reflections in *Négritude
et Négrologues*, Adotevi expresses doubt as to the existence of
lasting unity amongst blacks in the various countries: What
really unites them except the colour of their skin and "this
common foundation of three centuries of slavery or collective
subconsciousness"? And even in respect of this "common
foundation", Adotevi remains rather sceptical in view of the
variety of historical, geographical and sociological factors that
have created the different forms of expression in the arts of
the peoples of these two continents. And he adds: "Even in
Africa the problems differ as you pass from Dahomey to the
Ivory Coast, from the Ivory Coast to Ghana. And what about
South Africa, Kenya, Rwanda? . . . "[26]

The "howled themes" Adotevi refers to, that have travelled
to and from the U.S.A., the Antilles and Africa, constitute the
unity of the moment. Nothing but the common experience of
white oppression can make us generalize about the black
man, according to this writer. The Nigerian scholar and critic
Abiola Irele was opposed to this point of view for quite some
time; in his article *A Defence of Negritude*, he acknowledged
the revolutionary nature of the movement's literature but felt
there was more to it than mere protest: the negation of
Europe was also a search for the self and a return to the
sources. Like Senghor, he held the opinion that "the negro
being is rooted in African tradition which is unified by a
common philosophical conception . . . a common ontological
outlook which governs the African psyche and in which the
negro in America can rightly be supposed to share." And
further: "There is something in common: I find nothing to
contradict the thesis of a unified African universe." For Irele,
something like a *je-ne-sais-quoi-nègre* existed, which he called
the "total African cosmology", the whole scale of African
values, in the words of Senghor whose point of view he

shared; at least that was the case when he wrote this article in 1964.[27]

Adotevi on the other hand quotes Peter Abrahams and Richard Wright in defence of his ideas. Neither of these two writers experienced the unity of black brotherhood during their stay in West Africa. Wright remarked: "I was black and they were black but it did not help me at all", and Peter Abrahams stated:

The sharp black consciousness of the black American or the South African, victim of Apartheid is foreign to the African of independent Africa. Race and colour were his last preoccupations before he was forced to think of them. And "Mother Africa" is too vast to inspire him with a total feeling.[28]

Racial consciousness no longer preoccupies the inhabitants of independent African countries that much, but black Americans do continue to deal with it in their poetry because they are still an oppressed minority in the society they live in. The war cries of the people whom Pol Ndu has called "the new breed" echo in this literature today as they did in the past. Until their independence this was also the case in the Portuguese-speaking African countries. Mario de Andrade attested to the "unité certaine des thèmes" in the poetry of these countries, a poetry of combat, during the time of "winning or dying", but he also added that this poetry was written under specific circumstances.[29]

The themes of negritude are relevant to the people who are still oppressed by white rulers: I have already mentioned James Matthews of South Africa but there are many other poets who write in the same vein.[30] Outside South Africa there has been tendency to quote Mphahlele as the authentic spokesman of the South African attitude to negritude. Even though he somewhat revised his ideas on this subject in the second edition of The African Image, Mphahlele nonetheless maintained (in a chapter entitled "Negritude revisited") that

[41]

negritude as an artistic programme is "unworkable" for modern Africa and that the historical factors which had brought about the negritude movement did not exist any longer.[31] However, he wrote this pertaining to South Africa at a relatively early moment (in 1974) and from outside. He spent about twenty years in exile before he returned to his country in 1977 to deal, as he put it, "with the concrete reality of blackness in South Africa rather than with the phantoms and echoes that attend exile".[31]

Like their black American brothers and sisters, black poets in South Africa have indeed been dealing with negritude themes for a long time and found it quite useful. It would seem that white domination has stimulated the rise of black consciousness there since the early 1970s. Terms like *blackness*, *black culture* and *black consciousness* are a response to the oppressive situation in that country. In December 1974, the first Black Renaissance Convention took place in Hammanskraal in South Africa. The black delegates vigorously affirmed the solidarity among all Blacks in opposition to the whites of their country, now that it had become quite clear to them that all the efforts on their part to bring about an effective dialogue had been foiled by *apartheid*. Since the beginning of the seventies, the leaders of SASO (the black South African Students Organization), have been organizing popular cultural programmes consisting of poetry readings and theatre productions. These programmes, which were sometimes even entitled "Into the heart of negritude", included poetry by Senghor, Dadié, David Diop and the work of Mtshali, Serote, Sepamla, Gwala and other South African writers.

In an interview I had with some SASO leaders in 1972, they explained that negritude was an indispensable cultural phase that would not end until freedom had been acquired, at which point new perspectives would be opened. These "radicals", as they were called in South Africa, aligned the negritude movement with their struggle for liberation.

Since the start of the 1980s, however, some of the people involved have cautiously begun to question the emphasis on black-white polarity in that country as well. One of them is Njabulo Ndebele.

Without literally using the concept of negritude, he enumerated the above mentioned themes as *the* themes of South African poetry:

> What we have . . . is protest literature that merely changed emphasis: from the moral evil of apartheid, to the existential and moral worth of blackness; from moral indignation, to anger; from relatively self-composed reasonableness, to uncompromising bitterness; from the exterior manifestations of oppression, to the interior psychology of oppression . . . While the poetry turns its attention toward the self, it is still very much conscious of the white "other" . . . it is still rooted in the emotional and intellectual polarities of South African oppression.[32]

As Ndebele remarks in his very fundamental paper, a new collective power has come up in South Africa, reaching workers, students and school children. This implies a new challenge for literature:

> the challenge to free the entire social imagination of the oppressed from the laws of perception that have characterized Apartheid society. For writers this means freeing the creative process itself from those very laws. It means extending the writer's perception of what can be written about, and the means and methods of writing.[33]

According to Ndebele, reflections on art and its function are badly needed in South Africa, as a new process of cultural exploration and debate. The writers' tasks will then be to grasp in language hitherto unmapped areas of the lives of black people, leaving "the rhetoric of protest" behind.

Up to now we have hardly referred to the Senghorian theories that have probably contributed most to the founding of the movement and the publicity given to it. Senghor has added content to the concept of negritude as not being transient but lasting. In an interview I had with him during his visit to Holland some years ago, the father of negritude reaffirmed once again the unity of black civilization's values, although of course the circumstances and themes are subject to change today. According to him, it is no longer a question of a polemic against European civilization, but negritude nevertheless endures. In the "Civilisation de l'Universal", Europe and Africa would both have clearly defined contributions to make:

> L'Europe nous apportera, essentiellement, avec son esprit de méthode et d'organisation, ses découvertes scientifiques et techniques. L'Afrique, je veux dire l'Afrique noire, apportera ses vertus communautaires et artistiques, singulièrement sa philosophie de la vie, fondée sur la complémentarité, et, dans les arts, son sens de l'image analogique, du rhythme et de la mélodie.[34]

> (With its spirit of method and organization, Europe will bring us, mainly, its scientific and technical discoveries. Africa, I mean black Africa, will bring its communitary and artistic values, particularly its philosophy of life, based upon the complementarity, and, in the arts, its sense of analogical image, of rhythm and of melody).

Senghor believes certain characteristics of particular racial groups remain constant, for if Africa had been able to colonize Europe, the Africans would have treated the whites better than the whites have treated the blacks in Africa; evidence of this hypothesis is furnished by historical cases in which black groups conquered white populations, such as the Almoravides who conquered Morocco and parts of Spain. Blacks in position of power never practised racism against whites, according to the Poet-President. When asked whether there is an analogy between the position of women and of blacks in the world (according to Simone de Beauvoir

[44]

in *The Second Sex*, "both groups are today liberating themselves from the same paternalism", that is, of the white male), Senghor responded:

'Il y a, certainement, des similitudes, non seulement entre les conditions de la femme occidentale et du Négro-Africain, mais encore entre les vertus féminines et les vertus négro-africaines. Que les conditions de la femme en Occident et du Négro-Africain dans le monde soient semblables, c'est l'évidence même. L'Euramérique, on le sait, a commencé par nier les vertus du Nègre comme l'homme de l'Occident avait nié celles de la Femme. Ce qui paraît moins évident, ce sont les similitudes entre les vertus de la Femme et les vertus du Nègre. Et pourtant il y a, ici et là, le même besoin d'expression, exprimée par l'image analogique et le rythme. Il y a, surtout, chez le nègre, comme chez la Femme, la puissance d'émotion et, partant, d'identification. D'où la fausse impression chez l'Euraméricain, comme chez l'homme de l'Occident, que l'on peut assimiler le Nègre, comme la Femme".[35]

(There are certainly similarities, not only between the conditions of the Western woman and the black African, but also between the feminine virtues and the black African virtues. It is absolutely evident that the Western woman's conditions and the Black African's in the world are similar. Euramerica, as we all know, started by ignoring the virtues of the Black, just as Western Man ignored the virtues of Woman. What seems less evident, is the similarity between the Woman's virtues and the virtues of the Black. And yet, there is in both cases the same need to express oneself, to be found in the analogical image and the rhythm. There is, above all, in the Black, as well as in the Woman, the power of emotion and, thus, of identification. Therefore the Euramerican as well as the Western man has got the wrong impression that the Black can be assimilated just as Woman can be).

[45]

Western Women and Blacks may continue to be different from Western man or "Euramerican" man, but what about black women? On the other hand, if negritude is an eternal quality linking blacks in the whole world how can we explain the fact that Senghor accords a small nation like the Dutch a *Néerlandité* (based on the *robur Batavorum*, the strength of the Batavians to which reference was already made by Tacitus) and to another European nation, the Portuguese, the quality of *Lusitanité* which is derived from the Lusitanian energy, from its profound sensibility, its *gentillesse*, its sadness and its nostalgia, as it was formulated by him in *Jeune Afrique*.[36] "As long as a Dutch state exists there will be a *Neerlandité*" and "as long as there is a black *ethnie*, negritude will endure", Senghor stated while in the Netherlands.[37] What does his *ethnie nègre* then consist of and why is it not possible to attribute a characteristic "-ité" or "-itude" to the different black States as Senghor has done with respect to various European nations?

"Negritude? Don't know", comments Sembène Ousmane on my question, "to me it is like the sex of the angels." This Senegalese writer never accepted the concept of negritude. He admits, however, that it can play a positive role in a country like South Africa, but only temporarily:

> Ce n'est que demain que les Noirs sudafricains comprendront où se trouve le noyau du problème et alors ils ne continueront certainement pas à courir après la négritude."
> (Only tomorrow the South African Blacks will understand the core of the problem and then they will certainly stop running after negritude).

It is really a revolution that black South Africans need and negritude can never, according to him, bring about.[38]

This is the reproach very often levelled at negritude: it works at cross purposes with "the African revolution". According to Adotevi, negritude missed its political and revolutionary vocation: "Si la Négritude ancienne est un refus de l'humiliation, le nègre qui aujourd'hui parle au nègre, doit être au centre du drame de son peuple, conscient de soi, c'est-à-dire aux tâches de l'heure." (If the old negritude is a rejection of humiliation, the Black who addresses the Black nowadays must deal with the drama of his people and be self-conscious, that is conscious of the new tasks). And Mphaphele blamed negritude for telling the masses "how beautiful they are while they are starving, while they swelter under new lords".[39] For Adotevi, negritude today means the current discussion about neo-colonialism. Negritude is "the *black* way of being *white.*" Adotevi based his attitude on the ideas of Fanon, who always refused to belong to a particular branch of the human race, to be pinned down by history because human beings have the possibility of breaking through the historical situation and of introducing the cycle of their own liberty. Fanon also refused to draw up "the balance-sheet of black values", maintaining already in 1952:

Moi, l'homme de couleur, je ne veux qu'une chose: Que jamais l'instrument ne domine l'homme. Que cesse à jamais l'asservissement de l'homme par l'homme. . . . Qu'il me soit permis de découvrir et de vouloir l'homme, où qu'il se trouve. Le nègre n'est pas. Pas plus que le Blanc.[40]
(Being a man of colour, I want only one thing: that instruments never dominate people. That the bondage of man by man stop . . . That I discover and wish man, wherever he may be. The Black does not exist, nor does the White.)

The echoing of such words has constituted the basis for the decline of negritude. It goes hand in hand with the development of new forms and themes in present-day African literature.

IV. NATIONAL LITERATURES AND LITERARY HISTORY

It is often deemed unnecessary to define the concept of literary history, as if there were some definite unanimity as to what it entails. The same is then thought to hold true of its two components, "literature" and "history". Within any writing of literary history, however, very specific values shape the criteria of what is considered literature (the "masterpieces" only, or everything written, told, sung, or something in between), what is history or should be, and the resulting interrelations of the two.

Since no human being can study all the documents and facts in this field, selections are inevitably made on the basis of specific norms. Thus, one of the first questions to confront the literary historian is which economic, social and political interests and which cultural i.e. literary values he or she intends to confirm, to transform, to ignore, while (re-)constructing the history of literature.[1]

For anyone who wants to write a literary history of Africa, be it national or international, it is useful to examine what has been done in this field elsewhere. Which methods have been used, which problems have been dealt with and how have they been solved? What mistakes can be avoided this time? In some instances, I shall refer to European parallels. In European literary history, the problem of national literatures has led to discussions as to what to emphasize: the unity of Europe as a whole or the importance of each nation as an independent entity. In my opinion, one should never exclude the former for the benefit of the latter or vice versa.

[48]

The two perspectives – the national and the international – are indispensable because they are complementary in all literary history: national literatures influence and shape one another on the international level.

Polysystems

Literature as a semiotic model of human communication constitutes a heterogeneous, open-structured system, dynamic, rather than static, conditioned by the historical aspects of this communication. Nationally as well as internationally, one might therefore speak of a *polysystem* (PS) as defined by Even-Zohar,[2] who illustrated his view with the following example from the European literary context:

> Clearly, throughout the Middle Ages . . . the canonized system was controlled by literature written in Latin, while non-canonized literature consisted of spoken/written texts in the various vernaculars. Through a complicated process, this PS gradually collapsed, to be replaced about the middle of the 18th century, by a series of more or less independent uni-lingual polysystems, whose interdependencies with the other polysystems became more and more negligible, at least from the point of view of both current consumers and the dominating ideologies. However, it is apparent, for the PS theory, that in order to be able not only to describe the general principles of interferences, but also to explain their nature and causes with certain exactitude, a stratification hypothesis must be posited for them. For, when the various European nations gradually emerged and created their own literatures, certain centre-and-periphery relations unavoidably participated in the process from the very start.[3]

Of course, these centre-and-periphery relations not only exist on the national and international level, but also on the inter-cultural level; they influence each other in accordance with the various circumstances to be described on the basis of careful research.

It is obvious that the question of canonized versus non-canonized literature and the relations between them is also of primary importance within the national literary context. One could never write a complete national literary history while dealing exclusively with authors of "masterpieces", with authors belonging to the elite, because in general they represent only partly the national culture. The risk of neglecting such popular literatures, as for example the Nigerian Onitsha Market Literature, is all the more present since the national literary historians usually belong to this elite themselves.

Obviously, the most prestigious canonized texts are at the literary centre and they make every effort to retain all the critical attention. This elitist selectivity should be dismissed in literary history. In this respect, the following warning is very much to the point with regard to both Western and African literature:

It may seem trivial yet warrants special emphasis that the polysystem hypothesis involves a rejection of value judge-ments as criteria for an *a priori* selection of the objects of study. This must be particularly stressed for literary stud-ies, where confusion between criticism and research still exists. If one accepts the PS hypothesis, then one must also accept that literary historical poetics – the historical study of literary polysystems – cannot confine itself to the so-called "masterpieces", even if some would consider them the only *raison d'être* of literary studies in the first place. (This is an attitude we need not accept.) This kind of elitism should be banished from literary historiography. It should be remembered, however, that this has no bear-ing upon our standards as critics or private readers. It means, rather, that as scholars committed to the discovery of the mechanisms of literary history, we cannot use arbitrary and temporary value judgements as criteria in selecting the objects of study in a historical context. The prevalent value judgements of any period are themselves an integral part of the objects to be observed. No field of study can select its objects according to norms of taste without losing its status as an intersubjective discipline.[4]

National Feelings and Nationalism

In Europe national feelings developed with the social and cultural rise of the middle class. It was not until the eighteenth century that the word nation acquired the meaning it still has today. Literature certainly contributed to this process: Rousseau was one of the philosophers who related the collective will of the people to their geographical boundaries.[5] What had happened before then? In an article on dialectics in the concept of national literature, Niscov stressed that the European literatures written in Latin in the Middle Ages and later were rooted not only in Rome as the centre of classical tradition, but also in the new civilization that emerged after the wandering of nations. These migrations visibly marked the ethnic and later the national character of the contemporary European cultural constellation. Niscov prefers to underline the importance of individual nations rather than examining what the various European national literatures have in common.

The German scholar Ernst Robert Curtius, however, dealt with the latter question and ignored the former. In spite of his understanding of the historical circumstances that made him hesitate to broach the subject of national spirit or even nationalism because of its connotations in the German post world war context, Niscov criticized him for that.[6] This example illustrates that the ideological perspective and selection

[51]

of facts in literary history depend very much on the time, the background and the attitude toward nationalism of the literary historian concerned. But what is nationalism in the African context? Mudimbe gives the following definition:

> . . . nationalism can be defined as an ideological movement that is in practice established along the lines of theoretical choices posed by a ruling class. In order to mobilize the population, this ruling class tends to promote a new order of things and values such as undeniable socio-political originality, specific cultural features and so forth.[7]

Thus, when writing a history of national literature, one should analyze the specific unifying features as proposed or imposed by the critics of the ruling class as well as by those opposed to it, i.e. the polysystem as it functions on the national level.[8]

National Literature

A national literature exhibits certain features typical of a particular country. These features change in the course of national history.

A relevant issue is how the national features are related to the socio-economic, political and ideological changes that affect the history of the entire continent. In the case of Europe, for instance, the Roman occupation was an important event; in the case of Africa, the European colonization was. It goes without saying that a national language constitutes an essential instrument in any national literature. As far as the African countries are concerned, it will be necessary to describe the divergencies and the relations between the official, the national, and the other languages and their respective contributions to a national literature. When comparing the birth process of modern states in Europe and their respective national literatures with the same process in Africa, one finds a number of analogies. Classicism, the return to the classics in the European Renaissance, may have inhibited the birth of national literatures. In some respects, this phenomenon resembles the return to the pan-African past and the negritudinist inclinations which may have inhibited the birth or growth of national literatures in the independent African states, although they were also a prerequisite for it. One might add, in the case of Africa, the common colonial history that strengthened the pan-African movement, simultaneously hindering the national tendencies in the individual states. The same is true of the trade union leaders, who, by virtue of their very ideas, had an international view of human society. And then, the Western education of the African elites in European metropoles and the gap that separated them from their peoples was not favourable to the growth of genuine African national cultures. In spite of the nationalist movements that resulted in independence, the elites often preserved the existing connections with the culture of the one-time colonizer.

Cultural Nationalism

African cultural nationalism can be described as being based upon three pillars:
1. Cultural elements from the pre-colonial past; 2. national reactions vis-à-vis the economic, political and cultural [de]colonization (of course 1. and 2. have a dialectical relation); 3. the inventory of the national culture as it exists today (contributions by elite and other social and cultural groups, among them the "urban pop culture").[9] This type of inventory after about 25 years of independence could also help prepare guidelines for future national cultural strategies.

On the basis of the three above-mentioned points, the next step is to describe what a national population might have in

[53]

common culturally (and where the diversities lie). A related issue is the question of whether a national social reality exists at all and, if so, how to describe it (for that purpose lists of relevant questions should be prepared). Since our primary concern is literature, we shall have to study the relations between oral and written heritages and to devote attention to the history and liberation struggles of the peoples living in a particular country. The results could then be the object of a comparative study in various neighbouring countries. Of course a comparative study could be extended to an intercontinental level: in that case, the role of literature and the impact of the liberation struggle on the historical growth of independent states might be one of the subjects.

National Literature and Literary Relations

The work of a writer considered to be important exhibits the interplay of a number of universal factors, all belonging to broad fields such as myth, ritual, models of thought, world vision, models of literary syntax, language and the like. Common factors can also be found within the context of one individual culture, i.e. the national culture. Research is needed with regard to all these aspects. The national and the universal can influence one another dialectically, implying a confrontation possibly resulting in a new synthesis.

Every literary text relates to a number of frameworks to be taken into account when dealing with national literature and its historiography:

1. the complete works of the author concerned.
2. the context of the literary movement or period the work belongs to.
3. the framework of the entire body of literature written in the same language.

4. the framework of the literature of a particular culture (but written in different languages).

5. the literature of one nation.

6. the literature of one continent.

7. the corpus of world literature.[10]

All these points should be checked, but of course they are not always all relevant at the same time: some may deserve more attention than others, depending on the case. For example, if, in a particular national literature, an oral epic is essential (one might think of Shaka in South African literature), the epic then has links with numbers 3, 4 and 5, but it could also have links with 1 (if the author created or transmitted other epics or literary works). It has links with 2 if one wants to look at the contemporary literary context, or with 6 in the case of a comparative study of the epic in other African cultures (or other continents), if one wants to find out whether such epics have played a role in the growth of a national literature.

Or, still more concretely, take a well-known writer like Léopold Sédar Senghor: one would have to examine first the author, his poetry as well as his essays, and their critical reception. The biographical data cannot be neglected either.

Secondly, Senghor has to be viewed within the context of the negritude movement and the French surrealist movement. The latter is also inherent in the third point; literature of the same language includes francophone African and Caribbean literature as well as the literature of France.

The fourth point puts the author in the framework of West African literature in African and European languages, and the fifth refers to his place in Senegalese literature.

The sixth point links him to African literature in general and the seventh and last studies him in the context of the "Civilisation de l'Universel" to put it in his own words.

A number of related problems crop up when examining 2,

[55]

and defining national literature vis-à-vis world literature. A Eurocentric perspective has often prevented scholars from taking into account other aspects of the polysystem mentioned above, particularly the intercultural aspect. It is still true that Western norms and perspectives dominate world literary history, although there are signs of change.[11]

In African literature, Eurocentrism has meant that "the best" (according to Western norms, that is) francophone and anglophone texts have often been incorporated into French and English literature. There is also the danger that, as a reaction to this, the many relations existing between African national literatures and the literatures of the former colonial metropolis might be ignored completely. We'll return to this later.

National Literature and the Role of the Critic

In literature as a verbal communication process, texts can be viewed as an exchange of messages between the author and the audience. The functions of these messages can be either to strengthen or to weaken national literature. One function of the text as a message is its direct appeal to the reader. The second one is the emotional self-expression of the author. A third is the aesthetic attention drawn to the beauty of the text as such, "the focus on the message for its own sake", as Roman Jakobson put it.[12] The first function stresses the relationship between the text and the *reader*, in the second case the *author*'s role is emphasized and in the third the *text* is the main focus. In spite of one function being particularly focused upon in the whole of the communication process, the others continue to play a role in the background. Nevertheless, the text's appeal to the reading audience is essential if we are to discover whether literature has contributed to the rise of national literature. Among the readers, critics play quite a decisive role, because any influence the text is to have will largely depend on their comments. Like any other reader, the critic is conditioned by his or her cultural, social and ideological background. This is why historiographers of literature should not only study as many literary texts as possible, but should also be familiar with as many reviews as possible, discover the common denominators and understand their impact on readers in the national and international community.

Differing interpretations may have to do with whether the critic is a compatriot of the author or a foreigner, whether he or she belongs to the same or another culture, as we'll see later in chapter IX. Resulting differences can help to define the frontiers of national literature.

Writing Literary History

The job of the literary historian is quite complex indeed, since literature is related to so many fields, e.g. aesthethics, history, philosophy, linguistics, and sociology to name just a few. Furthermore, there is the rich and varied material in archives and libraries, and the data on distribution and bibliographical information to be taken into account. One risks getting lost in the overwhelming mountain of documents, and team-work is recommended. It has often been said that literary history should be grafted upon history, but what are we to choose in history? For us, the literary facts and conditions (and their changes in the course of history) are the point of orientation. In order to avoid getting sidetracked, literary historians should bear in mind the literary communication process, in which the sender (author) transmits his message (text) to the recipient (reader, auditor). Accordingly, they'll find firstly *the origin of the works*, that is the study of authors' lives and their contexts, in so far as these facts relate to the texts; and secondly, the structure and development of *the corpus of national texts*. Furthermore, this body of texts should be defined in terms of similarities and differences with regard to neighbouring national literatures (i.e. international and, if necessary, also intercultural comparative study); and thirdly *literature and public*, i.e. the norms of the critics, norm changes in the course of literary history, the function of texts in various contexts (readership, distribution circuits, relation to the authorities etc.).[13]

These three points should be carefully studied in order to guarantee thorough, in-depth description. It goes without saying that each national context will contain a number of unforeseen elements.

National versus International

A number of literary phenomena can be understood only within their context of synchronic and diachronic relations. Which texts have preceded contemporaneous ones and left their marks in the past, what contemporary influences, movements, and events have conditioned certain literary products? Thus, in the African context, for instance, the fact that a number of oral literatures are shared by people living in different neighbouring countries will have to be taken into account. Or, to give another example, colonial and non-colonial European literatures have influenced African literatures in many respects in most countries, not in the least because of the reactions these influences provoked. Take for instance the phenomenon of cultural renaissance manifested in Negritude or Black Consciousness. Its nostalgia for the precolonial past and its African romanticism were a logical reaction to European cultural domination.

The next question is whether such a movement, regarded broadly as inter-african and/or metropolitan, also influenced national unity within the nation-state. Here we are reminded of Frantz Fanon's scepticism with regard to movements like negritude which led, in his opinion, into a cul-de-sac. He

[58]

was convinced of the necessity for both the elite and the people to recognize themselves in the *national* context, hence his appeal for a real national literature.[14]

The diverse cultural mosaics inside the countries are now in the process of creating their own national culture and literature independently. In some cases, the general African opposition to Europe and the nostalgic and romantic myths of the past have probably been deliberately cultivated in the national context of independence by the authorities who, to maintain their power, try to divert the people's attention from the present with its unsolvable social problems.

Fanon, however, always stressed the importance of the question of where, in this review of the past, the link with the present, and especially the link with the future, is to be found. His claim has lost none of its relevance today.[15]

Apart from the international African unifying factor of the negritude and Panafrican movements, other factors also weaken the national aspect in literature. The use of such international languages as English, French and Portuguese, for instance, implies the contradiction between the national and the international:

It is the conflict within nationalism between modernisation and authenticity which produces the well-known phenomenon in developing nations of wanting western industry, science and material goods, while rejecting European culture or the kind of secular, rational, sceptical mentality that has usually accompanied industrialization. But as its claim to authenticity is the defence of traditional culture, and as it needs the symbols of tradition to obtain and remain in power, a nationalist movement will find itself imprisoned in a paradox which in turn provides its dynamism, its despair and its outburst of rage.[16]

Having rid themselves of the colonizers, the nation-states were even more exposed to political, economic and cultural influences from the international community. While they were colonies, the countries were still relatively isolated. After independence, the problem of authenticity became even more serious: the colonial system moved out, but its representatives were soon replaced by international development "experts" whose numbers far exceeded those of their predecessors, the colonial representatives. Bruce King rightly observes:

The new class and the industrial development with which it is associated is seen as a neo-colonialism and produces a neo-nationalist reaction. Because of the inherent dialectic between progress and authenticity within a new nation, there will be cycles of nationalism followed by internationalism, followed by more nationalism. Periods of rapid industrial growth, new wealth or disruptive social change will usually be followed by retreats into a search for roots, national values and traditions . . . With the expansion of international trade, nationalism is likely to occur in many countries simultaneously.[17]

In literary texts, such contradictions are broached when communal values in the villages are opposed to the decadence and degradation of city life. Examples are to be found in novels of Chinua Achebe and Ngugi Wa Thiong'd as well as in the poetry of Okot p'Bitek and in many African plays.

In general, the forces of change have had their impact on the cultural heritage from inside as well as outside the nation. An inventory of these forces will help us to answer questions relating to the visible manifestations of national culture. For us, the point of focus is again the place of literature in the culture context. In national literature, the established hierarchy often has to do with the language used in the texts. The literature of international language is often considered more prestigious than literature in languages of smaller use. This probably has to do with the prestige of "having been published abroad".

The language question is directly associated with the

[60]

national-international issue. Just as Latin was the official literary language in Europe for a long time, European languages
continue to play a significant role in African literature. Comparative research on the replacement of Latin in Europe by
the national languages and the positive or negative attitude
towards literature in African languages by national elites
would be interesting. Latin, once fashionable among the
European elites, was later replaced by French as the sophisti-
cated language. Differences between popular and official
literature have to do with the language they are in, and have
consequences regarding their introduction into the academic
curriculum, the genres practised and so forth (e.g. more
novels in international languages; more songs, stories and
theatre in local languages).

Apart from literature in either European or African languages, there is also a growing use of Africanized French or
English, for instance in plays by the Congolese Sylvain
Bemba or the works of Amos Tutuola. Thus, new forms of
verbal creativity are born which could not exist in European
literature written in the Queen's English or the French of
Voltaire. Finally, one shall have to find out whether, and
how, new language use contributes to a typical national
literature.

National Literature and Political Reality

To what extent is literature written by and for elites in contact
with what Fanon used to call "national reality"? Writers'
themes and motives can strengthen national identity or
undermine it. And what role is played by the State itself with
regard to literature?

Governments might wish to place literature at the service
of nation-building, or simply ignore this possibility. The
ambiguous relation between writers and authorities will be
further discussed in chapter X. In some countries, literature

[61]

is perceived by those in power as a threat to national unity. Writers who criticize the authorities there are considered enemies and encounter censorship, imprisonment, or exile. The stifling effect of these mechanisms seriously affects the national literature of any country with restricted freedom of speech. In some cases it leads to the paradoxical situation that about half the national literature is written, and still more published, in foreign countries.

This has to do with the function of the arts and literature in society. According to the classical European formula, art should teach and divert. Of course, this has meant different things in different historical, social and cultural contexts. Art has mostly been considered as *instrumental*.

From the nineteenth century onward, European artists have also developed an *intrinsic* view of art: art for art's sake. In this view, art has a value of its own. The value of the artistic object or text is contained in the object or text itself and art's value is not historically and culturally determined. The arts have become an institution and, as such, they have very little social influence in the Western world. The ideal of the autonomy of art has led to the artists' becoming a separate category.

The ideal was to be independent from academic, religious, moral and political pressures: art should not be an instrument of propaganda of any kind (art as opposed to mass culture and its economic interests). However, the arts have paid the price. Their influence seems largely limited to the arts themselves, the institution, their own area. This might well be one of the reasons why the authorities in the Western world accept the arts more tolerantly than in most other parts of the world; in the West politicians hardly fear the arts any more.

In African countries, art and society seem to be more strongly intertwined than in the West. The Nigerian writer Wole Soyinka once said: "The artist has always functioned in African society as the record of mores and experiences of his society *and* as the voice of vision in his own time".[18]

Today, Western mass culture has a tremendous impact everywhere in the world, because of the global reach of the international media. This will continue to have a number of consequences, leading to the uniformity of cultural patterns that are not only accepted but, in many cases, deliberately stimulated by governments outside the Western world.

Authorities seem to view this kind of Western culture as politically more innocuous than many of the domestic art forms. At the same time, political leaders reject, ban, arrest, and oppress writers who are critical of contemporary society, more than ever, because these artists still have an impact in their own society.[19]

Thus, there is a steady flow of artistic and intellectual talent to the West where free expression has fewer consequences. In many countries, the authorities are suspicious of any popular artistic experiments involving social or political criticism. This is particularly true as far as popular songs and theatrical performances are concerned, because these are understood and appreciated by "the masses".

Can contemporary writers still record "the mores and experience of their society"? And for whom are they still allowed to be "the voice of vision in their own time"? This is a very relevant question for anyone who wants to write a national literary history, with far-reaching consequences for the entire culture and literature rooted in the national soil. Indeed, when writing literary history, one must try and measure the extent of the cultural loss caused by the political reality of the country concerned. What will happen to national culture and national literature if the bulk of creators, authors and critics are absent from the national scene? Fanon was right once more when he said more than twenty-five years ago: "Se battre pour la culture nationale c'est d'abord se battre pour la libération de la nation".[20] (To fight for a national culture is first and foremost to fight for the liberation of the nation).

V. ORAL LITERATURE AND WRITTEN ORALITY

Can one speak of *literature* in the case of oral tradition? African scholars, e.g. the late Pius Zirimu from Uganda, have introduced the concept of *orature* opposite to *literature*. The former would then refer to oral "texts" and the latter to written ones. Most of the time we deal with oral literature only in transcribed, written form. In any case it seems to me that there is not so much of a problem in maintaining the concept of oral literature referring to orally presented "texts" as well as to texts transcribed *literally* from the oral performance. As literary texts they can be distinguished by calling the former *dicts* and the latter *scripts*. In the words of Monroe Beardsley: "scripts and dicts are both texts; moreover, a particular script and a particular dict may be the same text".[1] Whether oral materials have been changed or adapted – so that a new text in the written tradition has been created – can only be seriously checked when tapes of the performance are available.

In fact an oral "text" does not exist without the performance itself: the very presence of the performer, story-teller, singer, without whom oral literature cannot even exist, is a fundamental characteristic which in the past has often been overlooked. Oral literature has often been left by scholars of literature as a stepchild to anthropologists and folklorists who in general lack the literary perspective on these "texts". In her *Oral Literature in Africa*, Ruth Finnegan rightly stated that in oral literature research scholars have been wrong not to ask questions that are asked with regard to written literature:

There has been a tendency to play down the significance of the contemporary verbalization and performance of the story as a whole in favour of an attempt to trace back the detailed history of certain elements of its subject-matter.[2]

The artistic genius and the literary devices used by the author are hardly taken into account and all the attention is fixed on non-literary aspects. Writers are gifted or mediocre and this holds also with regard to oral story-tellers, as Obiechina tells us:

> The folktale . . . belongs in its bare outline to the community until the individual picks it up and, during the process of narration, makes it his own. There is therefore no single authentic text. The skeletal text which embodies the well-known motif is there and, sometimes, the underlying exemplum. The individual narrator using the former builds it up by the use of his own methods. There could therefore be as many texts for one story as there are narrators, some of them very good, some indifferent and others downright poor, depending on the competence or otherwise of the individual.[3]

In *Culture, Tradition and Society*, the same author described how much the oral tradition is still alive in Africa today, in spite of Western influence. The links between city-dwellers and villagers are very strong. A large number of West Africans are still illiterate; others read and write in their vernacular languages only and are thus not influenced by Western literature. According to Obiechina, the majority of the West African population continues to live in an oral rather than a written culture and to express itself within the norms of the oral tradition.[4]

In the following pages the relations between oral and written literatures in Africa will be investigated in written texts that have obvious links with oral literature. For that purpose, the works of the Nigerian writer Amos Tutuola will serve as

[65]

a reference point in this chapter, while some general influences of oral literature on contemporary theatre will be studied in chapter VI.

The West African oral culture referred to above is the fertile
soil in which the works of many contemporary African writers are firmly rooted. They are indebted to the oral tradition
for themes, images, characters, rhythms, expressions and so
forth.

In 1983, the oral tradition as a source of inspiration for the
contemporary writer was the theme of an important colloquium in Dakar where Bernard Dadié (Ivory Coast), Akin-
wumi Isola (Nigeria), Léopold Sédar Senghor (Senegal), Jean
Pliya (Benin) and other writers personally confirmed and
explained the impact of oral traditions on their own writings.
It was clear that they do not limit themselves to inspiration
from the particular tradition of the culture of their own
people.[5] As a writer one is completely free. "The author
chooses his own precursors", as the Argentinian Luis Borges
once said, and of course this holds for oral and writing
authors.

It is obvious that Amos Tutuola plundered his oral ancestors in a quite straightforward way. Therefore it is interesting
to analyze what I have called his "written orality". This
apparently contradictory expression came to my mind while
reading his works. In fact, the devices common to oral story-
telling that he uses in his written texts can also be found in
many other literatures. They are comparable to what the
Russian Formalists Eichenbaum and Vinogradov called *skaz*
in their own literature. *Skaz* is described as a narrative mode
which is inspired by the verbal art as practised by the popular
story-teller. The artistic prose structured according to the
skaz devices is clearly distinguished from the written Russian
tradition by its transposition of characteristic features of oral
discourse into the written text. In order to appreciate the
qualities of such texts adequately, one needs to study them
with "ear philology" as well as with "eye philology".[6] The
skaz analyzed by the Russian Formalists in the early decades

[66]

of the twentieth century corresponds with the written orality in so many works of African authors. Indeed, *skaz* and written orality feed on the same source: the art of the oral storyteller. However, it goes without saying that African written orality is born in a very different context than the Russian *skaz*, when looked at from the perspective of literary history. *Skaz* is a narrative technique which is a reaction to the written tradition of solemn nineteenth and twentieth century Russian prose, while written orality practised by African writers directly continues the often age-long tradition of fully alive African story-telling.

Amos Tutuola's works are respresentatives *par excellence* of written orality, in their language as well as in their composition. His particular language usage raised, right from the beginning, widely different comments, among his critics. They varied from a positive appreciation of his "young English" (Dylan Thomas in *The Observer*), or his "fresh West African idiom" (Ulli Beier in *Black Orpheus*), to a pitiless condemnation of his "incomprehensible" language by some bourgeois compatriots who felt embarrassed by the original use this "illiterate" made of the Queen's English.[7] In her article "The Palm-Wine Drinkard: A Reassessment of Amos Tutuola," Omolara Ogundipe-Leslie, whose mother tongue is Yoruba, underlined the personal nature of Tutuola's language, which she defined as an original mixture made of "scraps of language such as officialese, journalese, and ungrammatical English words of the Yoruba language: in fact, Tutuola speaks Yoruba using English words.[8] Many of his figures of speech (repetitions, puns, antitheses, metaphors, proverbs, riddles, and so on) come from his mother tongue and are not always easy to detect and understand for the non-Yoruba, who, as a foreigner, should be modest and cautious in interpreting Tutuola's texts. Nevertheless, there are many examples of his language usage which also strike the non-Yoruba: for instance, the puns and repetitions as in the quotation from *The Palm-Wine Drinkard*:

[67]

My wife had said of the woman we met: "She was not a human-being and she was not a spirit, but what was she?" She was the Red-smaller-tree who was at the front of the bigger Red-tree, and the bigger Red-tree was the Red-king of the Red-people of Red-town and the Red-bush and also the Red-leaves on the bigger Red-tree were the Red-people of the Red-town in the Red-bush.[9]

Or, in the story of Ajaiyi, with the antitheses and repetitions right on the first page:

This story happened about two hundred years ago when I first came to this world through another father and mother. By that time I was a boy and not a girl, by that time I was the poorest farmer and not as a story-teller, by that time I was the most wicked gentile and the strongest worshipper of all kinds of the false gods and not a christian, by that time there were no cars on the roads or the aeroplanes on the sky but to trek from village to village and to cross large rivers by hand-made canoes and not by steamships.[10]

The use of proverbs is a technique of verbal expression that helps to clarify a situation through metaphors. Ruth Finnegan demonstrated the mutual relations between proverbs and other oral forms of literature like tales, anecdotes, songs and riddles. Proverbs are also "part of conversation and palavers".[11] In all Tutuola's works proverbs are to be found, but he uses them in a special way in *The Brave African Huntress* and in *Ajaiyi and His Inherited Poverty*: they figure as chapter titles and are then repeated during the action they refer to. Sometimes these proverbs of Yoruba origin are not at all clear to outsiders, perhaps partly because of Tutuola's English translations, e.g. the meaning of the one quoted in the amusing story of the huntress Adebisi who became the king's hairdresser in Ibembe city: "The thief who steals bugle. Where is he going to blow it?" Ulli Beier explained that bugle is the English translation of the Yoruba word *akaki*, the bugle which can only be played in the presence of the king: so it is useless to steal it![12]

Other proverbs are less obscure like the following ones: "The rain does not know the honourable person apart. But the rain soaks anybody who comes out when it is raining"; "The rope of the truth is thin but there is nobody who can cut it"; "The rope of lies is as thick as a large pillar but it can be cut easily into a thousand pieces"; "No one claims relationships with a poor man, but when he is rich, everyone becomes his relative", and so forth.

The function of proverbs in oral literature in general, as well as in Tutuola's written works, is to reinforce the author's argument, to animate the story or to explain some situation or behaviour. Thus, a proverb is quoted after Adebisi's killing of the bird-monster; she receives wonderful gifts from the king and his subjects, who come and look at the corpse and take feathers from the voracious animal which they had never dared touch alive: "It is after the elephant is dead that everybody will go near it and cut its flesh" (p. 40).

In oral literature, there are often plenty of songs; in Tutuola's stories, however, they are quite rare. Here Tutuola has probably felt obliged to give in to the written form. As a matter of fact, this happens quite often when oral performance is written down, as one can see in most published collections of stories from the oral tradition. In reality, songs are much more common than those collections and, in our case, Tutuola's works would make us believe. Ruth Finnegan explains it this way: "Since the songs are almost always so much more difficult to record than prose, they are usually omitted in published versions; even when they are included, the extent to which they are repeated and the proportion of time they occupy compared to spoken narration is often not made clear".[13]

The lack of songs is particularly striking in the story of Simbi, the girl with the marvellous voice that enables her to resuscitate the dead. According to Obiechina, a story-telling

[69]

performance in which Simbi risks being sacrificed to the gods by the king of the fishermen's village would have produced an operatic effect which it no longer has in the written version, in spite of the description of the alternate songs:

"Please, the King, set the rest of us free."
    "Ha! -a! -a! don't you think you know you have become the slave of these gods this midnight!"
"Please, the chiefs, deliver us from these gods!"
"Ha! -a! -a! you chiefs, don't you hear her plead now!"[14]

The King, the chiefs, the high and the low people reply – also in the form of a song – that Simbi's death is imminent. When Simbi hears these words, she immediately starts another song, so gay and enjoyable that it makes everybody join in a dance. One can imagine that a good oral story-teller would succeed in making his audience sing while performing these scenes. Of course, in the written form such devices easily lose most of their effect.[15]

In *The Brave African Huntress*, there are also passages to be sung: the "singing gourd" (p. 129) is an example. Another one is of course the victorious song of Adebisi and her men, hale and hearty in their canoes on the way back home. It is an African adaptation of a "modern" Western song Tutuola must have known from the radio. Before their departure from the forest, Adebisi and her friends have eaten strange fruits, as sweet as chocolate and as creamy and cold as ice-cream. Adebisi tells:

As they were eating them at a time they formed a kind of song.
They first shouted greatly with great joy just to show that they were leaving this jungle safely. And as they were singing this song they began to paddle the canoes along homeward . . .
the song which they were singing went –
"Bulla-bul-laha: Shaka-bul-laha

With all chocolates: bullaha-bul-laha
Ice-cream: You scream: row o: row o o: row o o o
killed all the pigmies
Monday-Tuesday-with all Ice-cream:
for Ice-cream: row o: row o o: row o o o . . . " (p. 149)

Shakabulla is the name of the gun the huntress used in her adventures. The above quotation demonstrates the improvisational nature of such songs. It also illustrates the existence of happy marriages between traditional and Western dict and script elements in oral literature as well as in written orality. We'll come back to this point later.

Dilemma tales are a particular genre in the oral tradition. These are prose stories with an open ending, a moral problem for the audience to discuss; for example, who, among the characters, was most right behaving as he or she did, who has to be condemned, who has to be rewarded etc. Sometimes the solution is impossible or highly delicate:

> The choices are difficult ones and usually involve discrimination on ethical, moral or legal grounds. Other dilemma tales, which border on tall tales, ask the listeners to judge the relative skills of characters who have performed incredible feats . . . their special quality is that they train those who engage in these discussions in the skills of argumentations and debate and thus prepare them for participating effectively in the adjudication of disputes, both within the family or lineage and in formal courts of law.[15]

Tutuola inserts some of these tales in his books. The best-known are the moral dilemmas he describes in *The Palm-Wine Drinkard*: the hero explains that his wife has fallen ill and that they are forced to spend some time in the "mixed town". To amuse himself, the Palm-Wine Drinkard attends court cases and after a while he is asked to judge some cases himself. Thus, exactly as in an oral performance, the narrator creates an opportunity not only to present dilemmas, but

[71]

also to comment and reflect upon problems of lending and borrowing money, or relations between husband and wives. In the latter dilemma story, a husband has three wives who all love him very much. Unfortunately, "as they were travelling from bush to bush, this man . . . fell down unexpectedly and died at once" (p. 113). Immediately the senior wife dies too, out of solidarity, the second wife goes to find a "Wizard" whose work is "to wake deads", while the third wife stays near the bodies to prevent the wild animals from eating them before the Wizard's arrival. The husband is woken up by the Wizard who then wants one of the wives as a reward. However, the three of them all refuse to be separated from their husband:

> When their husband saw that none of his wives wanted to follow the Wizard, then he told the Wizard to take the whole of them, so when the three wives heard so from their husband, they were fighting among themselves; unluckily, a police-man was passing by that time and charged them to the court. So the whole people in the court wanted me to choose one of the wives who was essential for the Wizard. (p. 114)

The Palm-Wine Drinkard feels unable to solve the dilemma, because the three women have been loving spouses. So he adjourns the judgement of the case for a year. In fact, many dilemmas like this one cannot and are not meant to be resolved, as Obiechina indicates. In the oral performance, "the duty of the traditional story-teller is to enunciate it in the clearest way possible and to leave each individual to reach his own solution if he can".[16]

In his presentation of such dilemmas, Tutuola literally follows the oral tradition: he has succeeded in preserving their nature while writing them down. The end of a dilemma story is not an end, but a beginning of the inevitable debate among the audience, who try to find the best possible solutions. Of course, the arguments are strengthened all the time by means of proverbs. In the written presentation this part of the performance gets lost. Tutuola has got round this by using the very device of the written word: making the hero directly address his readers with the request to send him letters at home with comments on the dilemmas:

> So I shall be very much grateful if anyone who reads this story-book can judge one or both cases and send the judgement to me as early as possible, because the whole people in the "mixed town" want me very urgently to come and judge the two cases. (p. 115)

In the oral story-telling, descriptions are often quite limited. Here, I can make only some general remarks on that matter. In tales, if we get to know characters, it is through their actions: the personages are hardly described, even their names are often not mentioned.

The same holds for the setting: houses, villages, landscapes, members of the family, friends of the hero are not described in detail. They function as the point of departure or as a background of action for the hero: they are often there to be left behind, so to speak. The departure is the beginning of the action, the basis for the events to come. Parents, children, friends, enemies, animals, monsters, dwarves, giants, witches, wizards, objects, means of transportation are presented and summarily described only to the extent required for the action.

This economy of depiction is also typical of Tutuola's written stories. We do not get to know the wife or the monster-child of the *Palm-Wine Drinkard* through a description, and his father dies before we are really introduced to him. The mother of Simbi in the story of the same name, and the mother of the hero in *My life in the Bush of Ghosts*[17] are only there to be said goodbye to and to be found again at the end of the adventures. Nor is there any description of Adebisi's father: all that is mentioned is that he is too old to fight the pygmies of the forest, a piece of information we need in order to understand that now Adebisi has to do this in his place. The parents of the hero in *Feather Woman of the Jungle*[18] are too old and miserable to go in search of good luck and this also holds for the pitiful hunchback parents of Ajaiyi and Aina, who die even before the adventures of these children begin. Of course, these are all minor characters but the main characters are not presented in much more detail. Consider the famous presentation of the *Palm-Wine Drinkard* in the book's opening scene. The only information we get is that the hero has been an "expert palm-wine drinkard" since he was a boy of ten. *Simbi*, we are told, is beautiful and rich and she has a marvellous voice. The hero of *My Life in the Bush of Ghosts* presents himself, telling us only that he was seven years old when he began to understand the meaning of good and bad. Neither do we get to know the characters' physical appearance nor their nature. Their skill, cleverness, courage, perseverance and so forth become obvious through exploits accomplished in the course of painful tests.

Detailed descriptions are only presented when bizarre beings or strange situations are to be faced. Then there is a functional reason for description: it emphasizes the strangeness of the appearance or situation. If necessary, it can properly underline their horrifying aspects. Here is, for example, the description of the red fish that the Palm-Wine Drinkard meets:

Its head was just like a tortoise's head, but it was as big as an elephant's head, and it had over 30 horns and large eyes which surrounded the head. All these horns were spread out as an umbrella. It could not walk but was only gliding on the ground like a snake and its body was just like a bat's body and covered with long red hair like strings. It could only fly to a short distance, and if it shouted a person who was four miles away would hear. All the eyes which surrounded its head were closing and opening at the same time as if a man was pressing a switch on and off. (pp. 79–80)

[74]

Mysterious towns and palaces, terrifying forests and mountains are described to reinforce the supernatural elements in the story. In Tutuola's works one finds plenty of them: the monster of "Wraith-Island" in *The Palm-Wine Drinkard* (p. 47), the witch covered with soft feathers "really grown out from her body" in *Feather Woman of the Jungle* (pp. 14 ff.), the spirits in the *Bush of Ghosts* (passim), the pygmies in *The Brave African Huntress*, and so on.

Commonly, such descriptions present only the exterior of the marvellous world and its inhabitants. The latter manifest themselves through their actions: clearly good or bad. This also holds for the "normal", non-marvellous characters.

The expressive and fantastic form of images and comparisons is often surprising and fascinating. Like other Yoruba writers who follow the oral tradition, such as Fagunwa, Tutuola loves picking up words, repeating expressions, varying details and exaggerating dimensions. He loves impressive hyperboles, he creates humorous effects by enumerating in detail numbers, amounts, distances, hours, and so forth, next to completely unlikely events, which of course strengthens the contrast, as in this passage of the *Palm-Wine Drinkard*:

> I cut a tree and carved it into a paddle, then I gave it to my wife and told her to enter the river with me; when we entered the river, I commanded one juju which was given me by a kind spirit who was a friend of mine and at once the juju changed me to a big canoe. Then my wife . . . used the canoe as "ferry" to carry passengers across the river, the fare for adults was 3d (three pence) and half fare for children. In the evening time, I changed to a man as before and we checked the money that my wife had collected for that day, it was £7:5:3d. (p. 39)

This extraordinary way of combining two worlds, the natural – presented without digression – and the supernatural described abundantly constitutes one of Tutuola's strongest

[75]

artistic qualities. At the same time, however, he lets himself go in a flow of words, accumulating too many details and repetitions in his description of strange phenomena, so that the result is no longer captivating for the reader. In such cases, the author seems to address himself to an audience rather than to a readership, forgetting that his orality is limited by its book form: the resulting weaknesses of the written style would not strike one as such in an oral performance. This explains why critics have complained about his prolixity. It goes without saying that the written form requires a rigorous adaptation of orally acceptable devices. Tutuola, admittedly, has not always succeeded in aptly condensing the orality of his stories as a writer.

In the same way as the natural and the supernatural worlds are combined in oral story-telling, traditional and "modern" elements are mixed in performances. As Ruth Finnegan has already observed: "Not only are there multiple references to obviously recent material introductions – like guns, money, books, lorries, horse-racing, new buildings – but the whole plot of a story can centre around an episode like . . . a young hero winning the football pools".[19] Oral literature is full of this and one need not be astonished about the co-existence of magic and technology in one and the same story: both are part of life in contemporary Africa.

Reading Tutuola's works, we thus find cauri shells as well as English pounds as a means of payment; there are Yoruba Gods next to Christian influences. Obviously the past and the present both interest the story-teller and both provide him with inspiration. Bombs, telegraphs, electric wires, airplanes, telephones, radios, cars, steamships, methodist churches, photographs, guns, money, clocktime and so forth all parade in Tutuola's books, which have nothing out of the ordinary for a readership familiar with oral literature. Like any gifted story-teller, this Nigerian author varies and changes the available material, combining elements from memory, every-day life and phantasy to end up with personal, original, literary texts. The structure he imposes upon

[76]

his material is the novel form in the widest sense of the word: a long fictional prose story dealing with human relationships and actions. He achieves a certain unity thanks to the protagonist, who is the hero of the adventures. The latter often originate from traditional well-known stories. The structure of the episodes is rather vague and their order arbitrary: the author could have omitted some or added some. He could even partially have changed the order without thereby harming the line of action.

When Geoffrey Parrinder – who wrote an interesting introduction to Tutuola's second novel *My Life in the Bush of Ghosts* – asked him the reason for the apparently haphazard order of the ghosts' towns his hero goes through, the author simply replied: "That is the order in which I came to them" (p. 11). Such a reply indicates he proceeded according to the inspiration of the moment, just like the oral story-teller. A number of episodes function as independent stories in oral literature. In the text structure they are linked by means of one or two transitional sentences, and by the theme of human search through frightful adventures.

Gerald Moore and other critics after him have noticed that Tutuola's novel heroes and heroines "follow out one variant or another of the cycle of the heroic monomyth, Departure-Initiation-Return, as analysed by Joseph Campbell in *The Hero With a Thousand Faces*.[20] The oral pattern of this genre is found widely in cultures all over the world. The search of the protagonist is personal: he or she has to confront obstacles and find solutions to his or her problems, all the way to the destination. In *La mère dévorante*, Denise Paulme[21] analysed the initial situation in oral story-telling. According to her, the departure of the hero results either from the initial situation or from its disturbance: the situation is bad in the first case and euphoric in the second case, but that euphoria is quickly destroyed. An existing deficiency (*manque*) thus motivates the search in oral tales, as Paulme convincingly demonstrated. The same applies to Tutuola's books, e.g. the poverty (*manque*) of the hero's parents in *Feather Woman* provokes the

[77]

young man to depart with his brother: the search for wealth motivates the journey. The initial situation in *The Palm-Wine Drinkard*, on the contrary, is euphoric, because he has "no other work more than to drink palm-wine" in his life. The modification brought about by the sudden death of his palm-wine tapster provides the motive for the departure: the hero wants him back. Thus, each protagonist is in search of a new equilibrium as soon as he starts upon his wanderings through a world that combine natural and supernatural elements. Both of these determine human life, and the hero, in search of his equilibrium or identity, explores the two of them in a field of experience far beyond that of ordinary human beings.

In fact the protagonist's journey, his search in a foreign universe, represents at the same time man's descent into himself, his possibilities and limits in the eternal struggle against want and deficiency. Oral literature is probably as old as mankind, so obviously people feel the need to express in dict and script, in poetry and prose, their disguised dreams and the realities about the origins, condition and destiny of man. At the end of their imaginary wanderings the heroes know what life is.

As far as Tutuola is concerned, his world view is optimistic, his heroes don't lack confidence. This vision can be shared by his readership: with him they can become the "Optimistic, daring and defiant African of yesterday" as Taban Lo Liyong has put it.[22] It is significant that Tutuola's heroes always come back home to their unchanged traditional setting. From his perspective, the identity of traditional man is neither threatened nor called into question. In his view there are no things falling apart, there is no question of negritude nor conflict of cultures. Far from being abandoned in the cul-de-sac where certain critics would have liked him to be forgotten, his works are found fully alive at the crossroads where African oral culture meets contemporary writing.

VI. ORAL TRADITION AND AFRICAN THEATRE

The theatre is always a mirror of human existence, and theatrical expression always linked to a specific time and place and culture. Changes in societies generally lead to new forms of dramatic expression. African theatre today "reflects" a variety of societies, due to the simultaneous existence of so many different kinds of communities. In most contemporary African theatre forms, the oral tradition constitutes a source of inspiration to the playwright. This being the case, the question is, *in which ways* do playwrights use the rich oral material? The answer leads in many unexpected and often fascinating directions.

As far as the metaphor of the mirror is concerned, theatre does not "reflect" society in an objective manner. An objective reality does not exist. The theatre is an instrument by means of which dancers, singers, narrators, writers and actors interpret their own ideas about reality as they see it.

Oral literature is inseparable from its performance. Actually, there are strong parallels between oral literature, theatre, dance and music, which all depend on repeated performance for their continued existence. In this sense, plays differ from the rest of written literature.

It has sometimes been asserted that "real theatre" did not exist in precolonial Africa. In Robert Cornevin's book, *Le théâtre en Afrique Noire et à Madagascar* (1970),[1] dedicated, as we said earlier, to the father or "bon oncle" of African drama, Charles Béart (director of the Ecole Supérieure of Bingerville in the nineteen thirties) theatre is, for the most part, compared with theatrical practices introduced since French colonization. Within this perspective, religious plays such as *Les trois Mages*, *La Farce de Maître Patelin* and *Le Malade imaginaire* are merely seen as useful breeding grounds in which "the real African theatre" can begin to flourish. Leaving aside the Eurocentric nature of such thinking, it remains important to ask what the influence of Western culture on African theatre is, or has been. Béart compares the French role in the creation of African theatre with the role the Greeks and Romans played in the creation of theatre in Europe, and Cornevin refers to Béart with great approval.[1]

It goes without saying that it is erroneous to take Western theatre as it has developed in recent centuries as a criterion to determine whether or not theatre exists among other peoples. In Europe the verbal element has come to dominate all other aspects in drama. In other cultures this is not necessarily so: the word may be subordinate to other elements or it may form a harmonious unity with them. All people have dramatic forms of their own. It is always a question of norms within the society in which the specific forms developed. This is unfortunately not the only case of Eurocentric thinking in literary criticism and scholarship: we have dwelt on that point earlier in chapter II. Even in the European context it has represented a rather narrow and elitist view of theatrical forms for quite some time now. Indeed, during the thirties, Antonin Artaud already attacked the purely verbal and psychological character of Western theatre. In his famous *Le théâtre et son double*, written in 1934, he accused the West of having prostituted the theatre:

> Why is it that in the theatre, at least in the theatre as we know it in Europe, for that matter in the West, everything that is specifically theatrical, i.e. everything that doesn't obey expression by speech, by words, or if you wish, everything that is not contained in dialogue . . . is left in the background?[2]

Artaud became passionately interested in Asian theatre and was inspired by the Eastern forms of theatre he was able to see in France at the World Exhibition performances there. He was fascinated by the Eastern aspects of theatre which were not merely verbal: its wide range of facets allowed the Eastern theatre to retain the character of a total theatre – a total theatre as exemplified in so many African traditional· performances.

The ignorance in the Western world regarding traditional African theatre is partly due to a lack of transcriptions of these theatre forms. In his book *The Drama of Black Africa*, Anthony Graham-White gives the following reason for this neglect:

> Why has most traditional drama gone unrecognized? The brief answer is that most observers of traditional performance in Africa who wrote about them have, unfortunately, had no interest in drama. The ironic result was that at the very time that Europe was freeing itself from the restrictive dramatic conventions of the well-made play on the well-made proscenium stage, Europeans in Africa were unconsciously using such standards to judge African cultures as wanting in drama. Groups of performers and spectators roaming a village did not match the European observer's conventional image of theatre.[3]

Perhaps Western anthropologists looked with interest at theatre forms in Africa, but they looked with anthropological eyes and were not interested in theatre as an art form. However, observers, who are indeed interested in the dramatic arts as such are confronted with enormous difficulties. One must not only be fluent in the language of the performance, but also know the context in order to catch the meaning of all the allusions and jokes based upon situations and circumstances with which the audience is familiar. The transcription and description of such theatre is not easy at all.

Another question to be posed is: how to set the borders

between oral narrative and theatre? This is a very complicated point. Oral literature always contains elements of drama: the story-telling performance is a total happening, a total art form, in several ways. The narrator is often, at once, a *poet*, a *singer*, a *musician* and an *actor*. He is a *poet* because he re-creates in his own, improvising way, the traditional "texts". He is able to do so because of his knowledge, mastership and command of the traditional literature. He is a *singer* because he may sing the complete text, or parts of it, and a *musician* when he accompanies himself on his own instrument. Sometimes there is an entire orchestra of percussion instruments, drums, xylophones and so on, or a group of singers and/or dancers. The bard is also an *actor* because he interprets different roles with his voice and mimicry. The performance is total theatre in another sense too, involving as it does the active participation of the audience. Dancing, music and singing have a community aspect and are focused on the dialogue between two groups, or a single person and a group. Dancing, singing and music are still an important part of African written plays, even when the playwrights have been influenced by verbally dominated Western drama.

Very often oral tradition and written literature have been treated as if they were two completely distinct matters. Likewise, in the case of drama, it would be incorrect to treat traditional drama forms as one thing and modern drama as another. The oral tradition continues partly in written literature, and traditional theatre has a great influence on written drama in our time. In many contemporary written plays, the narrator functions very much as he did traditionally. The same holds for a number of other devices in present-day African theatre. On a general level, we can see that the contemporary playwright draws upon such varied oral genres as myth, epic, history, animal stories, popular comedies and farces. As regards *themes*, there are those which are borrowed directly from *literary genres*, for example myth or epic; others are based on *traditional cultural practice*, such as the dowry, fetishism, the authority of age over youth, rituals, etc. As far as *techniques* and *attributes* are concerned, here I consider *formal attributes* such as presentation by a singer or story-teller, inclusion of songs, singing by turns or in refrains, the use of choirs or a group response, the use of music and musical instruments, dance, mime, costumes, masks and so on. It is impossible within the scope of this brief study to consider all these aspects. In the following pages I will show, on the basis of examples from plays, how certain elements from traditional African culture have continued to play an independent role within the European-language theatrical context.

It is dangerous to impose a division of genres in oral literature. The existing European-orientated distinction is, as far as African material is concerned, both inadequate and inaccurate. In Africa, where does myth end and epic begin? What is a legend and what is an historical chronicle? Often all these genres are presented as "actual happenings". The terms "myth", "legend", "folk tale", "fairy-tale", cannot be strictly distinguished in oral literature, they often merge into one another. The proverb is a genre in itself. A story is sometimes based on a proverb, and conversely a proverb is sometimes distilled from a popular story. I cannot pursue this problem further but obviously, if classification is already problematical for the whole of oral literature, then in the case of borrowings from this literature, the characteristics of the original can dominate the characteristics of the genre to an even greater extent within the new literary context. This is no disaster and it can indeed lead to an exciting and enriching new literature, or, in this case, new theatre. Playwrights borrow in numerous ways from the oral genres, and most of them feel absolutely free in their own creative transformation of the original material. Nevertheless, I think that in the sphere of the theatre, it can generally be said that the oral genres to which playwrights return for their inspiration are above all *myth* and *epic history*. Plays are also, but less commonly, based on fairy-tales and animal stories.[4]

Myths are told everywhere in Africa. They are stories of

[83]

creation which explain why the world has become as it is. Real myths always have a deeper and more serious aim than merely telling a story. The myth comprises the "truth", has authority and is accepted as such within the group in which it is told. Myths explain not only the origins of the world, but also the relations between God or the gods and the original ancestors, the relations with the earth upon which life and work take place, along with the culture and customs as they have developed in society.

I'll give a few examples. The Ugandan playwright Tom Omara based the *theme* of his play *The Exodus* on the *myth*, the "story from the beginning", as he calls it, from the north of Uganda, Acholiland, which explains the original separation between the ancestors of the same clan that now live divided on opposite sides of the Nile. As far as the *form* of the play is concerned, he also draws heavily on devices from oral tradition: a narrator introduces the play up to the point where it is taken over by actors. An old song marks the transition from the first part to the moment the actors start. At the end, there is a ceremony in which the brothers swear on their crossed spears that they will never meet again. Another example of the use of myth, song and the narrative frame is the South African play *uNosilimela* by Credo Mutwa. After a short introduction and "The song of the children of the Sun", the story-teller enters and says:

> Ever since Man first began to think, he began to wonder about the origin of the stars, the sun, the mountains, the seas and the miracle of life in them, and he wove shining legends about all this. In the land of the Barotse there are those that say that Man originated from a great tree that grew in the middle of the desert, while in the land of the Batswana they say that Man and the animals crawled out of a great hole in the ground which is still to be seen today . . . And here in our own country, kwaZulu, we believe that man originated from a great reed, uHlanga, that grew on the bank of a mighty river. . . .[5]

[84]

The same myths are sometimes told and/or interpreted very differently in different places and at different times. The way in which the myth is told is closely bound up with the social situation in which it is told. The current situation has an influence on the mythical text which moreover may be manipulated by those in power. Ideology always plays a part. If writers concern themselves with material from the oral tradition, they also always consider the public they have in mind. The best authors know that returning to the roots of their culture does not of itself guarantee artistic success. They also know that simply transcribing the material without relating it to contemporary society may render it sterile. Just as oral literature is itself living and developing with the public for which it is intended, the same holds true for the authors who are inspired by the oral tradition. The art is to give the material a new contemporary reference. Naturally this holds for the use not only of themes but also of techniques.

Myth is often closely related to *history*, and the *epic* contains both mythical and/or historical elements. All three are well-known sources of inspiration for the playwright who of course interprets these sources in his or her own way. Heroes may rise above the historical reality and sometimes even be deified and granted almost mythological status.

In the epic, a mythical and a historical branch can be distinguished. The Mwindo epic of the Nyanga of Zaïre, for example, is a myth-orientated text which contains little in the way of historical elements: Mwindo appears neither in the genealogies of the first ancestors of the Nyanga nor in those of the grandparents or great-grandparents of the chiefs. However, a few aspects point to "the beginning", such as living in holes, the origin of fire, the first hunting dog and the way in which other practices were introduced into their culture.

The other branch of the epic is more historically determined. The hero actually lived and played a role in the history of his people. The epic is by no means always strictly distinguished from the historical chronicle. Where that is the

[85]

case, the historian restricts himself more to recalling the family tree of the ruler, the migrations, wars, conquests, defeats and victories of his own people; these "facts" he passes on to his contemporaries. The epic has another function. It devotes more attention to the artistic form; it is more than a presentation of the historical facts. In the first place, the reciter of the epic wishes to captivate the public. As author and artist, he subordinates his story to his own artistic conception, but a foundation of truth always remains if it concerns historical characters whose famous deeds live on in the memories of later generations. A hallmark of the "historical" branch of the epic is that the hero concerned actually existed: battles, conquests and such like are then authentic, but the figure of the hero is more heroic and his deeds more marvellous than they ever were in reality. Miracles and magical feats appear frequently, and gods and spirits often play an important role. The hero has become more than an "ordinary" ancestor, and often becomes revered almost as a god. An example of this is Chaka, the Zulu hero. There are many plays based on this epic, and a remarkable number are written in French by West Africans. Mostly, they only know Chaka through the French translation of the original by Thomas Mofolo, who first wrote the story in Sotho. The many dramatic versions attest to the great variety of treatment which the original theme can receive.

Senghor emphasised the passion and the spirit of sacrifice of Chaka, while Seydou Badian (Mali) chose the theme of his death and draws him as a black militant fighter. After them, Abdou Anta Kâ (Senegal) saw Chaka as the visionary who foresees the coming of the Boers to his land and so forth. Thus in the words of Ogunbesan, Chaka, the epic hero, became "a King for all Seasons".[6]

There are many other examples: the traditional epic hero Ozidi is the main character in J. P. Clark's play of the same name. Eugène Dervain (Ivory Coast) devoted two of his plays to Da Monzon, a hero from the Bambara tradition. More historically faithful are plays like Ebrahim Hussein's *Kinjeket-*

[86]

ile (1970) or Cheik Ndao's *L'exil d'Alboury* (1967), although both playwrights stress in their respective introductions that they have borrowed freely from imagination when the historical facts did not suit their purpose. History had to be reconstructed in order to have faith in the future restored, as Christophe Dailly put it in *Le théâtre africain*.[7]

One of the historical heroes of Kenya, who lives on in the memories and the oral history of the people, is Dedan Kimathi. In the introduction to their play *The Trial of Dedan Kimathi*, Ngugi wa Thiong'o and Micere Githae Mugo stated their view explicitly:

> The most important thing was for us to reconstruct imaginatively our history, envisioning the world of the Mau Mau and Kimathi in terms of the peasants' and workers' struggle before and after constitutional independence . . . We believe that good theatre is that which is on the side of the people, that which, without masking mistakes and weaknesses, gives people courage and urges them to higher resolves in their struggle for total liberation. So the challenge was to truly depict the masses (symbolised by Kimathi) in the only historically correct perspective: positively, heroically and as the true makers of history.[8]

Here again we see that oral tradition – Ngugi and Micere Mugo consulted people from Kimathi's surroundings to get their oral historical information – is moulded to the intention of the authors.

Traditional stories about animals, or fables, exist in large numbers everywhere in Africa. There are cycles of tales about the hare, the small antelope, the tortoise or the spider. However, plays based upon such animal stories are not that common. I only know them from Ghana. Efua Sutherland developed the oral Ananse stories into new plays. Ananse is a kind of Everyman. As a character he shows people who they are and how human qualities such as greed, ambition, foolishness or slyness affect the community. Efua Sutherland's *The marriage*

[87]

of Anansewa (1975) is an example of this kind of story-telling drama, as the author calls it. Here again the framework of the story-teller is used. He is as omniscient as he normally is in the oral story-telling situation: he knows what is going to happen, he intervenes in the action and comments upon the events. Efua Sutherland also introduces musical inter-mezzos called *mboguo's*, which traditionally may be contributed by people in the audience. A libation is necessary before it all can start, as is often the case in tradition. The singing of the mboguo is accompanied by handclapping and drum rhythms.[9]

Besides the four above-mentioned genres from oral litera-ture that serve as a source of inspiration for the writer, there are many others we cannot deal with here, e.g. all sorts of poetry, from elegies to love poems, riddles and dilemma tales. And of course, there is the *proverb* which is used time and again in contemporary African written literature in gen-eral and in theatre in particular. Here is just one example from Wole Soyinka's play *A Dance of the Forests*:

> If the wind can get lost in the rainstorm it is useless to send him an umbrella. Proverb to bones and silence . . . The eye that looks downwards will certainly see the nose. The hand that dips to the bottom of the pot will eat the biggest snail. The sky grows no grass but if the earth called her barren, it will drink no more milk. The foot of the snake is not split in two like a man's or in hundreds like the centipede's, but if Agere could dance patiently like the snake, he will uncoil the chain that leads into the dead. . . .[10]

Apart from themes from oral genres such as myths, epics and history, there are also *themes* which authors borrow from *traditional customs* and rules – respected, denied or rejected. For example, the plot in Oyono-Mbia's well-known *Trois prétendants . . . un mari* was inspired by the dowry custom; Guy Menga's *La marmite de Koka Mbala* by the old custom that

[88]

elders demanded unconditional obedience from the young. This latter rule led to excesses and abuses of power in the kingdom of Koka-Mbala. In this play, it is not the elders' authority that the younger generation wishes to attack; that remains accepted as is apparent in the Kikongo saying which one of the younger characters quotes with approval: "However big they are, the ears never stick up above their heads". It was only what followed from the exercise of authority that sparked off their opposition. It is the fetish priest who embodies the dictatorial lust for power and his attitude is rejected in the traditional society in which this play takes place. Here there is no question of a link with the contemporary situation: it occurs within the limits of a closed traditional society.[11]

Indeed, greatly diverse traditions exist, offering a wealth of material which can serve as the basis for plays. In the best plays, just as in all good literature, form and content cannot be discussed or handled separately from each other. In connection with the themes, there are a number of *techniques* and dramatic *devices* borrowed from the tradition: the *narrator/ actor* is a character *sine qua non* in oral literature as the presenter of the performance. In contemporary plays, this character is frequently used to provide a framework, an introduction, a link between the acts, or a continual comment on stage events. Omara's *The Exodus* or Mutwa's *uNosilimela*, referred to earlier, both make use of the story-teller to introduce the action, while Efua Sutherland's story-teller in *Anansewa* intervenes throughout.[12]

Just as with the function of the griot or story-teller, *dance* is used in very different ways. A relatively high proportion of plays in European languages include dance and other stylized forms of movement, such as mime, either as ornament or in order to achieve a smooth transition from one act to another. Dance can also form an integral part of a feast celebrated in a particular scene. Or dancers can be brought in to amuse the king, as for example in Guy Menga's *La Marmite de Koka-Mbala*, where the king and his wives enjoy

[89]

watching the two best young dancers from the entire kingdom. In the Zaïrian play *Pas de feu pour les antilopes*, the dance is even an essential part of the plot: in a conflict between two chiefs, a wise bard suggests a settlement not by fighting, but by means of a competition in dance. This is accepted, and while the drums sound and the people encourage the chiefs with song, Mukoko and Manga dance, first to a slow rhythm and then gradually speeding up, until Manga falls exhausted in the dust and Mukoko is applauded as the winner. Dance and drums are indispensable in this play, which ends with another formal feature borrowed from tradition, namely the enthronement ceremony of a chief in which the dance element is equally important. It ends in a "grand unity, in which the entire cast dances the final dance". Such an ending is not exceptional. Another well-known example is Oyono-Mbia's popular *Trois prétendants . . . un mari*, which culminates in a great feast where actors *and* audience dance together. Oyono-Mbia says in his introduction that his intention is to involve the audience as much as possible in the action: the people must be induced to join in the singing spontaneously and where possible to dance. It has naturally given him great pleasure that he has achieved these results in Europe, "and even in England!".[13]

The above examples illustrate how numerous the links are between oral tradition and modern drama, and the great extent to which playwrights have been influenced and moulded by genres, themes and techniques of oral literature.

On the other hand, present-day African drama, particularly the forms and performance of many written African plays, have undeniably been affected by Western influences:

1. The language used is in many cases a European language, although in recent years there has been a significant increase in writing in African languages, and in the use of more than one language in the same play.

2. The verbal element is more important than the music, singing or dancing.
3. The distance between the audience and the stage has increased and an elevated stage is used. The curtain emphasizes the distance between the performer and the audience.
4. The play is presented in a more concentrated form and in much less time than in most traditional performances.
5. Depending on the society, themes have changed.
6. Modern performances, especially if given in a hall in the city, are mostly attended by a small upper-class elite.

In the past, performances were meant for the entire community. Often, this is no longer the case. Referring to the gap severing African theatre in two, Eldred Jones has said that "popular plays never get published and plays which are published are never popular". In practice, the difference between popular theatre and literary theatre is becoming more and more evident. Literary theatre is usually limited to a small audience of schools and universities, but I won't go into that subject here.[14] Instead, I'll briefly talk about popular theatre as it has been developed in recent years by playwrights who have used it as a means of conscientization. Very often, popular productions are not offered to a publisher whereas, on the other hand, a number of published plays have never been performed. A systematic investigation of this phenomenon has not yet been conducted. It is obvious that a European publisher would see little profit in a popular play using different languages side by side, which are only understood by the audience in the area it was written for. The popular playwright takes advantage of the fact that his audience is bilingual or trilingual. This adds an extra dimension to his play which will be appreciated by the audience it is written for. A Christmas play I saw performed in Kisangani was in Kiswahili (the local language) but the soldiers spoke Lingala (the language of the army in Zaire), and the officials

[91]

spoke French (the language of the administration). In this way different languages are used to add to the realistic character of a work. The same use of different languages is to be found in many South African plays, where the police speak the language of the white Boers, whereas other languages, e.g. English, Tsotsi (a sort of city slang) and African languages, are used for other purposes.

The author of a popular play is inspired by the life of the ordinary people for whom he writes his plays. Etherton speaks of an "urban pop culture which has developed in the urban areas: it is a mixture of traditional and new elements".[15] The traditional elements in such plays are borrowed from different traditions and amalgamated into one new form. Unfortunately, the officials in charge of granting subsidies seem to lack enthusiasm for this new popular culture. In most independent African countries, the authenticity of "pure" ancient tradition is considered to be the criterion for artistic merit. Traditional dancing groups receive subsidies and are sent to the Western world as visiting cards from Africa, even though the dancing is adapted to the Western stage and performed out of context.

The ordinary people in the townships dance their own dances without wondering about their "pure" authenticity. For such an audience, a writer like the Zambian Kasoma has written his plays. His is the saying: "In Africa you must bring theatre to the people, not people to the theatre". This Zambian playwright also uses different languages in a play like The Long Arms of the Law (1968) which deal with life in a township in Zambia's Copperbelt. The play continually refers to local situations, popular songs, political leaders and events with which everyone in the audience is familiar.[16] People react enthusiastically. Such plays by popular playwrights are comparable to the Ghanaian Concert Parties and the Nigerian Opera. Alain Ricard described similar popular forms in Togo, where he distinguished between théâtre scolaire and théâtre populaire.[17] Comparable tendencies are to be found in South African theatre. Some groups there were founded by the black students organization SASO (now banned). Most of this popular theatre originates from a mixture of African and Western elements arising out of the social conflicts in the large African cities. The main theme is the pursuit of material security and human contact in the hard reality of urban society. The result of the amalgam of "traditional" and "modern" elements can be very original and, whether published or not, is applauded by the people about whom it is written and for whom it is intended.

To go into this briefly, in South Africa white domination has damaged traditional culture more than anywhere else in Africa. But there have always been counter-currents reacting against this domination, and theatre is an excellent form to bring new opportunities for self-affirmation to the people. All action for cultural freedom is risky and the South African laws are designed to control the lives of the black people in all respects, by the most unbelievable regulations, police intimidation etc.:

There are no black professional theatres in South Africa and no black drama schools. Under the Group Areas Act city centres and commercial theatres are zoned for white use. Blacks may only enter theatres, as players or as spectators, if a special permit is issued . . . Black actors, directors, musicians and others in the theatre are thus confined to their own areas – strictly speaking not just black areas, but African, Indian or coloured as the case may be.[18]

In spite of all the difficulties, black theatre in South Africa is very much alive. In the seventies it changed, in the sense that European theatre norms were abandoned and, whereas in the previous years black art had expressed sorrow and protest against white injustice, it now became more and more a theatre of anger, a theatre that speaks to the black audience about the ways and means to change their situations. Ever since '73, the Black Consciousness leaders have been almost systematically eliminated by the government by means of banning orders, house arrest and prison.

South African black artists have often felt closer to Afro-American liberation movements than to traditional African literature. For instance, after performances of Pinter's *The Caretaker* and Osborne's *Look Back in Anger*, or Anouilh's *Antigone*, the Theatre Council of Natal performed *Requiem for Brother X*, a Black Power play by the American dramatist William Wellington Mackay. This play is set in an American ghetto and the possible responses to oppression by the blacks are dealt with, from assimilation through collaboration to resistance. At the end of the sixties and the beginning of the seventies, plays became more and more radically committed to political change. At the same time there was a move from the black-white cooperation theatre in town centres to theatre for blacks only in the black townships. The theatre forms changed as well: from poetry recitals and concerts as separate identities until in fact the distinction between "drama" and "poetry" disappeared. In an introduction to a recent anthology of black literature, the editor, Mothobi Mutloatse, put it this way:

We are involved in and consumed by an exciting experimental art form that I can only call, to coin a phrase, "proemdra": Prose, Poetry and Drama in one! . . . We are not going to be told how to re-live our feelings, pains and aspirations by anybody who speaks from the platform of his own rickety culture. We'll perform all these exciting, painful, therapeutic and educative creative acts until we run out of energy![19]

The result is a literature in which the oral element becomes very important indeed. It is oral literature, as Mutloatse confirmed when I asked him during his visit to the Netherlands. But it is not so much oral *tradition*. It is essentially urban, and the inspiration comes mainly from the urban situation of people under the Apartheid system. The elements from oral tradition are often much less directly evident than in many plays elsewhere in Africa. One might bear in mind plays like Nkosi's *The Rhythm of Violence* (1964), Leshoai's *Revolution* (1972) or Mqayisa's *Confused Mhlaba* (1974) – which have all been banned in South Africa.

In his introduction to *South African People's Plays*, Robert Mshengu Kavanagh explains this as follows:

> Soweto and other South African urban townships contain the largest concentration of industrialized proletariat in Africa. It is this proletariat in Africa that gave birth to a new, urban, popular tradition of theatre. It is as important to comprehend the significance of this fact as it is to comprehend the extent to which the traditional structure in the rural areas has been shattered . . . To expect, therefore, in the context of such phenomena, a genuine modern traditional theatre with its roots in a vital rural culture is at present unrealistic. All the plays . . . are examples of the new urban, popular theatre that the largest proletariat in Africa has given birth to.[20]

What I said earlier about the export of so-called "pure" authentic tradition by African governments is all the more harrowingly true in South Africa. There, the racist government sponsors European tours of black dance-dramas like *Ipi Tombi* or *Kwa-Zulu*, entertainment with tradition misleadingly used and largely influenced by the Western demand for the exotic, in terms of tourist needs under white direction.

The question I asked earlier was: *How* is the modern playwright inspired by the oral tradition? The answer given dealt with *oral genres*, *themes* and *techniques* in modern plays. However, the question can also be asked and answered from an ideological point of view: how, with what intentions, serving what kind of interests, does the writer use the oral tradition in his texts? An example from the South African context illustrates the point. I referred to Credo Mutwa as one of the playwrights who used myth in his play *uNosilimela*. This play was, for a while, quite popular in South Africa, because it represented a re-evaluation of black culture, one of the ideas of the Black Consciousness Movement. The black cultural heritage had to be rediscovered and *uNosilimela* was considered by many people to be an important contribution to the theatre of Black Consciousness, although the author was never connected with the movement. The play suggests a way out of the destruction, symbolically, as uNosilimela leads the children of Africa "into a new Africa where peace and harmony, based on a revitalization of the old values, are restored, with the High Inyanga (traditional Zulu doctor) as their custodian".[21]

Language, songs, dances and music are beautifully and richly combined; however, Mutwa's ideas are rather romantic and also very conservative: he rejects the modern city and its inhabitants, replacing them by a mystical Eden with a religious hierarchical system. The first performance was in 1973 and the success was enormous, mainly because of the romantic black dream he showed. Then came 1976 and Credo Mutwa revealed on which side he stood: he rejected the militant youth of Soweto and he wrote an unsolicited letter to the Minister of Justice, Jimmy Kruger, in which he "compared Black Consciousness to Nazism and urged the government to suppress the June uprising by sending in the army. In retaliation the people of Soweto burnt his house down about his family's ears".[22]

Does idealization of traditional culture and rejection of the urban environment in the play have anything to do with the author's rejection of the militant students? Politically aware South Africans reproach Mutwa for wanting to present African culture as a "nice black culture for white people" instead of using black culture to bring about change in South African society. To a critic like the South African exile Lewis Nkosi, the question seems to be whether this is possible at all:

The question of a usable tradition still lies at the heart of the problem of South African literature . . . The question

[96]

is not whether Xhosa, Zulu or Sotho cultures exist, from which a writer might derive sustenance in the same way that a Soyinka might draw information from Yoruba lore or Achebe from the Ibo one; it is simply that the Black South African writer is engaged in a contest the nature of which gravely limits his ability to make use of the indigenous tradition . . . In South Africa the pressure of the future is so enormous that looking backwards seems a luxury. The present exerts its own pressures which seem vast, immanent, allconsuming . . .
The black writers' gruff impatience with models from old traditional cultures is due in part to the recognition that such models provide no clues as to how life is to be lived under apartheid conditions where survival is the only test of human intelligence. Without these clues, tribal morality, the grace and dignity of African traditional life, the severe ethical restraints such a way of life imposes, seem for the embattled city-dweller to have only an empty pietistic appeal.[23]

From Nkosi's statement, one might conclude that in a political situation like the one in South Africa it is almost impossible to link the oral tradition with the literature of the present. One might ask whether this is a result of the Apartheid system. Or does it actually have to do with the urban character of South African literature in general? The Mutwa case, on the other hand, shows how relevant the question of the author's intentions is when he makes use of oral tradition in his writing.

Unfortunately, this is also the question the censors ask themselves, and not only in South Africa. Censorship is suffocating many texts and performances, especially of the popular kind, because they reach too many people.

When considering the theatre in South Africa, I personally believe that Nkosi's statement is not as valid here as it is for the case of the novel (which was what he was specifically referring to), because in the popular theatre the traditions of

[97]

music, song, dancing and mimicry are very much alive in the township. Diviners, wakes, weddings, funerals and rural people coming to town, it's all part of the traditional culture preserving some of their characteristics in the urban theatre. Kavanagh described the township audience's expectations as follows: they want a play

> to teach, reveal, comment on either moral or political issues. They require a message. They expect the driving force of the play, its cohesion and its strongest channel of communication to be music and dance. They prefer large casts, many and varied characters, a multiplicity of incidents and a clear narrative emphasis. Playmakers and actors attempt to create plays of this kind usually through a mixture of writing, group improvisation and discussion. Their theatre is oral not literary, public not private. Acting is passionate and committed, energetic and heightened. Laughter is provoked in the midst of tragedy – comedy depends more on movement, gesture and facial expression than on dialogue. Tears are brought by prayer and song. Anger is expressed through purple passages in English. Joy is embodied in dance.[24]

All in all, this description does not seem to be so different from the developments in popular theatre elsewhere in Africa. My conclusion is that the oral tradition is linked by an umbilical cord to the present-day theatre, which continues to hold up the mirror of society to the audience, as it always has. Political authorities are likely to prefer a different reflection of reality than the one shown by the popular theatre and to criticize the way it relies on the oral tradition in its commitment towards change in today's society. In this and many other respects the African theatre is a rich source of inspiration for dramatists outside Africa who are in search of new theatrical forms and experiments in their societies.

VII. "WHO AM I?": FACT AND FICTION IN AFRICAN FIRST-PERSON NARRATIVE

Every day all sorts of narratives are presented to us, orally or in written form, be it comic strips, cartoons, jokes, newspaper articles, letters, tales or autobiographies. Some of these genres seem to adhere to a particular narrative form. Normally, "the news" on radio or t.v. is presented "neutrally", in the third person, while letters and diaries are typical first-person genres.

First-person narrative does not necessarily coincide with autobiographical forms of expression. The author may prefer to "neutralize" his personal autobiographical information by means of a third-person presentation or even by presenting it as a fictional text. However, real autobiographies which are presented as such are generally written in the first person: the subject and object of the narrative are the authors who "tell" and reveal themselves to others, or who wish to bring order into their own past and ultimately wish to explore themselves. There may also be other reasons for autobiographical writing.[1]

These days, a growing number of studies on autobiography are appearing, at least in Europe, and they all seem to agree about the origin of the autobiographical genre, confirming one after the other that the autobiography is a "purely European literary genre", a "creation of Western culture".[2] The English author Stuart Bates goes so far as to put it this way: autobiography manifests itself mainly in Europe and in the European sphere of influence – just like

[99]

syphilis. Or to quote Gusdorf: "If others than Europeans write an autobiography, then it is because they have been annexed by a mentality which was not theirs".[3]

Of course it is not easy to determine what should be defined as "the European mentality". However, one might try to find out whether first-person narrative in general, and autobiography in particular, is present in the literatures of other cultures. Not much research has been done in this field as yet. An exception is Milena Doleželová's *The Chinese Novel at the Turn of the Century*. She points out that obvious changes due to Western influences are to be found in Chinese literature. The tendency toward subjectivization had already been developed to some degree since the seventeenth century:

> Instead of editing various previous sources into sagas exemplifying Chinese history and accepted ideology, novelists began to relate their individual experiences and views drawn from personal observation of society or their own private lives.[4]

The author emphasizes that the first-person personal narrative model – that is the narrative in which the "telling I" is at the same time the main character – is undoubtedly an innovation in the history of Chinese vernacular fiction and she mentions Wu Woyao's *Strange events* as the first occurrence of first person narrative in *baihua* literature. Wu Woyao was an author who had read many Western novels and who always advocated the reading of foreign literature. According to Doleželová, the appearance of the first person personal narrative in the East is especially significant in comparison with Western literature "where first person narrative has been well established since classical Greece".[5] She then comes to the conclusion that the autobiographical first-person narrative as a distinctive genre in Japanese literature had a relatively late start as well. The first examples:

caused a sensation in Japanese circles because the hero

was patently a self-portrait of the author and because the real-life models of the other characters were readily identifiable.[6]

The first Japanese autobiographical first-person narrative was published in 1890. In China, these new forms manifested themselves around the turn of the century.

It has often been argued that the change from third-person to first-person narrative form is not a question of pure formality but indeed affects the text structure. Depending on the readers' norms it may underline the authenticity of the story or it may be used to reinforce the illusion of reality, as a realistic device in the first-person fictional narrative. However that may be, the first-person narrative in which the narrator is also the hero attests to a considerable basis of individualism, as it concentrates more on the narrator's personality and its growth than on the group to which he or she belongs.

In Chinese fiction, it represented a fundamental development which took some time:

it was only in the twenties and thirties of this century that the process leading to the full variety and artistic maturity of first person narrative was accomplished.[7]

This change in literary history was a product – as it always is – of the marriage between inside traditions and outside influences: elements, from the introspective and lyrical tradition of first-person narrative and the extroverted and social-minded tradition from the vernacular fiction were combined with the deeper psychological description from the Western and Japanese first-person novel.[8]

I have dwelt a little longer on this oriental development, to show how interesting it might be to do comparative intercultural research in other directions than the already well-treaded Europe/Africa paths.

My specific intention here is to discuss the first-person narrative form, its main genres and various techniques, as they are used in African literature. Not all the genres I am dealing with are fictional: the autobiography for instance is not, or at least is supposed not, to be fictional.

If we look first of all at the oral tradition, we could say that all oral literature is told in the first person, since, inevitably, the narrator himself is presenting his story to the audience which is on the spot. It is important to distinguish clearly between the *real author* who presents the "text" orally or in print, and the *narrator* who belongs to the text as a narrative transaction. At the other end of the communication line there are the *narratee* and the *real reader*. The narratee "is the agent which is at the very least implicitly addressed by the narrator. A narratee of this kind is always implied, even when the narrator becomes his own narratee".[9] An example of the latter is the diary novel. This may be schematized as follows:

TEXT

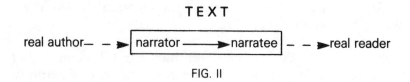

FIG. II

We can even go a step further and say that the real author is always a first-person "agent", whether announcing orally "I am going to tell you . . . " or, silently, in the written form, transmitting his text in book form as a gesture of "I am herewith presenting you my story . . . ". In both cases the text (the "message") can be presented either in the first or in the third person or, although that is much less common, in the second person. I propose that we leave the oral or written "I am going to present you my story" outside the literary texts we are to study here.[10]

The "frontiers" of the oral text are often marked by means

of special formulas or expressions which emphasize the real beginning of the narrative: "Here comes my story"; "Once, long ago"; "How did it happen?"; and so forth. The same is true of the end: "This was the story of hare and leopard" or "This is the end, not of me but of my story".[11]

The first-person presentation by the author is normally lacking in written narrative because the beginning and end of the printed texts make themselves clear without further notice. Thus the written text starts, hierarchically speaking, on the next level, the textual narrative level. The author's explicit "here comes my story" is felt as superfluous and is therefore omitted, but formally the I of the author lies behind every text. A distinction should be made between this "I" and the introduction of "the author" as a literary device *within* the text by writers, as for instance Fagunwa does when he presents his stories in *The Forest of a Thousand Daemons*. He starts his first chapter under the heading: "The Author Meets Akara-Ogun". The latter is presented as the narrator-hero of the story, who dictates it to "the Author":

> When he had spoken thus I hurried to fetch my writing things, brought them over to my table, settled myself in comfort, and let the stranger know that I was now pre-pared for his tale. And he began in the words that follow to tell me the story of his life.[12]

In the text itself, the real author should not be confused with the narrator, although they may be synonymous and coincide with the main character, as in the case of autobiographical writing. In the terms of Gérard Genette, one could say that a narrator who is "above" or superior to the story he tells, should be called an "extradiegetic" narrator (*diegesis* meaning the story) if he belongs only to the narrative level and does not participate in the story as a character. He is to be called an "intradiegetic" narrator if he also participates in the pre-sented story as a character.[13] This is the case with "the Author" in Fagunwa's *Forest of a Thousand Daemons*: the narra-

[103]

tor-character tells how he starts writing down Akara-Ogun's adventures. These adventures are told to him by Akara-Ogun who is himself the hero on the next level. Thus we find a narrator-character's presentation of a whole series of embedded stories in which the second narrator is the main character. At the end of each chapter the narrator of the first level "takes over" again and switches back to the frame of the first level narrative (see fig. III):

Fagunwa writes:	I First narrative level: "the Author" tells about meeting Akara-Ogun who introduces II	II Sec. narrative level: Akara-Ogun's (= hero's) adventures	I First narrative level: "the Author" becomes narrator again: back to the "embedding" first level

FIG. III

There are different types of narrators. The narrator is a device, a construction which is there to serve the specific needs of narration in a particular text. The first-person narrative can be presented in such different forms as a letter, an epistolary novel, a real or a fictional diary, an autobiography and many mixed or in-between forms. The narrator is an agent of the text which can be identical with the real author (as in the autobiography, for instance) or fictional.

The hierarchy of narrative levels can be used by the author in various ways. In the case of Fagunwa, it is clear that the use of the first narrator serves as a narrative framework only to present the character who is going to tell another (= the main) story consisting of the series of adventures. The latter is an inner narrative which is subordinate to the first-level

[104]

narrative in which it is embedded. The function of the embedded narrative in this case is a *function of action*.

The embedded narrative may also have other functions, for example *an explicative function*, like in Achebe's *Things Fall Apart* (p. 72), answering a question of the first level by telling a second story on a "lower" level ("hypodiegetic") embedded by the first one: Okonkwo suffers from mosquitoes whining around his ears and he suddenly remembers the story his mother once told him about why Mosquito always attacks Ear.[14] In the beginning of *Aké*, Wole Soyinka described the parsonage and the Canon's square white building as:

> a bulwark against the menace and the siege of the wood spirits. Its rear wall demarcated their territory, stopped them from taking liberties with the world of humans.[15]

This is followed by further allusions to spirits, ghosts and gommids together with references to the Bible. He then fits in his mother's experiences with spirits and daemons by means of an embedded, explicative narrative, in which Wild Christian is the narrator and the young Wole and his sister are the audience. It is an explicative, inserted story about the mixture of Christian and African beliefs in his mother's faith.

The third function an embedded narrative can have is *thematic*: "the relations established between the hypodiegetic and the diegetic level are those of analogy, i.e. similarity and contrast".[16] A good example of the thematic use of embedded narrative is to be found in Mariama Bâ's *Une si longue lettre*. In the main narrative level of this epistolary novel, another story is embedded, also in the form of a letter. Besides this formal analogy (and many thematic analogical elements), there is also a contrasting point vis-à-vis the main theme: the friend, Aïssatou, to whom the heroine addresses her long letter, divorced when her husband took a second wife, while the main character, Ramatoulaye, has swallowed her disappointment and accepted her husband's second marriage and his subsequent behaviour. The narrator-heroine quotes the

[105]

whole letter in which her friend tells her husband she wants to leave him. The thematic analogy gives an extra dimension to the main (Ramatoulaye's) story. The latter, who is the first narrator in the book, in this passage yields the act of narration to a character (i.e. her friend Aïssatou) who presents, on the hypodiegetic level, her narrative to another addressee (= the narratee): Mawdo her husband. The thematic parallel – the effects on a first wife of a husband's taking a second wife – in this "mirror story" is reversed by an opposite reaction: divorce in the embedded story versus acceptance in the main narrative.[17] Of course the transition from one level to the other is not always as clearly indicated as in the above examples.

"Who speaks?" and "Who sees?"

First-person narrators can take different positions with regard to the narrated events: First, they can tell a story in which they are or have been the hero/heroine; second, they can tell a story in which they mainly figure as observers; or third, they can tell a story which has been transmitted to them by somebody else in an oral or written form and which they are merely "presenting literally" on paper now.

In the first case, the "I" has a central position on the first level, as a narrator, and also on the second level, the level of the story itself where the "I" acts and is presented as the main character. In this case first-person narrators tell and observe; they express themselves and recall their past experiences, as in Tutuola's *Palm-wine Drinkard* or his *Feather Woman of the Jungle*.[18] An example of the second category is *The Poor Christ of Bomba*: in his diary Denis observes the Reverend Father Dumont, who is the main character in this diary novel, although we also get to know Denis himself as an important character through his comments and reflections. One example of the third category is Fagunwa's afore-mentioned book;

a second example could be Ferdinand Oyono's *Houseboy*. In Fagunwa's case, the main story has been transmitted orally to the first narrator on the extradiegetic level, while in the second case the first narrator functions as the translator and "editor" of the received manuscript.[19]

In the field of narratology, it is useful to raise two questions concerning the relation between narrator and character, namely Who speaks? and Who sees? In terms of concepts, a distinction is to be made between *narration* and *focalization*. The narrator tells the story but at the same time the events and situations are presented from a specific perspective, a point of view, which is not always necessarily the narrator's. For instance, in the scene in which Denis tells about the Father's quarrel with the chief whom he wants to forbid to dance, the focalization shifts from the Chief to the Father, while the narrator remains the same, i.e. Denis in his diary:

> The chief himself was still glaring murderously at the Father, but they gripped him tight. The Father looked back at the chief with a sort of amused pity, quite free of dislike. (p. 55)

In most studies about perspective or point of view,[20] narration and focalization have often been used confusingly, as is demonstrated convincingly, by Shlomith Rimmon (who uses the word "agent" instead of "character"):

> Obviously, a person (and, by analogy, a narrative agent) is capable of both speaking and seeing and even of doing things at the same time – a state of affairs which facilitates the confusion between the two activities. Moreover, it is almost impossible to speak without betraying some personal "point of view", if only through the very language used. But a person (and, by analogy, a narrative agent) is also capable of undertaking to tell what another person sees or has seen. Thus, speaking and seeing, narration and focalization, may, but need not, be attributed to the same

[107]

agent. The distinction between the two activities is a theoretical necessity, and only on its basis can the interrelations between them be studied with precision.[21]

The focalization can shift from one character to another and is therefore an important device in its contribution to the effect a character may have on the reader. If we are not aware of it, we are easily manipulated in our opinions, as Eleanor Wachtel stresses with regard to contemporary Kenyan autobiographical novels:

> As in nearly all third-world countries, most of the Kenyan novelists are men. Their central characters are preponderantly males. Further, the male viewpoint is underlined not only by the many characterizations of young men, but by the literary device of the first person protagonist . . . This is quite natural to the relatively inexperienced author who would tend to be somewhat autobiographical anyway. At the same time, however, it is also more intimate, personal, and hence, more explicitly male in outlook and tone . . . This device creates a rapport between author and reader and enlists the latter's sympathy. It does not allow for another point of view . . . Women are necessarily "the other". In Kenya, this male-focused lens on life is an accurate reflection of society. It is consistent with a society where men are the primary decision-makers.[22]

Although narration and focalization can coincide in first-person narrative, they can also be separate, as they often clearly are in first-person retrospective narratives. I give an example of both. In Mariama Bâ's novel, the following quotation shows how narration and focalization coincide (attributed to the same "agent", to use Rimmon's term):

> Modou Fall is indeed dead, Aissatou. The uninterrupted procession of men and women who have "learned" of it, the wails and tears all around me, confirm his death. This

condition of extreme tension sharpens my sufferings and continues till the following day, the day of interment (p. 3).

In *Aké*, the difference between narrator and character-focalizer is clear in the following lines:

> I lay on the mat pretending to be still asleep. It had become a morning pastime, watching him exercise by the window. A chart was pinned to the wall, next to the mirror. Essay did his best to imitate the white gymnast . . . There was a precise fusslessness even in the most strenuous movements. In . . . Out . . . In . . . Out . . . breathing deeply. He bent over, touched his toes, slewed from one side to the other, rotated his body on its axis. He opened his hands and clenched them, raising one arm after the other as if invisible weights were suspended from them. Sweat prickles emerged in agreed order, joined together in disciplined rivulets. Finally, he picked up the towel – the session was over. (p. 77)

In *Aké*, it is the (author-)narrator, the older Wole, who tells, but the (author-)character, the younger Wole, who sees, who focalizes his father's actions. Focalization has a subject and an object: the focalizer is the agent whose perception leads the presentation; the focalized object is (the selection of) what the focalizer perceives.[23] Focalization is not purely perceptive as in the *Aké* example; it is also psychological (cognitive and emotive) and ideological. All these aspects may harmonize or belong to different focalizers. An example of the psychological aspect is to be found in the following quotation from *Aké*, where the reactions the young Wole felt after his little sister's death are recounted by the narrator so many years later:

> Suddenly, it all broke up within me. A force from nowhere pressed me against the bed and I howled. As I was picked

up I struggled against my father's soothing voice, tears all
over me. I was sucked into a place of loss whose cause or
definition remained elusive. I did not comprehend it yet.
(p. 98)

The ideological facet of the focalization, or the norms of the
text, consists in the evaluation of events and characters. It
can be presented "through a single dominant perspective,
that of the narrator-focalizer". The latter's ideology is then
considered as "authoritative". In the first-person retrospective narrative, one often finds the latter's view as superior to
the narrator-character's earlier views recalled by the older I,
many years afterwards. If other norm systems are presented
as well, they are generally evaluated in comparison with the
narrator-focalizer's ideological authority.[24] In the following
example several ideological viewpoints are presented, but
the main perspective throughout the text is the narrator's,
who imposes himself at the end:

After dinner the Father set to work with the catechist. I
followed the interrogation as long as I could, then went to
bed. Zacharia exasperated me again with his uninvited
interventions. For instance, the Father asked the catechist
this question: "Why is it, do you think, that so many
backslide from the true religion? Why did they come to
Mass in the first place?" The catechist answered: "My
Father, at that time we were poor. Well, doesn't the Kingdom of Heaven belong to the poor? So there's nothing
surprising in many of them running then to the true God.
But nowadays, as you know yourself, Father, they are
making pots of money by selling their cocoa to the Greeks;
they are all rich. Now, isn't it easier for a camel to pass
through a needle's eye than for a rich man to enter the
Kingdom of . . . ?" But just then Zacharia blurted out,
interrupting the wise words of the catechist: "Get away
with you! That's not the truth of the matter at all. I tell
you just how it is, Father. The first of us who ran to your

religion, came to it as a sort of . . . revelation. Yes, that's it, a revelation; a school where they could learn your secret, the secret of your power, of your aeroplanes and railways . . . in a word, the secret of your mystery. Instead of that, you began talking to them of God, of the soul, of eternal life, and so forth. Do you really suppose they didn't know those things already, long before you came? So of course, they decided that you were hiding something. Later, they saw that if they had money they could get plenty of things for themselves – gramophones and cars, and perhaps even aeroplanes one day. Well, then! They are turning from religion and running elsewhere, after money, no less. That's the truth of it, Father. As for the rest, it's all make-believe . . . " And speaking in this fashion, he put on an important air. I was boiling with indignation when I heard this illiterate gabble, this "bla-bla-bla" . . . I was hot with anger. I would gladly have slapped his silly face. But the Father listened to him with great attention. (pp. 29–30)

Thanks to the irony of the author this assertive ideological main perspective is, after all, effectively undermined. The norms of the text may be presented through statements by the narrator and or one or more characters; norms can also be implicitly given with events and behaviour as they are narrated and perceived by narrator or characters. The device of shifting the focalization among the different characters or from narrator to character always affects the meaning of a text. When the focalization shifts regularly in the text, we may get a rather broad idea of the various aspects of a conflict or problem. This technique may produce the suggestion of the narrator's neutrality vis-à-vis the various characters and their relations: this is often the case in the realistic novel (subject of the next chapter). The way the focalization is handled definitely contributes to the effect a character (and in fact the whole text) has on the reader, e.g. we are more inclined to share views or to sympathize with a character when the story is presented mainly from his or her particular view, feeling, ideology. The fact that in *The Poor Christ of Bomba* the missionary's servant Denis is the first-person narrator as well as the main focalizer in the text results in a specific view and coloured information.

Different first-person genres

Without pretending to give a complete and detailed inventory of the various first-person narrative forms to be found in African prose, I will try to present a brief description of the main genres as they are mentioned in figure IV.

FIRST-PERSON NARRATIVE

FACTUAL	FICTIONAL
a. Diary	a. Diary novel
b. Letters	b. Epistolary novel
c. Autobiography	c. First person memoir novel

FIG. IV

In African literature, many first-person narratives are presented as autobiographical. The construction is often that of the older I who looks back to his/her earlier life and who, usually years later, narrates what he/she remembers from the past. Many texts of this kind deal with the theme of colonialism, e.g. in *Cette Afrique-là*, the old Mômha tells his experiences which, in a foreword, the author, Ikellé-Matiba, authenticates as "real events". Mômha was born before the colonial occupation of his country, Cameroon, by the Ger-

[112]

mans and in this book he presents his life and "cette Afrique-là que nous ne verrons plus".[25]

Before giving a brief description and some examples of the above-mentioned genres, I should like to look more closely at the opposition between "facts" and "fiction" as it has been used here. This point always raises more questions than can be answered. Sometimes authors pretend to speak the truth while in fact they are telling lies or producing phantasies. Others pretend to be writing fiction while they are telling the story of their own life. Of course, some of the facts are verifiable, notably when the author refers to concrete places and well-known events. However, thoughts, dreams, feeling and beliefs are never controllable. Some scholars have pointed out that an autobiography may contain only historical, biographical material about the author, while others claim that the autobiographer should have the right to see and express himself as subjectively as he pleases. In all this confusion, the real autobiographical narrative must meet one overall minimum requirement, i.e. the *autobiographical pact* as it has been defined by Philippe Lejeune: in his view the autobiography is a retrospective narrative in prose told by an existing person about his or her own existence, when his/her personal life is emphasized and particularly the story of his/her own personality. From that definition we may deduce the following:

1. the form is a prose narrative
2. the subject is the life story (the growth of the personality)
3. author and narrator are identical
4. author and main character are identical and the story is retrospectively told.[26]

The "pact" is realized when the reader gets the guarantee from the text that the author, narrator and main character are one and the same person. This is a formal, verifiable criterion on the basis of which one can determine whether a given text is autobiographical or not. For the rest, it is seldom possible to establish exactly to what degree invented or untrue elements have been introduced in the autobiographical text. Taking this pact as our starting point, let us now look at the different genres, on the factual and the fictional side. I will deal briefly with each corresponding pair on the comparative level.

Diary and diary novel

In Western literature, the diary has been regarded as a literary genre only since well-known writers, such as André Gide, began to publish their diaries. In Africa, very few diaries have been published as yet. Like the autobiography, the diary respects the pact: author=narrator=character. The time aspect distinguishes the diary from the autobiography most clearly, although the contrast is sometimes less extreme than one might think at first sight. In the autobiography, as we have seen, the story of the author's life is told, at a much later moment in life. Conversely the diary follows the events very closely. Nevertheless, the diary is not very often kept conscientiously day by day: it covers recent events, thoughts, feelings which are still there, fresh in memory.

The difference in time distance between the experiences and the moment of writing, in the diary and the autobiography respectively, has certain consequences. In the diary, there is much uncertainty or even confusion about the question of how things will go on, what will happen next: the author is as ignorant of the future as the reader. In the autobiography, however, the author looks back from the perspective of knowing what happened next and how his life went on since. Both perspectives have advantages and disadvantages. The autobiographer's looking back allows him/her to introduce lines and structures which he/she alone is able to see (or construct) from his/her later perspective. This is not possible at all in the diary: in the intimacy of day by day writing the elements of the narrative cannot be structured. Even if many things happen in the author's life, their story-telling value is parcelled out by the diary principle which does not allow an overall view of the course of events, according to Béatrice Didier.[27]

Well-known examples of published diaries in African literature are Amadi's *Sunset in Biafra* and Ngugi's *Detained*. The same applies to them as to the diary as a literary phenomenon in Europe: when their diaries were published, both authors were already known to large numbers of readers, Amadi as a novelist and Ngugi as a novelist and playwright.

Their diaries are quite different in intention, although they both deal with tragic events. Amadi gives his book the subtitle *A Civil War Diary* and in a foreword he emphasizes that he is not reflecting the views of the Federal Military Government of Nigeria but that his opinions are strictly personal: "This is not a story of the war; it is an intimate, personal story for its own sake."

In his *Detained: A Writer's Prison Diary*, Ngugi puts it otherwise:

I have . . . tried to discuss detention not as a personal affair between me and a few individuals, but as a social, political and historical phenomenon. I have tried to see it in the context of the historical attempts, from colonial times to the present, by a foreign imperialist bourgeoisie, in alliance with its local Kenyan representatives, to turn Kenyans into slaves, and of the historical struggles of Kenyan people against economic, political and cultural slavery.[28]

Both writers follow the events very closely, and they do not know that they will survive and be free in the end. As writers they are interested in literature and in their diaries they both

[115]

insert other literary texts. Amadi for instance quotes among other texts an Ibo song (p. 59), a Shakespeare love poem (p. 117), Keats's "Ode to the Nightingale", and Shelley's "Ode to the Night" (p. 118), but he also quotes other sorts of texts, e.g. from the minutes of the Advisory Committee "charged with the restoration of normalcy" (p. 155ff) at the end of the war.

Ngugi too quotes a number of literary as well as other texts, ranging from Kwame Nkrumah's autobiography (p. 6) to Dennis Brutus's *Letters to Martha*; he also quotes Shakespeare (p. 9) and Margery Perham's diaries (1920–1930) (p. 30), and so forth. The effect of such quotations on a literary text in general and on autobiographical works in particular still needs to be much more carefully examined in European as well as in African literature.[29]

As far as the *diary novel* is concerned, it has some advantages for writers: the very form allows them to hold back information from narrator and reader, although they themselves know what they want their narrator/main character to become, in the course of the story. Of course, the autobiographical pact does not exist here, since author≠narrator=main character. As in the real diary, the narrator in the diary novel has no or very little distance from the events he/she records in his/her notes. In Europe, the diary novel came into existence near the end of the eighteenth century, with a few rare earlier exceptions. Well-known examples in African literature are Ferdinand Oyono's *Houseboy* and Béti's *Poor Christ of Bomba*. *Houseboy* is presented "hypodiegetically" as a second level in the hierarchy of the narrative: the first pages of the book are told by the first narrator – in the first-person presentation – who explains how he got the two notebooks containing this diary written by another author whose name was Toundi Joseph. We get to know how this Toundi, dying, entrusts him with the manuscript written in Ewondo. This first narrator ends his (first level) introduction to the second and main part of the text (i.e. the diary notebooks) as follows:

[116]

I opened the packet. Inside there were two worn exercise books, a toothbrush, a stub of pencil and a large native comb made of ivory. That was how I came to read Toundi's diary. It was written in Ewondo which is one of the main languages of the Cameroons. In the translation which I have made and which you are about to read, I have tried to keep the richness of the original language without letting it get in the way of the story itself. (p. 8)

Here I cannot go into the details of this interesting novel or of the diary novel in general. I will just mention briefly a few points which are typical of this novel form, as distinct from the other first-person genres. The narrator of the diary novel is his/her own (fictional) narratee. They address themselves, talk to themselves, ask questions, express their thoughts to themselves as in the following lines:

For the first time Madame had a visit from her lover while her husband was here. M. Moreau at the Residence; my stomach was uneasy all the evening and now I am furious with myself. How can I get rid of this ridiculous sentimentality which makes me suffer over matters which have nothing whatever to do with me? (p. 82)

The diary is divided into two "exercise books". Very few dates are marked. In the beginning, it is "August" (p. 11); another time indication is "After the funeral" (p. 23). In the Second Exercise Book, allusions to "real" time do not occur, except for one, i.e. "Second night at the police camp" (p. 132). The fact that dates are not mentioned underlines that such official time indications are of little importance to the narrator/main character, who in his social context has learned to follow the time of sun, moon, seasons rather than to respect the European calendar as his white boss does.[30]

Typical for the diary novel as well as for the epistolary novel is the lack of distance between the time of narration and the narrated events. This distance is considerable in first-person adventure stories like Tutuola's and Fagunwa's and in first-person novels like Camara Laye's *L'enfant noir*. In the "factual" diary as well as in the fictional, the narrator knows no more than the reader how the subsequent events will take place. The narrator-hero writes down events and experiences in proportion, as he lives them. The reader becomes aware of this nearby situation through many indications. In *Houseboy* for instance, Toundi notes down immediately what he has experienced that day or the previous night, as the following quotations show:

> At midday I watched my master from the kitchen window (p. 26). Last night the location had a visit from Gullet, the Chief of Police (p. 28). My master is off into the bush again this morning (p. 86). I was arrested this morning. I am writing this sitting on bruised buttocks in the house of the chief native constable (p. 120).

The narrator uses various tenses: present, past, future. The narrator/main character presents, interprets and participates in the events – it is clearly a personal narrator like the one in the above-mentioned adventure stories by Tutuola. Through the naïve perspective of Toundi, a boy from the Cameroonian countryside – whom the author uses as narrator-focalizer – the mentality and manners of the colonial whites are presented in all their oddness. Thanks to this "close-following" first-person presentation, the immediate contrast between the African and the European world pervades the whole text, and the diary novel form as such is certainly quite appropriate, as Oyono's book shows so clearly.

Letters and the epistolary novel

Up till now, very few "collected letters" by African authors have been published. I mention here Ngugi's letters from prison, which constitute the second section of his *Detained*. This second part consists of a compilation of letters he sent to his wife, to the Security Officer of Detained and Restricted Persons, the Minister of Home Affairs, the Chairman of the Detainees Review Tribunal. All these letters relate to his imprisonment, although in different ways: they do not form a coherent structure as the epistolary novel does. Ngugi just adds these letters to his prison diary as an appendix of documents to show aspects of the Kenyan reality as he has experienced it.

Another example of "factual" letters is Zamenga Batukazanga's book *Lettres d'Amérique*: travelling to the United States, this Zaïrian author writes letters to his son at home, in which he describes his impressions of the New World and in which he especially links his own Africa to the "Africa" elements he encounters in the U.S., as, for example, when he tells about his visit to the house of Alex Haley, the author of *Roots*. This book is full of anecdotes, but there are also reflections on differences and similarities between people.[31] As stated, the epistolary novel resembles the diary novel in the absence of time distance between the moment of narration and the actual events: here too the narrator/main character who writes the letters knows no more than the reader what is going to happen next.

The letter-writing novel form as a particular genre of first-person narrative is no longer as popular in Europe as it was in the eighteenth and nineteenth centuries. It is supposed to have its origin mainly in posthumously published authentic letters, such as the famous letters Madame de Sévigné wrote to her daughter in France in the seventeenth century. Little by little, the letter-writing culture disappeared, being replaced by the telephone as a medium of communication in the Western world. In Africa, the telephone is still less gener-

[119]

ally available and the letter a much used means of communication with which the letter-novel could link quite naturally, but it is not very widely practised yet.

Theoretically, a distinction can be made between books with one or more letter-writers as narrator-characters in epistolary fiction on one hand, and books containing letters written by one author-character to one or more addressees on the other. African literature, however, has not (yet?) produced many epistolary novels, and the few that exist mostly concern one fictional letter-writer/narrator writing to one or sometimes two different addressees. It is striking that the genre is almost nonexistent in anglophone literature: all my examples are therefore taken from texts by francophone writers. Epistolary novels have been written by, among others, Bernard Dadié from Ivory Coast, who in his *Un nègre à Paris* adopts the same attitude as Montesquieu did in *Les lettres persanes*, that of the naive outsider observing "the Others", their customs and behaviour. Dadié's book consists of one long letter signed by the narrator/main character in which he describes his Parisian experiences and observations to a friend in Africa. Other epistolary fiction is to be found in one of Sembène Ousmane's short stories, entitled "Lettres de France". Henri Lopès' novel *Sans Tam-tam* consists of five letters written by a certain Gatsé followed by one last letter – as an epilogue – written by the addressee to the publisher. Both narrators are fictional as it is stressed in the "avertissement" which precedes the letters:

> De ce qui va suivre, seul le pays est vrai: le mien.
> Le peuple aussi. Mais j'ai laissé ce dernier dans l'ombre, craignant de mal transmettre son message sacré et de dénaturer sa voix.
> Pour le reste, tout est fruit d'une imagination fantaisiste: le lieu, les personnages, les situations, leurs pensées, sentiments et paroles. Si d'aventure ils coïncidaient avec un vécu réel, je jure que ce serait pur hasard.[32]
> (In what follows, only the country is true: my own. The

[120]

people too. But I have left the latter in the shadow, afraid to wrongly transmit its sacred message and to distort its voice. For the rest, everything results from a whimsical imagination: the place, the characters, the situations, their thoughts, feelings and words. If, by chance, they concur with reality, I swear it is pure coincidence.)

Such statements are not exceptional in African novels in general. The fictional character of the novel is already formally clear from the lack of the pact: here, author=narrator=main character. Forewords like the above one, however, in fact strengthen the suggestion that there are indeed more "facts" in this novel than fiction and that the author wants to protect himself from possible consequences of the publication of his book.

The best-known epistolary novel is Mariama Bâ's *Une si longue lettre*, which was awarded the first Noma Prize for African literature. It is a good example of the most outspoken characteristic of the epistolary novel, notably the very personal character of this narrative form. This personal character is due to the fact that the narrator addresses the narratee directly and continually, this narratee being a concrete fictional character mentioned in the text. In *So long a Letter*, the female letter-writer Ramatoulaye addresses one long letter to her old friend Aissatou and as readers we get acquainted with both when the former, at the time of the death and the funeral of her husband, confides her thoughts, memories, experiences to the latter.

Although it is presented in the letter form, the first paragraph shows that it is very close to the diary, at least in the narrator's intention: she wants to share not only her present sorrows with her friend but also their common memories of the past:

Dear Aissatou,

I have received your letter. By way of reply, I am beginning this diary, my prop in my distress. Our long association has taught me that confiding in others allays pain.
Your presence in my life is by no means fortuitous. Our grandmothers in their compounds were separated by a fence and would exchange messages daily. Our mothers used to argue over who would look after our uncles and aunts. As for us, we wore our wrappers and sandals on the same stony road to the koranic school; we buried our milk teeth in the same holes and begged our fairy godmothers to restore them to us, more splendid than before. If over the years, and passing through the realities of life, dreams die, I still keep intact my memories, the salt of remembrance. I conjure you up. The past is reborn, along with its procession of emotions . . .

Modou is dead. How am I to tell you? (pp. 1–2)

This presentation serves at the same time as motivation for the writing of the letter. It also shows the closeness of the diary and epistolary forms with regard to the handling of time referred to above: the time of the story and the time of the narration are sometimes so close as to almost coincide. The letter-writing first-person narrator in both genres can permit herself not only to tell what she has lived through quite recently, but also to express what she feels, sees or thinks at the moment of writing. This is very significant in Mariama Bâ's book. An example:

I take a deep breath.
I've related at one go your story as well as mine, I've said the essential, for pain, even when it's past, leaves the same marks on the individual when recalled. Your disappointment was mine, as my rejection was yours. Forgive me once again if I have re-opened your wound. Mine continues to bleed. (p. 55)

[122]

While writing to her friend she recalls, too, common memories from the distant past, from childhood and adolescence. In the whole of this book, memories do indeed play a quite important role, which is not always the case in the epistolary novel. In general, both diary novel and letter-novel deal with a short and recent period from the life of the narrator; rarely is a whole life told retrospectively as in the case of Ramatoulaye by means of long flashbacks; thanks to her flowering memories at the moment of her husband's death we get all this information about her earlier life. At the same time, we receive information about recent events and about the present. In that sense, the book forms a sort of bridge between the diary novel and the retrospective first-person novel in which the narrator-hero recalls his life from the beginning until adulthood or old age. The difference between the two is that in *So long a letter* (as well as in the epistolary novel in general), the narratee occupies an important place, because she is addressed directly, for instance, when the narrator reminds her friend of how she decided to divorce her husband:

And you left. You had the surprising courage to take your life into your own hands. You rented a house and set up home there. And instead of looking backwards, you looked resolutely to the future. (p. 32)

This presence of the narratee sometimes leads to a "narrative dialogue", a common device in the epistolary novel. A real dialogue is not possible, since the addressee is not on the spot. Therefore the friend's answers are given indirectly and we get to know Aissatou as a character through the narrator's memories, questions and comments.

Why aren't your sons coming with? Ah, their studies . . . So, then, will I see you tomorrow in a tailored suit or a long dress? I've taken a bet with Daba: tailored suit. Used to living far away, you will want – again, I have taken a bet with Daba – table, plate, chair, fork.

More convenient, you will say. But I will not let you have your way. I will spread out a mat. On it there will be the big, steaming bowl into which you will have to accept that other hands dip.

Beneath the shell that has hardened you over the years, beneath your sceptical pout, your easy carriage, perhaps I will feel you vibrate. I would so much like to hear you check or encourage my eagerness, just as before, and, as before, to see you take part in the search for a new way. (p. 89)

There have been numerous discussions about the advantages and the disadvantages of the epistolary novel form: disadvantages such as the implausibility, the risk of annoying repetitions and prolixities due to the letter-writing method as such. The advantages are obvious too, as Ian Watt has already made clear with regard to the works of Richardson; in his view

> the major advantage, of course, is that letters are the most direct material evidence for the inner life of their writers that exist. Even more than the memoir they are, to repeat Flaubert's phrase, 'le réel écrit', and their reality is one which reveals the subjective and private orientations of the writer both towards the recipient and the people discussed, as well as the writer's own inner being.[33]

The epistolary novel is still little practised in Africa and its particular characteristics in African literature as a whole have hardly been studied as yet.

Autobiography and the memoir novel

The autobiography is sometimes considered as a completely different genre from memoirs, but in practice this distinction is hardly possible since it is made on the basis of "verifiable facts" as characteristic for the memoirs and "the growth of the personality" of the author in the case of the autobiography. Or, in other terms, the memoirs supposedly deal with external events and the autobiography with the development of the author's personality. It is usually a matter of emphasis: memorialists may be tempted to become autobiographer and to express their thoughts and feelings and their personal growth and, on the other hand, autobiographers may feel the need to tell about the VIPs they have met or the political events which marked their country and which they have lived through or helped shape. An example of more emphasis on events than on personal elements is certainly Oginga Odinga's *Not Yet Uhuru*, although it is presented as "an autobiography", Oginga Odinga gives the following introductory comment on his book:

> I have told frankly the story of my life and political activity, admitting my mistakes and miscalculations, and trying to write about the early days without too much hindsight – though this might be difficult for anyone to shed completely. I have tried to show that there have been consistent threads running through our struggle from the early days until the present.[34]

In his book, the anecdotal is intertwined with well-known events from Kenyan history, and less attention is paid to the very personal aspects of the author's life.

The emphasis on authenticity in the autobiography and the striving for the illusion of authenticity in the fictional first-person narrative genres is very much en vogue in African literature. A well-known device to guarantee the illusion of reality is the device of the fictional editor who happens to

[125]

lay his hands on letters or a diary, Henri Lopès' *Sans Tam-tam* and Oyono's *Houseboy* being, respectively, cases in point.

Parallel to the realist "autobiographical" fiction there are the first-person fictional adventures of the marvellous genre. Tutuola's adventure stories are good examples: no facts, only fiction and everything is plausible and believable; the natural and the supernatural are linked without any problem. The narrator/main character tells his own adventures from the past, but this sort of narrative is quite the opposite of the memoir novel which tries to convince us of its authenticity. In such a realist fictional memoir novel, a whole life is presented from early childhood to old age by a first-person narrator who is at the same time the main character looking back as far as his/her memory reaches. It covers quite a long period of time if it is fully developed, as in Jean Ikellé-Matiba's *Cette Afrique-là*, in which the whole life of Frantz Mômha is told by himself in the first person: it cannot be called an autobiography, since the author's name is not the same as that of the narrator and main character.

It is clear that the autobiographical form is much used in fiction as a sort of certificate of reality. The only formal point of reference we have is the presence or absence of the auto-biographical pact as mentioned above. This pact does not apply to the fictional genres dealt with, because there the name of the author is not the same as that of the narrator-hero. For the real autobiography in its conventional form, the subject is the growth of the author's personality from early childhood to adulthood and it must be retrospectively told, from a comparatively long distance in time. In the latter sense, it is clearly distinct from the epistolary and diary genres. A number of questions arise here: what about autobi-ographers who only narrate a short period? According to Philippe Lejeune, one writes one's autobiography only once in a lifetime.[35] Why should that be? Writers are completely free from whatever prescriptions literary traditions seek to dictate, although most of them respect at least quite a number of these. In order to distinguish the genres on some formal points, I have made the following chart:

FIRST-PERSON NARRATIVE PROSE

	narrator=main[36] character	author=narrator	whole life told	fiction
Letters	+/−	+	−	−
Epist. novel	+/−	−	−	+
Diary	+/−	+	−	−
Diary novel	+/−	−	−	+
Autobiography	+	+	+/−	−
Memoir novel	+	−	+/−	+

FIG. V

For the purpose of analyzing first-person narratives more thoroughly, the following questions and criteria might be of some help in distinguishing and determining the genres and their possible mixtures.

1. Is *the autobiographical pact* concluded between author and reader? In agreement with Philippe Lejeune's definition we mentioned four points concerning this pact. These do not apply to the same degree to all the genres of the first person I have been dealing with. Are there other indications in the text or possibly also outside the text (e.g. interviews with the author) about the "factual" or fictional character of the text? Is verification possible? Are there many or few unverifiable matters dealt with in the text (feelings, beliefs, thoughts, dreams etc.)? Does the author confirm that he/she speaks the truth and

[127]

nothing but the truth or does he/she on the contrary confirm that the whole story has been invented? Of course, in both cases, the opposite of what is said may be true. The question of "truth" in fiction will always be a complicated matter. The author's own conception of truth can sometimes be construed from statements in the text.

2. Selection of *the time period dealt with*: some days/months/ years/a whole life recalled? Is the selection motivated? Is there a chronological or a thematic order? How relevant is what is left out for the ultimate meaning of the text? Is time otherwise dealt with when the author talks about childhood or adolescence, e.g. from youth to adulthood with a growing consciousness of one's own identity, or, conversely, from confidence to uncertainty? Which are the main narratological devices regarding the time factor, e.g. anticipation and flashbacks in relation to the story moment, the interrelationship between past, present and future in the text as a whole?

3. What are the relations between *narration* and *focalization*? Is it always the "older I", that is, the narrator, who focalizes the past events or is it the "younger I" who observes, or do they tend to merge into one? The answer to this question has consequences for the interpretation of the text: for example, the author may have the idea that past and present are inseparable in his/her mind and that he/she is unable to look at the past through the younger I's eyes. Or, on the contrary, he may want to present the past as something completely detached from the present and may therefore use the younger I as focalizer, while the older I who is the narrator tells the past events. It is also possible that the narrator makes a problem of recollection as such. In African autobiographical texts this is quite exceptional, while in recent European autobiographical literature

[128]

such texts quite often focus on the very impossibility of autobiographical writing.

4. Does the text contain explicit *motivation*, explaining why it was written? Above, such motivations were to be found in some of the mentioned texts: the narrator in *So long a Letter* answers her friend's letter as a "prop in distress" (p. 1). If it is not explicitly formulated in the text, there are sometimes indirect indications in the text or in other sources such as interviews and letters.

5. The *reader* can be addressed directly in the text, in general as an unspecified category. There is sometimes a specific fictional character whom the narrator addresses in person, like Aissatou, the narratee in *So Long a Letter*. Narrators may also address themselves, as in the diary or diary novel.

6. *Quotations and references*: these may be borrowed from literary or other texts, from different genres, by the author himself/herself or from other sources. The question one could ask is what effect do they have on the meaning of the concerned text?

7. What is the *relation between the author and his/her society*? Is a harmonious image produced or is the author critical of his society? It is also possible that the older narrators looking back are highly critical of themselves and their behaviour in the past and conclude, in retrospect, that they fit better into society now that they have found their identity, and say "yes" to their society. More often there are conflicts between authors and their society, like the political controversies between e.g. Oginga Odinga or Ngugi and the authorities in Kenya. The image the author, or (if author≠narrator=main character) the narrator, presents of himself/herself and the image society has formed of him/her may be quite different: if so, the 'I' will try to prove that he/she is

right and that the others are wrong: the book then
becomes a sort of apology.

8. *How is the story presented*: in short fragments or long
   chapters or in just one long piece? In what mode:
   assertively? Or hesitantly, with many adverbs, verbs and
   auxiliaries which express doubts or questions? Or just
   by stating firmly without any problem? What is the effect
   of the use of direct, indirect, or free indirect speech?

In the above we have discussed some aspects of different
first-person narrative genres as they are practised in African
literature – although some genres are less popular than
others, as we have seen. In Western literature, the intense
preoccupation with the self has led to what Christopher
Lasch called *The Culture of Narcissism*, in which:

> the convention of a fictionalized narrator has been aban-
> doned in most experimental writing. The author now
> speaks in his own voice, but warns the reader that his
> version of the truth is not to be trusted.[37]

It then becomes a sort of a parody in which the author no
longer wants to be taken seriously – if one is to believe Lasch,
who therefore sees confessional writing "degenerate into
anti-confession" (p. 54). This is certainly not (yet?) true in
the case of African autobiographical first-person narrative.

It might be interesting to compare African first-person narrative forms with similar genres in Asian or Latin-American
literature, with regard to this particular point. Is the responsibility of the writer and the function of literature in society
there taken more seriously than in the contemporary Western
world, where art for art's sake is looked on with less sus-
picion than commitment in literature?

With regard to Chinese literature, Ms. Doleželová stated
that:

> the first-person narrator's experience is combined with the

search for his own identity in a world wider than his private universe. The basic question "Who am I?" obsessive in Western fiction, is in China overshadowed by the query "Who am I in my society?"[38]

This question is also a central one in African literature, where the search for identity is an important theme and quite often moulded in the first-person narrative form. I am convinced that more systematic intercultural research in the field of literature will throw new light on the mysteries of the phenomenon of the first-person narrative and hence, perhaps, on the eternal human Who-am-I? question.

VIII. SHATTERING THE FALSE IMAGES: TOWARDS A DEFINITION OF REALISM IN THE AFRICAN CONTEXT

In different times and cultures, "reality" is experienced and expressed by artists and writers in different ways. Reality and knowledge about it are socially determined and therefore relative. Our problem is here: How and to what degree does the writer succeed in making us believe that literature "copies" reality?

The aim of the realistic writer is constant: to write, with respect to the valid norms of his/her time, more veraciously and to put reality more directly into words than his/her predecessors have done. The word *realism* however has been so randomly applied to all sorts of texts and literatures that we must very carefully define our use of it. The question remains *how* realistic literature succeeds in producing an "effect of reality".

Realism does not just mean "true to the hard facts". It is not possible to determine it quantitatively in the sense of the more facts in a text, the more realistic that text will be. What is true is not always probable (in the sense of credible) – and therefore realistic – in the eyes of the readers, who use their own experience of reality as a touchstone.

Realistic writers destroy certain norms of their time (and their social group) in writing more truthfully than their predecessors. Therefore Harry Levin called the literary realist "a professional iconoclast, bent on shattering the false images of his day".[1] Sometimes the destruction of norms in the

[132]

realistic novel only strikes the literary system, but in many cases it also touches the social and political system. A concrete historical situation, a datable and locatable frame, are conditions for the realization of realism. The urge for liberty, which is often associated with the rise of a class or group, and the "view from below" of society are realistic features as well. These constitute a latent threat to the existing order and the ruling authority. Censorship, persecution or imprisonment are there to prove that the writer's realism can be effective, that this verbalized reality has been recognized (but not accepted for that matter) by the authorities. This is not a phenomenon of the past, as appears from the numerous cases of dissident and imprisoned writers in our own time, throughout the world, who describe their contemporary reality so realistically that the political authorities recognize their writings as realistic experiences and therefore as threatening. There are the many bans on realistic black writers in South Africa and the well-known case of Ngugi wa Thiong'o's imprisonment in Kenya (cf. chapter X).

In the author's point of view towards reality, there are two main possibilities:

1. He/she believes in the existence of reality in itself as an object of knowledge and he/she feels confident about knowing and representing it even better than other writers have done before him/her.

2. He/she does not believe in the existence of objective reality as it happens in Western Europe where there has been a growing uncertainty among writers and intellectuals about the human possibility of objective perception since the beginning of the century.

Language, according to the latter, seemed inadequate and insufficient to imitate the "objective" reality. As a result, the writers fixed their attention on their own person: they believed that the only reality left was the one they experienced in their own consciousness. The inter-subjective dimension got lost in the view of such authors who no longer believed in the possibility of describing the world outside. They withdrew into a personal consciousness without any concrete context of reality.

My starting point is that only the first conception – the author's belief that reality exists in itself as an object of knowledge and that it is possible to represent it "as it is" in literature – is to be called realistic and its product realistic literature. After these preliminary remarks, we'll now turn to the author's realistic intentions, themes and techniques in the African novel in general, and to the case of the Senegalese writer Sembène Ousmane and his *God's Bits of Wood* in particular.

The theme of Africa and the African has been frequently used in European exotic and colonial literature. It has inspired many European writers with all the stereotypes and exoticism it entailed. Emmanuel Obiechina ascertained that a novel like Daniel Defoe's *The Life Adventures and Piracies of the Famous Captain Singleton* (1720) already "embodies most of the stereotypes which were to characterize later European writing on Africa".[2] More and more fascinated by the African theme, many European writers gradually considered themselves "specialists on *Africana*". However, these novels did not yield any "real" information about Africa.[3]

Therefore, many African writers wanted to give their own views on the European presence in Africa and the colonial "reality". Later, other realistic themes were chosen in conjunction with contemporary society. The European character no longer played the important part it had in African literature – especially in the Francophone novel about the colonial era – for some time. In the sixties this radically changed. Other themes became central in the novels of African writers who were more and more preoccupied with their own present society – with all the risks their criticism implied. They committed themselves to criticize the social norms upheld by a new group, the political authorities of their own countries.

Broaching new themes, they destroyed at the same time the convention of formerly fashionable themes like the image of the European, the colonial times and the precolonial African paradise, as I have examined in my book *Le Blanc vu d'Afrique*.[4]

In Africa, the first generation of novelists reacted in various ways to the prevailing European conceptions of culture and civilization and the romantic view of Africa, by "a fictional documentation of cultural and sociological details", as Dan Izevbaye put it in an interesting article entitled "Issues in the Reassessment of the African Novel". Their "narrative strategy" reminded this Nigerian critic of the way Western realistic writers reacted to European Romanticism in literature in the nineteenth century.[5] Of course, the essential difference is the fact that the destruction of norms did not occur in the same cultural context as in Europe between Romanticists and Realists in the nineteenth century.

In European as well as in African literature, the "sociological" information has to be brought into line with the other elements of the literary text. The author's information, his "file cards", should not be too evident as such. If they are, "sociology" has not been forged into literature. The evaluation of the question of whether an author has succeeded in creating a literary text depends on the reader's criteria which in turn – as we have seen – depend not only on his/her own cultural background but also on the sociological knowledge he/she can bring to bear on the cultural background of the literary text.

Many African novels refer "realistically" to African history, mainly recent history. They often do this quite directly, mentioning historical names and places, referring to well-known events like wars, battles, conflicts, strikes etc. This is what Philippe Hamon, in his essay on realism, called "mega History", the corresponding real history which doubles the (illusion of) reality of the literary text.[6] There are many examples of such references, whether in East, West or Southern Africa. One might think of Sembène Ousmane's *L'Harmattan*

[135]

(1964), which is based closely on the theme of the "Référendum" of 1958 organized by the French authorities in order to keep the French colonies under French rule, and the struggle of the young Africans against voting in favour of the new Constitution and the French *Communauté*.

The novel is preceded by a very interesting preface by the author, who states: "I do not practise the theory of the novel. Yet I remember that in the olden times the story-teller was not only the dynamic element of his tribe, clan, village, but also the patent witness of each event. He was the one who recorded, putting down, in front of all, under the palaver tree, everybody's doing. The idea of my work derives from this teaching: to keep as close as possible to reality and the people".[7]

One of the chapters of *L'Harmattan* is entitled "Le Référendum" and the historical date is stated: 28th September 1958. It is then related how the people had been bribed to vote "yes" by gifts of wine and beer, money, French flags, and the women in particular by kilometres of material with the printed image of General de Gaulle to dress themselves in favour of the French government (pp. 285f).

Another well-known example comes from Kenya on the eve of Independence: Ngugi's *A Grain of Wheat* (1967). In this novel, there are frequent historical references to the colonial times, the Resistance, the Mau Mau movement, the fight for freedom, the "party", the World Wars, the Queen of England, leaders like Harry Thuku and Jomo Kenyatta, the ceremony of Independence itself. Two fragments:

So in Harry Thuku, people saw a man with God's message: Go unto Pharao and say unto him: let my people go. And people swore they would follow Harry through the desert
. . .
But the whiteman had not slept. Young Harry was clamped in chains, narrowly escaping the pit into which Waiyaki was buried alive. Was this the sign they waited for? People went to Nairobi: they took an oath to spend their days and

nights outside the State House till the Governor himself
gave them back their Harry.
Warni, then a young man, walked all the way from Thabai
to join the procession. He never forgot the great event.
When Jomo Kenyatta and other leaders of the Party were
arrested in 1952, Warni recalled the 1923 Procession. "The
young should do for Jomo what we did for Harry. I'd never
seen anything to match the size of that line of men and
women," he declaimed, gently plucking his beard.[8]

In this quotation the historical facts are related to the memories and experiences of the people in general and those of
the novel characters in particular. In the second example, the
importance of real history as a factual frame of reference for
the personal story is obvious. The fourteenth chapter tells
about the ceremonies of Independence. The author first presents his "file-cards" of the real objective facts, how it went
in reality, how it has been told in the newspapers. In the
next section the narrator, changing from third-person to first-
person narrative technique, recalls his own experiences, the
independence festivities in the village:

Kenya regained her Uhuru from the British on 12
December 1963. A minute before midnight, lights were put
out at the Nairobi Stadium so that the people from all over
the country and the world who had gathered there for the
midnight ceremony were swallowed by the darkness. In
the dark, the Union Jack was quickly lowered. When next
the lights came on the new Kenya flag was flying and
fluttering, and waving in the air. The Police band played
the new National Anthem and the crowd cheered continu-
ously when they saw the flag was black and red and green.
The cheering sounded like one intense cracking of many
trees, falling on the thick mud in the stadium.
In our village and despite the drizzling rain, men and
women and children, it seemed, had emptied themselves

into the streets where they sang and danced in the mud. (p. 177)

The "authenticity" of history emphasizes indeed the effect of reality on the reader: this is how it went, the author seems to say, on the general and the personal level – let there be no doubt about it.

In the historical framework which is so often alluded to in the African novel, the author then situates the weal and woe of the group which lives the historical events in its own community: the traditional village in Camara Laye's *L'enfant noir* (1953) or Chinua Achebe's *Things Fall Apart* (1959), Ferdinand Oyono's *Le vieux nègre et la medaille* (1956) or Ngugi's already-mentioned *A Grain of Wheat* (1967). Of course, the traditional community is only one of the possible themes. We also meet communities in the cities, for example, small groups of progressive youngsters as in Sembène Ousmane's *L'Harmattan* or trade union leaders as in his *Les bouts de bois de Dieu*, who confront the assimilated majority; groups of colonial whites as they are so unforgettably depicted, for instance by the Cameroonese writers Oyono and Béti, but one finds them as well in Ngugi's and other East African writings and, of course, in many South African novels. Other groups include the students, the politicians, the business-men, the new elite.

In his interesting book *The Novel and Contemporary Experiences in Africa*, Shatto Arthur Gakwandi distinguished two types of realism:

The first type concerns itself primarily with the behaviour of man, the individual being treated as an autonomous entity. The second type takes the whole breadth of society as its subject matter and examines how the customs, conventions, social institutions and individuals inter-relate. The first type is what has come to be known as psychological realism, the second as social realism. With social realism, the individual is treated as a social unit; most often he is silhouetted against the institutions, traditions and general behaviour of his society so as to underscore his insignificance. His aspirations, achievements and disappointments are seen as conditioned by his place in a given society and can be used to raise wider ethical, moral and social issues. Social realism became a major fictional technique in nineteenth-century Europe and it may be said to constitute the central inheritance of the African novel from its European ancestor. In essence and technique the African novel has borrowed heavily from the European novel . . . the leading African novelists have been satisfied with employing the techniques developed by European realism and having used them to comment upon African experience.[9]

The techniques of this social realism are now to be described in the African novel. Are the above-mentioned general characteristics of the European (mostly nineteenth-century) realistic novel really the "unaltered basic form with a local colour" the African novelists worked with, as Gakwandi believed? Or is there something else to be seen as well? It seems most practical to turn now directly to the author chosen for our purpose and generally recognized as an African realist: Sembène Ousmane, and more specifically to one of his novels, *God's Bits of Wood* (*Les bouts de bois de Dieu*).

We'll look first at the *author's intention*, his use of *mega History*, the *social context* and the *setting* of his works. Afterwards, we'll turn to the *techniques, language* and, later, *intertextuality* in his novel *Les bouts de bois de Dieu*.

In an interview I had with Sembène Ousmane some years ago, I asked him whether his work is to be viewed as belonging to Socialist Realism. He said no, because he felt Socialist Realism belonged to the socialist countries only, although he had nothing against the movement: "What I want to represent is a social realism. I have no intention of creating great heroes, on the contrary, I am concerned with everyday reality: the woman who struggles for life and toils to nourish

[139]

her child, her sorrows, her hopes, I work with the material of everyday life of ordinary people. They recognize themselves in my works and identify with my characters". For Sembène Ousmane, there is no question about the describability of reality. He believes in it, and he sees the task of the writer as that of putting reality into words "as it is":

The African writer must stand in the midst of society and at the same time observe this reality from the outside . . . I participate in the developments of society and note these. I am a fighter, I know what I want to change in society and this facilitates my work as a writer. You are right in stating that my works develop along with the society in which I live, with its ups and downs, its defeats and its victories . . . We started from a colonial system. This system is now partially hidden behind the façade of the black bourgeoisie. My work as a writer is narrowly associated with the struggle for real independence. In Africa, we first thought that in 1960 with Independence paradise would come. Now we know better. The whites have left indeed, but those in power now behave in exactly the same way . . . We are faced with the reality of our own bourgeoisie in power which wants to be exactly like the white bourgeoisie. These people are easy accomplices of imperialism in Africa. We must have the courage to denounce their practices.

These quotations make the author's perspective of reality quite clear. Ever since he started to write novels, he has wanted to describe the social reality of everyday life and has referred to concrete historical situations, in a datable and locatable frame.

Le docker noir (1956) depicts the life of the black dockers in the port of Marseille and racism in French society. All Ousmane's other novels are situated in Africa. Before the historical context of Independence, O pays, mon beau peuple (1958) is set in the Casamance in Senegal; Les bouts de bois de

Dieu in the cities of Bamako, Thiès and Dakar; *L'Harmattan* (1964) in an unnamed African francophone country voting in favour of the Referendum of 1958. In *Xala* (1973) we meet the post-Independence African bourgeoisie in the well-to-do business man El Hadji Abdou Kader Bèye and his colleagues. El Hadji's "xala" (Wolof word for impotence) symbolizes the bourgeoisie's impotence in dealing honestly with its deprived fellow citizens. It is interesting to see how Sembène himself explains the meaning of this last novel with respect to today's African reality:

> *Xala* is, in a certain way, the story of a true segment of history: the history of the contemporary bourgeoisie of the Third World whose representatives have, after the past struggle against colonialism, turned themselves into new classes which can only imitate the bourgeoisie from the Western World . . . I wanted to emphasize that only the masses possess the real solution to our problems. That is the meaning of the last scene: you have to spit on the new bourgeoisie and to vomit on them, starting with ridiculing them. This is our indispensable task if we want the new Africa we dream of to become real.

Sembène Ousmane's intention as an author is quite clear: he wants to show the *real* Africa, his Africa, that is the people's Africa. According to him, the only thing writers or filmmakers are entitled to do if they want to be social realists is to reflect the ordinary people and their problems.

This leads us to the *social context* of his works. In the framework of contemporary or immediate history in practically all his works, he refers to concrete events in the setting his characters move around in. These characters are portrayed in their milieu and linked to social groups which are in opposition to one or more other social groups in the novel. Thus we meet for example the black dockers versus the racist French, or the progressive youngsters versus the assimilated corrupted African clergymen and politicians in *L'Harmattan*,

[141]

or the employers versus the employed in *Les bouts de bois de Dieu*; the rich elite versus the army of the poor in *Xala*. Of course, there are many more oppositions between different social reference groups than the ones I mentioned here.

In all Sembène Ousmane's novels we see *the urge for liberty* and the efforts of a rising group viewing society from below, that is, from the side of the oppressed who react to their situation, be it as blacks or as workers, as women or as youngsters, in their opposition to whites or bosses or husbands or the elder generation.

Like many other African authors of his generation, Sembène Ousmane feels committed to portraying African life as an integrated reality viewed from the inside and from the people's perspective. Listening to the people is essential for him, or, in his own words: "I put to the test the impact of what I have written, I want to verify the truth. I spend hours discussing with the people . . . especially on very precise points. Thus, I have learnt a lot, especially from the peasants".

Sembène Ousmane does not pretend to work *for* the people, but he wants to belong *to* the people (*non pas travailler pour le peuple, mais rester du peuple*).

Next question: Where is his work to be situated in the historical evolution of literary and social features? There are several lines meeting at a crossroads, literary lines, cultural lines, ideological lines, and so forth. There is, first of all, *the oral literature line*. In the interview I had with him, he answered my question about the function of oral literature for modern African literature as follows: "The oral literature is vanishing. The modern writers are turning to it more and more as a source of inspiration. However, we must not forget contemporary reality, and let us no longer dream sentimentally about dear old Africa in the past, like some people, especially Europeans, still do. Very soon Africa will no longer orally transmit its old stories to the younger generations. On the one hand this is sad, of course, but on the other hand it is very comprehensible: . . . the ambition of the young generation reaches much farther than the horizon of the village".

Obviously, Sembène Ousmane grants a less important function to the oral tradition than a number of other African writers. It might entail the danger of concealing contemporary reality as he wants to reveal it in his novels and films. Nevertheless, the oral tradition line is present in his works in the language of the characters who represent the old people. We'll come back to this point later, with the intertextuality. The oral literature in his view will be increasingly replaced by the modern media like radio, film, television. The effectiveness, the link with the largest possible audience, is what counts most. A book has more readers than an oral tradition in the village has spectators, but a film has a larger audience than a book has readers, especially in Africa. This made Sembène Ousmane say that for him today "the cinema replaces the palaver tree".

The other literary line is the *line of written literature*, especially the novel. Sembène Ousmane has been influenced by Western novelists: the French such as Balzac, Zola, and Flaubert, and the Russians Dostoevsky, Gogol and Chekhov. It is the line of the traditional European novel, not the experimental *nouveau roman* genre, which would not correspond with the author's intention of reaching a large audience.[10]

Sembène Ousmane is mostly an autodidact. After primary school he had his trade union training, so that he has not been very much influenced by the "intellectual milieus in France" as were most Francophone African writers with a university education. Sembène Ousmane considered the Paris intellectual to be "too bourgeois to be interesting".[11]

A next step is to find out which *norms* Sembène Ousmane destroyed by writing his novels. First of all, the *literary norms*: being a written and partly western-influenced genre, the novel as such constituted a break with tradition from the African point of view, by its form. As far as the literary themes were concerned, his novels reacted against the norms of the European exotic and colonial novels about Africa. Secondly, the destruction of *social and political norms* of the ruling classes – first of the Western colonial rulers, then of the African élite in power: Sembène Ousmane's perspective is not the power perspective but the people's view of African society, which is to be seen in a different light.

Our next question is: How is the author's information about his reality – the "truth" as he called it – conveyed throughout the text. In order to answer this, we'll try to describe the *realistic devices* he is using in his novel *Les Bouts de bois de Dieu*.

Sembène Ousmane describes the weal and woe of the group whose "truth" he wants to reflect, the community life, its social coherence, the fact of belonging to the same clan, class, nation, or continent. In this respect, the author's note to *God's Bits of Wood* is significant:

The men and women who, from the tenth of October, 1947, to the nineteenth of March, 1948, took part in this struggle for a better way of life owe nothing to anyone: neither to any "civilizing mission" nor to any parliament or parliamentarian. Their example was not in vain. Since then, Africa has made progress.[12]

At the same time this note announces the mega History which doubles and predetermines the text, referring closely to the well-known historical "facts" and consequently creating a clear pattern of expectation in the reader's mind.

Another realistic aspect of this note is its *authenticating function*: thus the author guarantees the truthfulness of the story beforehand. The beginning of a realistic text often has such a "probabilizing" function, being a foreword, a dedication (Sembène Ousmane dedicates his book as follows: "For you, GOD'S BITS OF WOOD, and for my comrades in the unions", underlining once more its truthfulness), a first paragraph, a footnote on the first page, and so forth.

The above-mentioned author's note has yet another function: it is a good example of the *prediction* device, one of

[144]

the common realistic techniques in the novel. Here the note announces the story's happy ending; it is full of confidence in the future of Africa. The historical time of the author's writing is the fifties, that is, before independence. Other devices of prediction, foreshadowing developments in the text, include the lucidity of the leader Bakayoko, the group awareness of the railway workers and the African community, the fixing of the syndicalists' negotiation program, and the counter-projects of the white inhabitants of the quarter called "The Vatican".

On the other hand, numerous *flashbacks* are there to give concrete information and to strengthen the coherence of the text. They are produced in various forms, in the form of *memories*, for instance old Niakoro's memories right in the beginning about the previous strike of 1938, in which she had lost a husband and a son; or Doudou's memories at the moment of meeting Isnard who tries to bribe him (pp. 2, 146ff). Other flashbacks take the form of *summaries* of past events. Sometimes a chapter begins that way – for example, the chapter entitled "Tiémoko" (p. 78) or the one called "The Meeting" (p. 203). We also find flashbacks in the form of *references* to an ancestor, a clan, the mentioning of heredity, a tradition or a family: the case of Ad'jibid'ji and her mother for instance:

Ad'jibid'ji must have been eight or nine years old, but she was tall for her age. She had the same features as Assitan, her mother, and the same fine nose, for they were nobly descended, from the Peuls and the Berbers (p. 4). By the ancient standards of Africa, Assitan was a perfect wife: docile, submissive, and hard working . . . One night her father had told her that her husband was named Sadibou Bakayoko, and two months later she had been turned over to a man whom she had never before seen. The marriage had taken place with all of the ceremony required in a family of ancient lineage, but Assitan had lived only eleven months with her husband when he was killed in the first

[145]

strike at Thiès. Three weeks later she had given birth to a daughter, and once again the old customs had taken control of her life; she had been married to the younger Bakayoko, Ibrahim. He, in turn, had adopted the baby and given her her curious name, Ad'jibid'ji. Assitan continued to obey. With the child, and the child's grand-mother, Niakoro, she had left Thiès to follow her husband to Bamako. She was as submissive to Ibrahim as she had been to his brother. (p. 106)

The *interrelationships* are very close, generally speaking, not only within the small family circle – as in the European realistic novel – but in the whole community. It is social realism indeed, because the characters function as social units in the present, as defined by their historical condition. The social units meet in this novel in their function as trade unionists, as a group of white colonials, as members of the same family, as neighbours in a township, as old people, women, or prisoners.

As readers we are introduced to scenes in which the characters manifest their belonging to their social group(s) by their *language* as well as by their *behaviour*. Thus we are informed about the different social groups. The *names* by themselves are significant: on the African side, we find African names – and for those who know the respective languages, differences will be noticed between Bambara and Wolof names – like Bakayoko, Niakoro, Boubacar, Penda; in the white group we find French names like Dejean, Monsieur Edouard, Leblanc, Dr. Michel, Béatrice, and so forth.

It is not only characters' names that refer to "reality", but also names of places like Dakar (n'Dakarrou), Thiès, Bamako, Le Vatican, France, Les Vosges. Such geographical names are to be recognized as proper names by the way they are written with capitals. They are not necessarily followed by descriptions, because the proper names of places are able to guarantee the reference effect by themselves. Besides the denotation of such proper names referring to the context in a direct and literal way, they are at the same time heavily loaded with connotations full of social content: this is already clear in the implications of the use of African and French names, respectively. The names are associated with milieus and activities. The colonial whites are neither workers nor syndicalists, they are not victims of inequality and do not suffer materially from the strike. The Africans are just the opposite. This is what Hamon called "onomastic transparence".[13] It is reinforced by the filling-in of the characters and milieus. In the realistic novel, this leads to the creation of *social types* and *characteristic behaviour*, in professional activities as well as in the *couleur locale* setting. Here, the realistic writer sees his opportunity to convey part of the knowledge about African social life, groups, trade, milieus, and so forth, to the readers. He wants to convince the reader of the authenticity of the information within the framework of the story and keeps himself outside. Therefore "specialized" characters are introduced to present or represent a milieu, a situation, a profession.

Niakoro, for example, represents the old African woman, her way of thinking, her behaviour, her reactions in the African community where tradition is no longer respected as much as before. N'Deye Touti is the prototype of the French-influenced young generation of African schoolgirls, while Béatrice Isnard has all the characteristics of the white colonial woman.

The same holds true for the men: Bakayoko is the social type of the male visionary leader – almost too romantically idealized to be realistically acceptable. Two other types are: Hadramé the Moor, the shopkeeper, and the white "commandant" of the detention camp, Monsieur Bernadini – but there are many more in this novel. Here is one example from the text to illustrate the way it works: one of the women, Ramatoulaye, has decided to go and find food for her twenty "bits of wood". She enters the shop of Hadramé the Moor, the "hen roost" as it is called "because of the dirt that pervaded everything in it". The detailed description of the shop

[147]

starts at the moment Ramatoulaye enters. Later, other bits of information are given in between her conversation with the shopkeeper:

There were three entrances from the street, and an enormous wooden counter, covered with a mixture of grease and dust, ran the entire length of the store. On either side of a haberdashery showcase there were scales, of different sizes. At one end of the counter there were fly-specked jars of sweets, and at the other a sort of cage of metallic gauze, containing loaves of stale bread. A cockroach was climbing slowly up its inner frame. The whole rear wall of the shop was covered by rickety shelves, held together with wire and piled with rolls of cloth of every kind, from the cheapest calicoes to silks, side by side with boxes of candles and squares of tallow. Between the counter and the row of shelves there was a narrow pathway, littered with bags of rice and salt and cases of tinned sardines and tomatoes. The floor surrounding the big cask of oil was thick with grease. And, as if this glut of merchandise was not enough, Hadramé had succeeded in wedging three tailors into a corner at the back. They sat in the shop all day, measuring, cutting, and sewing. (p. 41)

Hadramé is clearly the type of shopkeeper who only thinks of his own interests. His behaviour is adequately rendered in the scene following the shop description.

Exactly the same method is applied in the presentation of the Corsican Bernadini. Before we see him in action, the detention camp is described, first from the outside, then from the inside, at the moment when old Fa Keita is locked up and joins the other prisoners. Setting followed by action is also the order in which the "Vatican" and its inhabitants are presented (see pp. 162ff). The combination of description of setting and a character's adequate behaviour contributes highly to the "probability" of the story. One of the elements in this probabilizing technique is what one could call the "pretext function": that is, the motivation of the information by first, the attentive look, e.g. Ramatoulaye's entering Hadramé's shop; second, the explanatory speech: the trial of Diara the ticket collector is a good example (p. 91ff); and third, the technical act: Niakoro designing a gourd (p. 3) or Bernadini torturing the prisoners (pp. 231ff).

All this is utilized by realistic writers who want their text to be an "ostentatious discourse of knowledge" (the descriptive file card, knowledge being equal to reality) which must be shown to the reader.[13] Thus they conceal their pedagogical intention and their well-documented file card system and technical vocabulary behind their characters' conversation and behaviour in their proper environment. Of course, the three above-mentioned motives – the attentive look, the speech and the technical act are often combined for the same purpose. Sometimes look and speech manifest themselves in a sort of pseudo-monologue in a semi-direct style, e.g. Sounkaré, *The Watchman* (p. 127ff).

One might wonder to what degree such characters are functional actors in the story and to what degree they are no more than agents of communication, transmitters of information. Hamon qualified them as "defunctionalized characters" from the narrative point of view.[14] If reality *is* knowledge for the realistic writer, the constraint is evident: the characters constantly risk being sacrificed for the benefit of the distribution of the author's knowledge.

Miracles, doubts, uncertainties, ambiguities, ironies are problematic in a way, because they can be detrimental to the seriousness of the story. This clearly distinguishes the realistic text from "strange", "marvellous" and fantastic literature, where such devices are optimally exploited.[15] *God's Bits of Wood* is an unambiguous text. For the purpose of neutralizing his information, the realistic author often aims at keeping himself, as well as the reader, outside the text, suggesting therewith perfect objectivity. However, this leads to that other constraint, the *problem of the hero* in the realistic novel. The constraint consists of realism requiring the absence of a genuine (idealized and/or romantic) hero on the one hand, and the literary text needing one for its coherence and readability on the other hand. Now, the central character of *God's Bits of Wood* is Bakayoko, but this militant leader is often kept offstage. For realistic reasons? Probably. The reason might well be to compensate for the romantic, epic, almost mythical features the author also clearly wants to attribute to this character. The list of personages is quite long; there are more than forty in all: the social group is more important than the individual character. In my opinion, Sembène has often succeeded in keeping the balance of realism in his novel stable, especially through the device of the characters' defocalization, that is the shifting of point of view among the different characters. In the field of narratology one can ask two questions as far as the relation between narrator and characters is concerned: Who speaks? and Who sees? The first question concerns *narration*, the second *focalization*. The narrator tells the story, but at the same time the events and situations are presented from a specific perspective, a point of view, and this is not necessarily the narrator's. The subject of focalization is called the focalizer.[16] It is important to distinguish between the two, because focalization or shifting of focalization contributes to the effect a character has on the reader. We must be aware of it because if we are not, we are easily inclined to share views or to sympathize with him or her. Technically speaking, the focalization might be to his/her advantage, if a view is presented via this character only. There are stories in which we meet only one character-focalizer throughout the text, which consequently leads to partiality and restriction. This is for instance the case in Mongo Béti's *Poor Christ of Bomba*, where we are allowed to see the events only from Denis's particular point of view, although the reader will do more with the given information than this narrator-character does. All the same, this has a special effect on the reader.

More often than not, the focalization shifts from one character to another, or from narrator to character(s) in a

[150]

novel. In this way we get a rather good idea of the various sides of a conflict or confrontation. This technique leads to, or at least suggests, neutrality vis-à-vis the different characters and their relations. The realistic writer will often use defocalization for his/her purpose, and Sembène Ousmane has not hesitated to do so. There is shifting in all his novels, but *God's Bits of Wood* is certainly one of the clearest examples of the kind: right from the beginning one finds focalization shifting from the narrator to the character and vice versa. In the first chapter, for instance, we first look at the setting with the narrator, then focalization shifts to Niakoro, after that to Ad'jibid'ji, and so on, creating the effect of reality and "objectivity".

To conclude, I should like to mention another very important realistic technique Sembène Ousmane uses effectively: *language*. The realistic writer is forced to bring a personal style into harmony with the different sociolects of the characters which require the actual effacement of that personal style. As we said, Sembène Ousmane always stressed the importance of the writer's being *of* the people and not writing *for* the people. The interesting thing is that his personal style is very close to the ordinary everyday language of the African community he lives in, thus creating an effect of coherence. On the other hand, he also handles quite easily other languages such as the syndicalists' jargon and the white colonial sociolect, knowing the former from his long trade union experience and the latter from having lived half his life under colonial rule.

The only possible "literal", concrete imitation of reality, is in fact the imitation of language. This brings us to the phenomenon of intertextuality.[17] Out of different oral and written "texts" (fixed forms of language) a new text has been forged which lays claim to unity – it is an intertext, the result of an intertextual process. In a text, different sociolects meet, reinforce or confront each other – for example, greetings, religious formulas, songs, stories, speeches, novel forms – the use of which is no longer the same: they have new

[151]

functions in the new text. All these parts of the intertext share the feature that they refer to similar "texts" in reality, "texts" which express social, ideological and historical positions. The text is based on a variety of these positions, as a realistic text should be. Constituting a multicoloured mosaic of sociolects, each referring to a specific group in reality, the denotation is quite easy, but denotating does not cover the whole signification of the text. The very fact of intertextuality, the being together in one coherent text, brings about lots of connotations at the same time, similarities and oppositions being created by this very fact.

Unfortunately, I cannot go into that subject here, but I am convinced that interesting possibilities for research are to be discovered in this direction. Interesting and useful – not only in the field of realism and the African context.

IX. CRITICAL PERSPECTIVES AND HIDDEN IDEOLOGIES: AN INTERCULTURAL APPROACH

In Western literary criticism, the starting point is still apt to be "real" literature with a capital L, the body of texts known as World Literature. As I have pointed out above,[1] the texts that are part of this literature have been selected on the basis of Eurocentric norms by Western critics from works of literature that are exclusively or mainly Western.

As a body of texts, this literature with a capital L forms a literary system maintained and protected as an institution in its own right, by the bodyguards or critics who keep a vigilant eye on something they consider very beautiful indeed. Sometimes "the body" is slightly altered by critics to suit changing circumstances – historical or political, aesthetical or social – inside the Western world itself.

As far as the present-day global literary bulwark is concerned, the Western cultural domination cannot be ignored. If writers from other cultures want to be taken seriously outside their own cultural context, they have little choice but to take into account Western literary taste and criteria. The problems inherent in these relations are reflected in criticism.

How Western is literary criticism? How aware are Western critics of the limitations of their own perspective? According to Wellek and Warren, the value of a text exists potentially in the literary structures, and texts are valued "only as they are contemplated by readers who meet the requisite conditions".[2]

What, however, is a competent reader? Are there different

competences or only one, and on what terms? Does it mean that there is only one value system for all the literature of the world? What about literature other than what is produced in the West? Wellek was too conditioned by his own cultural context to ever ask himself these questions. For him, art is autonomous, and cultural relativism fatally results in "anarchy":

> Relativism in the sense of a denial of all objectivity is refuted by many arguments; by the parallels to ethics and science, by recognition that there are aesthetic as well as ethical imperatives and scientific truths. Our whole society is based on the assumption that we know what is just, and our science on the assumption that we know what is true. Our teaching of literature is actually also based on aesthetic imperatives even if we feel less definitely bound by them and seem more hesitant to bring these assumptions out in the open. The disaster of the "humanities" as far as they are concerned with the arts and literature is due to their timidity in making the very same claims which are made in regard to law and truth . . . The concept of adequacy of interpretation leads clearly to the concept of the correctness of judgment. Evaluation grows out of understanding; correct evaluation out of correct understanding. There is a hierarchy of viewpoints implied in the very concept of adequacy of interpretation.[3]

"We know what is just, . . . we know what is true . . . and thus we know what is beautiful". This kind of positiveness sounds amazing from an intercultural point of view, which rejects the belief in an eternal canon of literary texts for all times and all places. Even within one culture or social group, the fixed body of favourite texts selected by the most prominent critics is modified in the course of time.

This is why it would be better, as I explained earlier, to start from a semiotic point of view and consider literature and literary texts as signs in a particular communication situation.

Messages in the form of texts are sent by the authors and appreciated by the recipients as literary, only if their social, cultural, intellectual and aesthetic norms and knowledge more or less coincide. In this communication, the literary codes used by the "sender" have to be at least partially decoded by the recipient in order to enable him/her to appreciate the literary aspects of the sender's code. The code that makes a text be experienced and appreciated as a literary one is based on certain conventions that can be studied. The reconstruction of the authors' or readers' reactions which do make them accept certain texts as literary, and reject others, can tell us as much about the readers' background as about the texts themselves.

The Russian Formalists noted that texts have to be read and viewed against the background of the literary and other traditions they result from or react to: there has been a rise and fall of literary systems throughout history. Literary systems are appreciated or rejected by readers and critics on the basis of contextual norms. The evaluation of texts and the values that readers attach to texts are interesting objects of research, and grant us better insight into the functioning of literary texts in their own and other social, cultural, historical and political contexts.

Literary criticism becomes part of literary research in the larger framework of communication. A rather new aspect of the comparative study of text interpretations is the intercultural comparison of critical texts. The world has become too small for the monocultural Western approach and this approach has received more and more critical, sometimes quite negative, comments from critics and scholars in other cultures. A study of the influence and impact of certain values on authors as recipients of texts (from their own and other cultures) on the one hand, and as producers of texts on the other hand, may well deepen and widen a scholar's insight into the way literature functions in today's cultures, where cultural autonomy is threatened by cultural synchronization.

At a Commonwealth Literature Conference in 1974, the well-known Nigerian writer Chinua Achebe read a paper entitled "Colonialist Criticism", in which he denounced what he called the colonialist mentality of the Western critic:

This attitude and assumption was crystallized in Albert Schweitzer's immortal dictum in the heyday of colonialism: *The African is indeed my brother, but my junior brother.* The latter-day colonialist critic, equally given to big-brother arrogance, sees the African writer as a somewhat unfinished European who with patient guidance will grow up one day and write like every other European, but meanwhile must be humble, must learn all he can and while at it give due credit to his teachers in the form of either direct praise or, even better since praise sometimes goes bad and becomes embarrassing, manifest self-contempt.[4]

Achebe advocated banning the word *universal* from discussions on African literature "until such a time as people cease to use it as a synonym for the narrow, self-serving parochialism of Europe, until their horizon extends to include all the world". The word has sometimes been used by Western critics to encourage African writers whose works they valued – in relation to other writers' works – as "almost universal".[5]

In fact its use illustrates critics' evolutionist thinking. Another point broached in the same article is the effect of this mentality on Third World writers themselves. Achebe wanted to know "on whose ideological side they are playing".

Critics and their Criticism

According to Abrams in *The Mirror and the Lamp*, the four salient features generally distinguished in the study of literary texts are the work, the artist, the universe and the audience:

> Although any reasonable adequate theory takes some account of all four elements, almost all theories . . . exhibit a discernable orientation toward one only.[6]

Thus Abrams distinguished four different kinds of art theories: mimetic theories, pragmatic theories, expressive theories and objective theories. In the critical texts from different cultures, one might try to find out which particular theory is favourite. To what extent do critics use one or more of the same kind of arguments in their criticism? These arguments may be useful for the scholar who wants to deduce the norms that some critical text is based on. One might check whether the following main categories are to be found in critical texts to be studied:

1. The literary text in its relation to reality.

2. The literary text in its relation to the author.

3. The literary text as an autonomous entity.

4. The literary text in its relation to the reader.

5. The literary text in its relation to other works.[7]

To these quite obvious aspects, I should like to add:

6. The critical comment on other critical perspectives originating from different social, cultural, historical and political backgrounds.

All the six points reflect value judgements by critics. There is never any question in their statements about the reality, the author, the work *as such*, but about the reality, author, work and so forth *as seen by* this or that particular critic belonging to this or that culture, nation, gender, social group, political party and so on. Ideology and group-interests are

[157]

hidden under the surface all the time. Our task is then to trace in critical comments the cultural differences behind the critics' basic norms and values.

As Marx and Engels put it in 1848, "the ruling ideas in every epoch have always been the ideas of the ruling class". There is a dialectical process going on between literatures and counter-literatures, criticism and counter-criticism, bringing about changes in the world-wide "mega-polysystem" of literature as described by Even-Zohar.[8] He rightly stated that criticism can be used either to support and reinforce a ruling literary system or to weaken and undermine it. The phenomenon Even-Zohar described, giving examples from within the Western culture, also applies to the global literary polysystem. Literature functions more as an overall semiotic system than as an exclusively literary one: "As systems are governed by those who control them, the tools fought for will depend on their relative efficacy in controlling the system . . . The constraints imposed upon the "literary" polysystem by its various systematic co-systems contribute their share to the hierarchical relations governing it". This is not only valid for the correlations within a community but also for those between different communities:

Just as an aggregate of phenomena operating for a certain community can be conceived of as a system constituting part of a larger polysystem of "total culture" of the said community, so can the latter be conceived of as a component in a "mega-polysystem", i.e., one which organizes and controls several communities in history, such "units" are by no means clear-cut or finalized for ever. Rather, the opposite holds true, as the borders separating adjacent systems shift all the time, not only within polysystems, but between them. The very notions of "within" and "between" cannot be taken statically. Such an approach, as the static a-historical approach in general, has been a major obstacle in the adequate understanding of the various historical facts . . . Literatures which developed before others, and which belonged to nations which influenced, by prestige or direct domination, other nations, were taken as sources for younger literatures. As a result, there inevitably emerged a discrepancy between the imitated models, which were often of the secondary type, and the original ones, as the latter might have been pushed by that time from the center of their own PS to the periphery.[9]

In cross-cultural relations, the power factor always plays an undeniable role.[10] Looking at comments by a critic from one culture on a text written by an author from another culture, this factor has to be taken into account, particularly if the critic belongs to a globally dominant country and/or culture and the author to a dominated country and/or culture, or the other way round. The critic may not be aware of his own lack of modesty, the superiority complex expressed in his critical comment, even though it might have been written with the best of intentions. In reaction, counter-criticism is produced, commenting on the same text from the other (i.e. the author's) culture, and the differences in view and background can be striking. Sometimes there is an obvious incompatibility of norms. Looking carefully at the critical texts from an intercultural comparative point of view, we must constantly take into account the possible cultural differences with all their ideological connotations, expressing group interests and values.

I shall illustrate the intercultural oppositions and reactions expressed by critics from Africa, the West, and the Caribbean in comments upon texts and critics from these same areas. Although cultural differences can be found in all the categories, I cannot go into more than one point here, viz the first one – text and reality – and only as far as the intercultural implications are concerned.

Text and Reality

One of the main issues in the intercultural comparison of critical texts has to do with this category: different cultural contexts seem to lead to different views of reality. I shall mention three arguments related to this point:

a) The *reflection argument*: it points out that a book is good if reality is well reflected. The idea behind it is that literature has to reflect reality correctly according to "the truth". It can be found in many critical texts, where reality in the text and reality in the context are compared. The book is appreciated positively if it is credible, probable, truthful, convincing.

Another argument concerning this point is b) the *commitment argument*: a book is "good" if it is committed to social or political change. The critic might or might not appreciate the committed nature of a text and the fact that the problems of the contemporary situation are recognizable. Either that or the author is reproached for refusing to commit himself/herself, for presenting events without taking sides.

c) The *moral argument* also belongs to this category: a book is good if the critic agrees with its moral tendency. In order to appreciate a literary work, the critic has to be able to agree with the moral norms in the book. Thus judgement is based upon the extent to which a critic shares the author's political, religious, social, and moral views of reality.

ad a): Commenting on the phenomenon of the European colonial novel set in Africa, the Nigerian critic Professor Echeruo once said that:

if there is anything 'true' of such novels, it is not essentially (or properly) in its setting or in its depiction of character and personality, but in the accuracy of its reflection of the imaginative temper of the author's culture.[11]

Against this exotic and colonial perspective of the European novel about Africa, a whole generation of African writers started to give their own version of the same reality. The

[160]

Eurocentric version had to be corrected, for example, in a novel like Joyce Cary's *Mister Johnson*. Chinua Achebe stated in an interview that "this was a most superficial picture – not only of the country, but even of the Nigerian character, and so I thought if this was famous, then perhaps someone ought to try and look at it from the inside".[12] And he did.

How can the difference be described? For the European critic, unfamiliar with the African cultural background, the "otherness" of the depicted milieu, customs, everyday life and so forth, had an effect it did not necessarily have in Africa. Dan Izevbaye made the point that an African might notice a comparable abundance of sociological details in European novels. One simply overlooks this fact if one is familiar with a cultural context. One's own culture, of course, is taken for granted by the reader. Izevbaye concluded:

For any one of Sir Walter Scott's historical novels of Scotland or the fairly contemporary account of London life which we find in Virginia Woolf's *Mrs. Dalloway*, a truly African reader – if it were possible for him to read English without a good knowledge of its cultural background – would require as full a glossary as the average English reader would need to enter the literary world of *The Interpreters* and *Petals of Blood*.[13]

The European critic who blames the African writer for giving too much realistic information about his/her own society probably never thought of that when reading Virginia Woolf or other British writers. Different cultures lead to different appreciation of "the other's reality", as we have already seen in the previous chapter.

ad b): The commitment argument has become somewhat dubious in the Western context since, in the words of E. D. Hirsch, the instrumentalistic conception of literature has been replaced by the intrinsic.[14] In Africa this is very different. The artist has always had a social role and this is generally considered very positive and necessary. The Kenyan critic Micere Githae Mugo noted:

No apology is made for treating politics as a valid content of African literature. Being committed spokesmen of their societies, writers like Chinua Achebe, Ngugi wa Thiong'o and others cannot avoid engagement with politics or indeed with other force that affects the lives of the people . . . The militant African writer has become quite a formidable figure among the ruling elite and such a force in society that he is beginning to unsettle apathy and complacency at many levels . . . the good African writer has grown progressively radical in his denunciation of plunder, enslavement, inhumanity, corruption, oppression and other twin forces of destruction that have crippled his society and disfigured his people's image.[15]

Such an outspoken positive approach to committed literature is not easily found among Western critics as far as contemporary Western literature is concerned.

ad c): *The moral argument*. Earlier in this paper, I quoted from Achebe's essay on colonialist criticism. Here I should like to refer to a critical essay that the same writer wrote on Joseph Conrad's *Heart of Darkness*. The whole essay is, in fact, based upon an analysis of the text-reality relation. For Achebe, the most serious negative point in Conrad's *Heart of Darkness* is what he calls "the dehumanization of Africa and Africans which this age-long attitude (of Western arrogance) has fostered and continues to foster in the world". And the question is for him "whether a novel which celebrates this dehumanization, which depersonalizes a portion of the human race, can be called a great work of art", and his answer is no. He deplores the fact that the book is described by a serious scholar as belonging to "the half dozen greatest short novels in the English language", and is required reading in 20th-century literature courses in English Departments everywhere. His conclusion is that *Heart of Darkness* is an

[162]

objectionable book and he reproaches the critics for not having clearly made this point:

> . . . namely that Conrad was a bloody racist. That this simple truth is glossed over in criticism of his work is due to the fact that white racism against Africa is such a normal way of thinking . . . The time is long overdue for taking a hard look at the work of creative artists who apply their talents, alas often considerable as in the case of Conrad, to set people against people.[16]

It is an eloquent example of the moral argument based upon the relation between text and reality. Not all, or rather only a few Third World critics, agree with Achebe's view of Conrad. Although at first sight the selection of quotations he presents may seem significant, they are quoted out of context as both Wilson Harris (Caribbean) and Peter Nazareth (Goa) have convincingly demonstrated. Nazareth has written a fascinating critical essay on Conrad, "Out of Darkness", in which he compares this author with the controversial Trinidadian writer whom he has inspired, viz. V. S. Naipaul, who like Conrad was "missing a society".[17]

V. S. Naipaul is an interesting "case" indeed for the intercultural comparative study of critical texts. The fact that he is originally from the Third World has been used by critics in the Western World to label him a "specialist" on that world. As the Moroccan writer Tahar Ben Jelloun once said, V. S. Naipaul confirms the Western status quo, which is why Western critics are preparing him for the Nobel Prize.

In almost all the important Western literary magazines and supplements to newspapers, his books have been praised. His view of Third World "reality" has rarely been challenged in these reviews. The American critic Robert Hamner admired Naipaul's realism and the fact that he introduces "a significantly new environment (and) details necessary to an understanding and acceptance of the exotic (sic!) situation".[18] "Significantly new" to whom, one might ask, and exotic from

[163]

whose angle? He clearly speaks from a Western reader's perspective.

Hamner does not question Naipaul's selection of details and their ideological implications, but the Third World critics Peter Nazareth (Goa) and Mpoyi-Buatu (Zaïre) do. I shall summarize their main points with regard to the relation between text and reality.

Having read a large number of critical comments by Western critics, who glossed over the problem, it struck me that the African Mpoyi-Buatu immediately drew attention to the core of the matter, viz. the conflict between the two value systems: Naipaul constantly refers to universal civilization but what does he mean by it? Nonetheless, Mpoyi-Buatu agreed that Naipaul is an excellent writer, "unfortunately", he added, but that was not the point he wanted to discuss. For him, Naipaul's talents are undeniable and he disconnects them from his ideological objections to this author. Neither does he deny the author his freedom and his right to look at any society he wants and pass it through his moral filter. He also stated that as a critic he would not deny Naipaul the right to criticize the Third World. These three remarks are followed by counter-remarks, in which he demonstrates *how* Naipaul uses his filter as a mechanism to condition his views of the Third World; views that are not the only possible views nor necessarily the most correct ones of Third World reality. The key concept in Naipaul's work is civilization, it is introduced to underline and stigmatize the absence of it in a number of societies. Thus all people, things, and situations that do not belong to what this novelist considers "universal civilization" are just the opposite: "primitive", "elementary", "barbarous", "savage", "bush", and he refuses to see any wisdom or intellectual life in such societies. This is exactly the way colonization dealt with "universal civilization". Mpoyi-Buatu analyzed the oppositions in Naipaul's travelogues as well as in his fiction – constructed around the poles city/disinfected universe/Western world versus primitivism/barbarity/Africa/Third World. The Third World is eternally damned in Naipaul's eyes.[19]

In his review of *A Bend in the River*, the same critic used arguments with regard to the category of the text-reality relation and the category of the author-text relation. His conclusion was that Naipaul refuses to know Africa because his only intention is to rescue "Western civilization". He compared Naipaul with the European colonial writers in the past who used their colonial novels to nurture the Western world with their prejudices against people in other continents: Naipaul as a "technical assistant for propaganda on behalf of the West" and "a huge entertainer of the Western Gallery".[20]

Peter Nazareth made a comparative analysis of Conrad's *Heart of Darkness* and Naipaul's *A Bend in the River*. Naipaul's interpretation of Conrad's book had been that the Africans are to blame for Kurtz's own unrecognized darkness. Naipaul himself is obsessed by a terror of the bush. In *A Bend in the River*, his protagonist Salim is horrified "not at the way the West has exploited the colonies but at how the Arabs with their oil are going to bring down the West . . ." Naipaul refuses to show what the West was really doing out there.

Conrad tells the truth through his novella, although he did not have the opportunity to read Achebe's *Things fall Apart* . . . or other African novels that show that the 'bush' was not just 'bush'; there were people living there with their own cultural matrix and their own relationship to the environment before the white man came and tore them apart. V. S. Naipaul had that opportunity and made nothing of it.[21]

In closing I should like to link up the points I have made on the intercultural comparison of critical texts from different cultural value systems. Values are expressed in language, in the texts we study. Here I have not been able to present a detailed analysis, but the texts present ideological and cul-

[165]

tural views of society on the basis of a particular sociolect which can be described on three levels:

1. as a *lexical* repertory (the selection of a specific vocabulary).

2. on the *semantic* level (i.e. the relevance of certain classifications and oppositions resulting in a code which is the model for a corresponding view of "reality" and thus of culture).

3. on the *syntactic* level (i.e. the level of the discourse as the concretization, actualization, realization of semantic oppositions within the code of a sociolect).[22]

In critical texts, examples of selections on the basis of oppositions with regard to different cultures can be contrasts like civilization vs. barbarity, aesthetics vs. politics, world literature vs. local literature, light vs. darkness, intellect vs. emotions and so forth, as well as reactions to these views.

The critic's cultural norms can be discovered in his criticism. Its meaning will become much clearer when compared with a critical text coming from a very different cultural value system. Along the lines of the above mentioned six categories to be found in critical texts, the critics' own selected relevances can be compared and may provide better insight into the complex phenomenon of intercultural communication.

X. FREEDOM OF EXPRESSION AND THE "CULTURE OF SILENCE AND FEAR"

Article 19 of the Universal Declaration of Human Rights rightly states:

> Everyone has the right to freedom of opinion and expression: this right includes freedom to hold opinions without interference and to seek, receive and impart information and ideas through any media and regardless of frontiers.

How far we are from the ideal freedom that George Orwell once defined as "the right to say what people do not want to hear". Throughout the world, the freedom of expression is inhibited to one extent or another by censorship and self-censorship. Unfortunately, Africa is no exception to this sad rule.

Nowadays, censorship certainly affects the growth of literature north and south of the Sahara in many ways. However, it is difficult to measure the consequences this has had, and very little systematic research has been conducted on the subject. The media and the press are barely interested: in Europe due to indifference, in Africa for fear of reprisals.

What is censorship? The official banning of books and other publications, plays, films etc. which contain material "of an immoral or seditious nature"; and in wartime it is the examination of "private correspondence and newspapers to stop information reaching the enemy," as the dictionaries put it. Of course, in a number of cases writers might foresee what would be considered immoral or seditious by their censors, and where war threatens to begin for them personally. The next decision to make then is how to react to such a situation. Censorship means fear. Fear on the part of the people in power, since they dread the power of the word. Fear on the part of the people whose work is censored, fear of the possible consequences: prosecution, imprisonment, disappearance, exile, murder. Many African writers live in exile, either voluntarily or involuntarily, sometimes temporarily, often permanently. Officially, there is little question of censorship in independent Africa. The number of writers imprisoned or disappeared isn't considered spectacular (if the world knows about them at all), in comparison to those who have fled or those who have disappeared in Latin America, for instance.[1] Nevertheless, many African writers are afraid of the censorship in their native countries, and it is this fear that sooner or later makes them opt for self-censorship or exile.

Given the wide range of cultural and social forms on the vast continent of Africa, one finds an equally wide variety of literary forms. Yet many African cultures have certain aspects in common, such as the oral literature of pre-colonial times and the colonial experience.

From times immemorial, the poet often had the role of society's critic, and in that delicate role he had the support of the community he belonged to, the village, the clan. The singer, the narrator, the poet, the author in the Latin sense of *auctor* – which means artist and storyteller at the same time – contributed to the group's power over the individual or the abuse of that power by the group, the community. In this sense the word could serve as a weapon. Poets, or "griots", as they are called in West Africa, have been known to cause the downfall of a chief or king by way of their critical poetry. The word of the artist had to be reckoned with in traditional society. If the man in power asserted himself too

[168]

much, the author could use his influence against him and provoke protest, or even a revolt, by the people.

Colonization became a general factor of change: all across the greater part of the continent, it led to some common characteristics in African history. The colonial epoch contributed to the widespread destruction of traditional cultural systems. The occupiers imposed new life styles, which were often strongly criticized by the majority of the local population. This is why certain popular folk songs were gradually banned. A well-known example is the blind Acoli singer Adok-Too in Uganda, who protested against the forced labour introduced by the chief, who was the representative of the British colonial authorities in the village. He was sentenced to two years of imprisonment: although he couldn't read or write, his voice was still feared. Here is a passage from one of his songs that became very popular and was considered "dangerous":

I become Death
I fall on the Chief
I take a bicycle
I go to Gulu
I fall on the District Commissioner
I become Death
I enter the aeroplane
I fly to England
I fall on the King.[2]

During the colonial era, the writings of dissident African or European authors considered subversive by the colonial authorities were regularly censored. In those days, there were very few independent publishing houses. The majority of them were controlled by the political authorities or run by missionaries. Now, about twenty to thirty years after independence, there are many local publishers but they are often small and vulnerable, and are faced with the overwhelming competition from the grand European publishing houses.

What about the freedom of expression of today's African writers living in Africa? Like their colonial predecessors, a growing number of post-colonial African governments do not tolerate "subversive" literature and try to suppress it any way they can. This has serious consequences for the culture and literature in countries where all forms of legal opposition are often lacking. If the press and media are almost entirely controlled by the rulers, then literature and other art forms are in principle the only non-conformistic means of expression left. But as soon as artists utter their criticism, they risk being labelled subversive and undesirable.

Due to the widespread illiteracy in Africa, writers didn't have any problems in the first years after independence, the more so because they usually wrote in foreign languages not mastered by the great majority of the population. Moreover, books were (and still are) expensive and therefore hard to come by. That state of affairs hasn't changed since.

Books from abroad have to be paid for in hard currency, which restricts the amounts imported, and local publishing houses are often forced to import their paper from abroad. To do so, requests have to be submitted to the government, since imported paper first goes to the government departments and scarcity of paper is not exceptional. All these facts inhibit the development of national literature in a good number of countries.

There was a time when written literature wasn't regarded as being very dangerous and it didn't seem necessary for rulers to take any systematic measures against writers. If literature criticized society in the 1960s, it was most often in novels, plays and poetry on colonial society. Since then, the literary themes have gradually changed: nationalism and opposition to white oppressors have now been virtually abandoned as principal themes. Instead of opposing the West, many writers now turn to their own countries and express their discontent with the ruling elite and the one-party system. This has made the rulers more apt to be the target of contemporary writers who are increasingly confronted with the difficult choice of either remaining silent and conforming, or braving the risks and exposing themselves to the possible consequences. There are certainly differences between one state and another, but the freedom of people involved with literature and theatre in Africa is in ever more danger.

Rather than presenting a long list of censorship cases – a complete list has yet to be drawn up – it seems more appropriate to give concrete examples from different countries to illustrate how freedom of expression has been suppressed, and how far censorship can go if literature is perceived by political authorities as being a threat to the establishment. For that purpose, I have selected three well-known writers unfortunate enough to have had the experience of being censored: Mongo Béti of Cameroun, Ngugi wa Thiong'o of Kenya and Abdellatif Laâbi of Morocco.

The case of Mongo Béti is not unknown in the French-speaking world. I have chosen him because his experience clearly demonstrates the links between Africa and the West in this matter; certain African writers have suffered not only from African censorship but from European censorship as well. Mongo Béti has lived in France for more than thirty years, having settled there after completing his studies because his ideas were not welcome in his native country. In the 1950s, he wrote a number of novels about the colonial era, presenting and judging the French authorities from an African point of view. In certain colonial and missionary circles, these books were condemned because of the "ingratitude" the author exhibited.

After a long silence on Béti's part, *Main basse sur le Cameroun. Autopsie d'une décolonisation* was published by Editions Maspéro in 1972. The censorship record of this book is interesting for various reasons. It was immediately banned in Cameroon. The author lived in exile and thus had no problems in his native country. The book describes Cameroon's evolution, the growing repression, and prison conditions. It also deals with Cameroon's post-colonial history, and shows

[171]

how little interest the Western media had in the violation of human rights in Africa, except when a white nun was raped or a French citizen abducted. The French press remained silent, in order not to harm the relations of interest that unite France to its former colonies. By government order, the book was also banned in France and all the copies were confiscated. According to Béti, there were expulsion procedures against him, and police in uniform and in plain clothes came to his home to find him. The writer started a lawsuit against the authorities and won it four years later. His book was published again in 1976. Maspéro claimed damages, and on 9 July 1981, the Court sentenced the Ministry of the Interior to pay 10,000 francs damages to the author.

How had the Minister been able to censor the book? Section 14 of a French Act dated 1881 allows the Minister of the Interior to ban "foreign books". This happened on several occasions, even in the 1970s, with books written by Africans or about Africa. It shows that the freedom of African writers can depend on the caprice of Western countries, be it for economic or political reasons.[3]

What is more, African writers who wish to publish in Europe have to take into account the techniques and literary norms fashionable among Europeans and comply with the criteria set by the multinational publishing system. Otherwise, they risk being ignored. Or they are manipulated in spite of their own intentions. As Mongo Béti put it:

Our writings are at the mercy of the exclusive dictatorship of the non-African critics, the commentators, the interpreters, the chroniclers of the Francophone world. Even if the good faith of the latter is total, how could they not draw our works, unconsciously, in the obligatory directions, the tunnels, the deadlocks, the side-tracks that French culture has engraved in their conscience and where we, the others are driven aside and consequently are adulterated. . . . After having first tried to fight me, their next strategy became to appropriate me. But that means viol-

[172]

ence and repression since such enterprises can only succeed to the extent to which the writer is powerless to
disavow the almighty critics working through the media
and the untouchable university mandarins.[4]

In independent Africa, the English-speaking countries seem
to enjoy greater freedom of expression than the ones where
French is spoken, though a number of writers in such former
English colonies as Kenya, Sierra Leone, Malawi, to mention
only a few, have their complaints too. They prefer to compare
their liberty to that of the British press, rather than to that
of papers in the French-speaking countries of Africa. There
are also numerous forms of censorship that hardly manifest
themselves at all on the surface: publishing restrictions are
not solely due to material problems. Publishers often follow
a policy of extreme prudence as they sometimes run even
more risks than writers. Where censorship rules, writers have
to make concessions if they want to have their books published. Self-censorship is often necessary if they are to avoid
repressive measures. It is almost impossible to investigate
this matter, because how are we to know whether a writer
has given in to the establishment?
    The cases of writers who refused to censor themselves are
more spectacular, since a confrontation with the authorities
inevitably has ensued. The Kenyan Ngugi wa Thiong'o has
had that experience. The history of this novelist, playwright
and essayist of international renown sheds an interesting
light on the plight of African writers using African languages
to reach their compatriots. From the outset of his career,
Ngugi adopted a critical attitude toward society. However,
since he wrote in English, he didn't represent much of a
threat to the government, even when his plays and novels
contained passages about corruption, pillaging by the elite,
and acts of popular resistance. Whatever the case may be,
for a long time he didn't encounter any obstacles. Things
only changed when Ngugi started writing in Gikuyu, his
mother tongue. His first play in that language was *Ngaahika*

Ndeenda ("I Will Marry When I Want"). This incriminating play relates the story of a farmer chased from his patch of land by a rich landowner who wants to build an insecticide factory with the aid of foreign investors. The enthusiasm of the audiences was immediately so overwhelming that the authorities took fright. Ngugi rehearsed the theatrical performance in the village of Kamirithu with the inhabitants, farmers and workers. Together they focused on the text, the participants adding ideas and suggesting changes taken from their own experiences, because the village actors were very well aware that their own situation was being dealt with. Thus a true popular theatre was born: theatre by the people and for the people.

Shortly after the first performances, Ngugi was arrested without any charge ever having been brought against him. Apparently the play was subversive in the eyes of the authorities, because it had been presented in the language of the oppressed about their situation and with their collaboration. And because it was theatre, even illiterates had easy access to it. For his democratic ideas about literature and society, Ngugi paid the price of one year in prison without trial. Following protests from all over the world, he was released, but was not allowed to continue his professorship at the University of Nairobi. In 1982 another work, the musical *Maitu Njugira* ("Mother, Sing for Me") was already banned during the rehearsals. Since then, all community activities have been forbidden in the village of Kamirithu. Three trucks with policemen were sent to destroy the open air theatre, which had been built by the villagers with their own funds and their own hands. Ngugi had to flee from his homeland and now lives in exile in London.

Popular theatre is obviously feared by the authorities if it deals with the problems of people in poor city districts or in the countryside where people have no fewer sorrows. Theatre performances reach a large audience and make people aware of their situation. Since the events in Kamirithu, laws have increasingly restrained the production of popular theatre in Kenya. The authorities now prescribe which themes are allowed to be used by pupils at the School Theatre Festival. No controversial subject is tolerated and the approval of the authorities is required for every new theatrical production. This is how self-censorship starts to play its role. Creativity is muzzled by the instructions and prohibitions of the state. The alternative is a life in exile. This doesn't hold true only for Kenya and Cameroon, but for a great number of African countries, as is evident in the monthly journal *Index on Censorship*, which compiles the gloomy balance sheet of censorship all over the world.

The third example I have chosen, is that of the Moroccan writer Abdellatif Laâbi, who was in prison for eight and a half years. A professor of French, he has published prose and poetry and was French editor of the literary journal *Souffles*, which later came out in an Arab version called *Anfas*. It published the texts of young Moroccans, full of ideas on society and the changes they thought should be brought about.

In January 1972, Abdellatif Laâbi was arrested and tortured. He complained about this treatment and was released on bail. He was arrested again in March of the same year. Once more, he was severely tortured and was left in the hands of the special branch of the Security Police known as the "second bureau". After his release from prison, he was still not allowed to travel for several years: the authorities refused him a passport. It wasn't until the end of 1984 that he was able to travel with the right to return to Morocco, where he lives. Life for Mr. Laâbi has not been easy, but he continues to believe in his duties as a writer. During a recent visit to the Netherlands, he explained that, much to his regret, there is no organization in his country to record, reveal and review cases of censorship. Thus one never knows what is going to happen before someone publishes something. Nevertheless,

a writer who loves his profession and who is experienced,

[175]

knows almost instinctively which words and expressions he may use to say what he finds essential without becoming unfaithful to his principles . . . Writing with his body and blood, with his entire cultural and historical memory, he takes risks. But at the same time, writing is a strongly pleasurable profession, an invigorating act, breaking the law of silence . . .
My offence happened to be in the domain of freedom of expression. As a matter of fact, it was not only a question of my incarceration, of my freedom at stake, but a concern for all those who are preoccupied with the freedom of expression: the moment one person's liberty is injured anywhere in the world, that implies an injury to all of mankind.[5]

For literature, the most serious danger is undoubtedly the impoverishing stifling of every opposing voice. In 1978 Wole Soyinka told me, not without pride, that in his country, Nigeria, there was no censorship and that not one writer or journalist was in prison. Of late, he has fiercely criticized the restrictions on the freedom of expression in Nigeria. His own film *Blues for a Prodigal* was temporarily banned before the official première in Lagos in February 1985. He was allowed to show it only after having deleted certain passages. Nigeria used to be exemplary in the field of free expression in Africa. At a conference in Nsukka some years ago, however, Chinua Achebe expressed his concern as follows:

My concern is not what politicians say or do, but the absence of a countervailing tradition of enlightened criticism and dissent . . . In this situation a writer who must be free, whose second nature is to dance to a "different drummer" and not march like a boy scout, such a person has no choice really but to run great risks. And we had better know it and prepare for it.[6]

Literature is most threatened by being reduced to silence,

[176]

by what Ngugi has called the "culture of silence and fear", according to him the most dangerous cancer in the Third World. It is this cancer that visibly threatens African literature more and more today.[7]

Because of the serious risk, many writers and critics in Africa prefer to remain silent, simply because their survival is at stake. This situation poses serious problems to artistic work, problems ranging from the destruction of literary works to physical harm to authors.

At the Institute of Contemporary Arts in London, Wole Soyinka recently blamed Western intellectuals, who are in a position to express themselves freely, for not raising their voices in protest against the state of affairs in Africa. Why are they so indifferent about the violation of free expression in Africa, while they do not cease to protest against what is happening in the Soviet Union or what happened in Greece some years ago?

The artistic community knows no bounds and the fight against injustice is indivisible. Terror is terror and the artist and his craft are open to the same dangers under the Greek colonels in the world's oldest democracy or under a despot in the so-called Third World.[8]

What conclusions can be drawn? As scholars and critics, it goes without saying that we are concerned about the stifling censorship of African literature. As with the iceberg, just a small tip of the matter is known to us, the greater part being hidden under the surface. We can but recommend and encourage systematic and serious research. Indeed, the first thing to be investigated is how the lack of freedom of expression has affected and continues to affect literature in Africa. The following elements may serve as guidelines:

1. *Inventory*: the first task is to collect all the available data (number of writers in prison, books banned, and writers living in exile, for each country concerned).

[177]

2. *Effects of imprisonment*: interviews with formerly imprisoned writers, and the study of documents written in prison or works written after and about imprisonment. An entire prison literature has begun to develop in Africa and a serious comparative study on this subject has never been conducted.
3. *Exile and its consequences*: a) for the writers concerned (change of themes and/or language, the exile's perspective on home countries etc.); b) for the country or origin: are the author and his work ignored, opposed, tolerated, or banned? c) for the literary tradition of the country and for the new generation of writers being formed (e.g. South Africa where an entire generation of writers left the country in the 1960s; most of their works were banned or made inaccessible, while the young writers had to start from scratch).
4. *Reception of texts written by writers in exile or in prison, in their own countries and elsewhere*: what is the attitude of the critics? Are they positive or negative, for literary or for political reasons? In a great number of countries, being a literary critic can have political implications and unpredictable effects. To give just one example: the adversaries of Ngugi wa Thiong'o who were severely critical of his literary work became the cherished ones of President Moi. On the other hand, certain writers may receive special attention from the foreign press, for reasons that have nothing to do with the literary qualities of their work.

It should be clear that these four points are not the only ones, but they might serve as a starting point for more research on the vast subject of censorship. Thus, hopefully, these scholarly activities may increase awareness of and concern for the threats it represents, not only to the richness of African literature, but, even worse, to the life and well-being of its creators, critical witnesses of their countries' realities or absurdities, and defenders of the freedom to write.

[178]

NOTES

Notes to Chapter One

1. Henry Louis Gates Jr (Ed.), *Black Literature and Literary Theory*, Methuen, New York/London, 1984, p. 3.
2. Jonathan Culler, *The Pursuit of Signs: Semiotics, Literature, Deconstruction*, Ithaca, Cornell University Press, 1981, p. 5.
3. Umberto Eco, *A Theory of Semiotics*, London, Macmillan, 1977, pp. 61 f.

Notes to Chapter Two

1. René Wellek and A. Warren, *Theory of Literature*, Harmondsworth, Penguin Books, (1949) 1973.
2. Haskell M. Block, *Nouvelles tendances en littérature comparée*, Paris, Nizet, 1970; René Etiemble, "Littérature comparée, ou Comparaison n'est pas raison", in: Idem, *Hygiène des lettres*, tome 3, *Savoir et goût*, Paris, Gallimard, 1958, pp. 154–174. See also Etiemble, *Essais de Littérature (vraiment) générale*, Paris, Gallimard 1974, pp. 9–35, and in this book chapter IX.
3. Roy Harvey Pearce, *Historicism Once More. Problems and Occasions for the American Scholar*, Princeton University Press, 1969; D. W. Fokkema, "Cultureel relativisme en vergelijkende literatuurwetenschap", Inaugural Lecture, Amsterdam, Arbeiderspers, 1971.

[179]

4. Ruth Benedict, *Patterns of Culture*, London, Routledge and Kegan Paul, (1935) 1971; Melville Herskovits (ed.), *Cultural Relativism. Perspectives in Cultural Pluralism*, New York, Vintage, Random House, 1973. See also Ton Lemaire, *Over de waarde van culturen. Een inleiding in de cultuurfilosofie. Tussen europacentrisme en relativisme*, Baarn, Ambo, 1976.
5. E. B. Tylor, *Primitive Culture* (2 vol.), (London, Murray, 1871), New York, Harper Torch, 1958.
6. Arnold Toynbee, "Widening Our Historical Horizon", in Martin Ballard (Ed.), *New Movements in the Study and Teaching of History*, London, Temple Smith, 1970, pp. 50–62.
7. E.g., Ruth Finnegan, *Oral Literature in Africa*, London, Oxford University Press and *Oral Poetry. Its Nature, Significance and Social Context*, Cambridge University Press, 1977.
8. See also chapter VII.
9. Pierre V. Zima, "Les mécanismes discursifs de l'idéologie", in *Revue de l'Institut de sociologie*, 1981 (4), pp. 719–740.
10. Bernard Mouralis, *Les contre-littératures*, Paris, P.U.F. 1975.
11. Itamar Even-Zohar, "Polysystem Theory", in *Poetics Today*, vol. 1, number 1–2, autumn 1979, p. 290.
12. Ibid., p. 291.
13. Ibid., p. 292. See also chapter IV in this volume.
14. Isidore Okpewho, "Comparatism and Separatism in African Literature", in *World Literature Today*, 1981, vol. 55 (1), p. 26.
15. Cf. Mineke Schipper (Ed.), *Text and Context. Methodological Explorations in the Field of African Literature*, Leiden, Afrika-Studiecentrum, 1977.
16. Gérard Leclerc, *Anthropologie et colonialisme*, Paris, Fayard, 1972; Roy Preiswerk et Dominique Perrot, *Ethnocentrisme et histoire*, Paris, Editions Anthropos, 1975; Bernard Mouralis, op. cit. cf. note 10.
17. Robert Cornevin, *Le théâtre en Afrique Noire et à Madagascar*, Paris, Le livre africain, 1970. Cf. in this book chapter VI.
18. Cf. Okpewho op. cit., p. 27.

[180]

19. Alejo Carpentier, Problemática de la actual novela latino-americana, in: *Tientas y diferencias*, La Habana, Cuba, 1974.
20. Cf. note 6.

Notes to Chapter Three

1. E. Mphahlele, *The African Image*, Revised Edition, New York, 1974, p. 79.
2. See my article "Littérature zaïroise et société décolonisée", in: *Kroniek van Afrika*, Leiden, 1972-4, pp. 187-194.
3. L. Kesteloot, *Les écrivains noirs de langue française: naissance d'une littérature*, Brussels, 1963; J. Jahn, *A History of Neo-African Literature. Writing in Two Continents*, New York, 1968; R. Depestre, *Bonjour et adieu à la Négritude*, Paris, 1980; M. Towa, *Poésie de la négritude. Approche structuraliste*, Sherbrooke, 1985.
4. In: *Caribbean Studies*, vol. 8/1, April 1968, p. 46.
5. R. Poggioli, *The Theory of the Avant-Garde*, Cambridge, Mass., 1968, pp. 17-40.
6. R. Wellek, *Concepts of Criticism*, New Haven, 1963, p. 151.
7. In: *Présence Africaine*, 54, 2nd trim. 1965, pp. 99-100.
8. Wellek, op. cit., p. 151.
9. Quoted in Mphahlele, op. cit., first edition, London, 1962, p. 50.
10. In *Situations III*, Paris, 1949, p. 270. (This and other translations of French quotations are mine.) This phenomenon is not unknown; other peoples have also believed that they had to play a similar role, for example the Jews, the Poles, the Russians.
11. Aimé Césaire, *Et les chiens se taisaient*, Paris (1946) 1961, pp. 151, 186.
12. J. Matthews and G. Thomas, *Cry rage*, Johannesburg, 1972.
13. N. Gordimer, *The Black Interpreters*, Johannesburg, 1972, p. 70.
14. D. Diop, *Coups de pilon*, Paris, (1961) 1973, p. 48.
15. P. Ndu, article in *Présence Africaine*, 86, 2nd trim. 1973, pp. 130ff.

16. See my article "Noirs et Blancs dans l'oeuvre d'Aimé Césaire", in: *Présence Africaine*, 72, 4th trim. 1969, pp. 124–147.
17. Clark, op. cit., p. 102; F. E. K. Parkes, "African Heaven", in: *An African Treasury*, selected by L. Hughes, New York, 1961, pp. 170–172; O. M. Mtshali, *Sounds of a Cowhide Drum*, in the volume of the same name (1971), London, 1974, pp. 71–72; D. Kadima-Nzuji, Afrique, in: *Anthologie des écrivains congolais*, Kinshasa, 1969, p. 235.
18. L. Damas, *Black Label*, Paris, 1956, p. 52.
19. L. S. Senghor, *La littérature africaine d'expression française*, in Idem, *Liberté I, Négritude et humanisme*, Paris, 1964, p. 401.
20. Idem, *Poèmes*, Paris 1964, pp. 92–93.
21. M. Towa, *Léopold Sédar Senghor: négritude ou servitude*, Yaoundé, 1971, p. 72.
22. A. Césaire, *Ferrements*, Paris, 1960, p. 85.
23. J. Roumain, *La montagne ensorcelée*, Paris, 1972, pp. 306.
24. Ibid., pp. 234–235.
25. F. Fanon, *L'An V de la Révolution Algérienne*, Paris, 1959; O. Sembène, *Le Mandat*, Paris, 1965, p. 15.
26. S. S. K. Adotevi, *Négritude et négrologues*, Paris, 1972, p. 306.
27. A. Irele, A Defence of Negritude, in *Transition*, 13, March–April 1964, pp. 9–11. He has changed his views since, as he told me in a discussion on the matter at the University of Mainz in 1975.
28. Adotevi, op. cit., pp. 47, 48 (my translation).
29. M. de Andrade, *La poésie négro-africaine d'expression portugaise*, Paris, 1969, pp. 26–28.
30. See for example the anthologies *Poets to the People. South African Freedom Poems*, B. Feinberg (Ed.), London, 1974; *To Whom it May Concern*, A. Royston (Ed.), Johannesburg, 1973.
31. Mphahlele, op. cit., p. 81; id., "Africa in Exile," in: *Daedalus*, 1982, p. 48.
32. Paper read at the Second African Writers' Conference in Stockholm (April 1986) entitled: "Beyond Protest: New Directions in South African Literature", p. 11.

33. Ibid., p. 12.
34. Interview, October 1974.
35. Letter of 21 November 1974.
36. L. S. Senghor, "Lusitanité et Africanité", in: *Jeune Afrique*, 21 March, 1975, pp. 22–25.
37. Interview, October 1974 in Amsterdam.
38. Interview, February 1975 in Rotterdam.
39. In: Adotevi, op. cit., pp. 151, 152, 207.
40. F. Fanon, *Peau noire, masques blancs*, Paris, 1952, pp. 206, 207.

Notes to Chapter Four

1. Cf. G. Plumpe and K. O. Conrady, "Probleme der Literaturgeschichtschreibung," in: H. Brackert and J. Stückrath (Eds.), *Literaturwissenschaft. Grundkurs 2*, Reinbek/Hamburg, Rowolt, 1981, pp. 373–392.
2. I. Even-Zohar, "Polysystem theory", *Poetics Today*, vol. 1, no. 1–2, autumn 1979, p. 290. This article is very relevant to the topic of literary historiography.
3. Ibid., pp. 301–302.
4. Ibid., p. 292.
5. Cf. Richard Björnson, "Nationalliteratur und nationale Identität in Afrika: Kamerun als Beispiel", *Komparatistische Hefte* ii (1985) p. 70.
6. Viorica Niscov, "Bemerkungen über die Dialektik des Begriffes Nationalliteratur", *Synthesis X*, 1983, p. 13 ff.
7. V. Y. Mudimbe, *Autour de la "Nation". Leçons de Civisme*, Kinshasa/Lubumbashi, Editions du Mont Noir, coll. "Objectif 80", 1972, p. 23 (my translation).
8. For theoretical aspects of the "national question", see the useful article by Nsame Mbongo, "Problèmes théoriques de la question nationale en Afrique", in: *Présence Africaine*, 136, 4th trim. 1985, pp. 31–67.
9. The expression is Michael Etherton's and refers to new cultural forms developed in the city, a mixture of

[183]

traditional and new elements, the results of which are sometimes very original. See his "The Dilemma of the Popular ᴾlaywright", *African Literature Today*, 8, 1976, pp. 26–41.

10. For this list I am indebted to Niscov, art. cit., p. 16.
11. See chap. II in this volume.
12. Roman Jakobson, "Linguistics and Poetics", Thomas A. Sebeok, Editor, *Style in Language*, Cambridge, Massachusetts, M. I. T. Press, 1960, p. 356.
13. See for general comments on these three points: Felix Vodička, *Die Struktur der Literarischen Entwicklung*, München, Fink Verlag, 1976, pp. 30–86.
14. Cf. Frantz Fanon, *Les damnés de la terre*, (1961) 1968, Paris, Maspéro, p. 147.
15. Fanon, op. cit., chapter 4.
16. Bruce King, *The New English Literatures. Cultural Nationalism in a Changing World*, London, Macmillan (New Literary Handbooks), 1980, pp. 43–44.
17. Ibid., pp. 44–45.
18. Wole Soyinka, "The Writer in a Modern African State", in: Per Wästberg (Ed.) *The Writer in Modern Africa*. Uppsala, the Scandinavian Institute of African Studies, 1968, p. 21.
19. For the effects of censorship and research on the subject, see chapter X.
20. Fanon, op. cit., p. 162–163.

Notes to Chapter Five

1. Monroe C. Beardsley, "Aspects of Orality": A Short Commentary, in: *New Literary History*, 8, 1976–77 (3), p. 521 f.
2. Ruth Finnegan, *Oral Literature in Africa*, Oxford, Clarendon Press, 1970, p. 322.
3. Emmanuel Obiechina, "Amos Tutuola and the Oral Tradition", in: *Présence Africaine*, 65 (1), 1968, pp. 86–87.
4. Obiechina, *Culture, Tradition and Society in the West African Novel*, Cambridge University Press, 1975, ch. 2.

5. A selection of the Colloquium papers has been published by ICA, the African Cultural Institute, under the title *La tradition orale, source de la littérature contemporaine en Afrique*, Dakar, Nouvelles Editions Africaines, 1985.
6. In his collection of texts by Russian Formalists, *Théorie de la littérature*, Paris, Editions du Seuil, 1966, Tzvetan Todorov translated *skaz* by "récit direct", but in Striedter's collection *Russischer Formalismus*, Munich, UTB, Fink Verlag, 1971, it is explained that *skaz* has a different meaning. It is related to *skazat*, "to say", and to *rasskaz*, "tale", and *skazka*, "folk-tale" (= "*Märchen*") Cf. J. Striedter, "Zur formalistischen Theorie der Prosa und der literarischen Evolution," in: Idem (Ed.), op. cit., p. xliv; see also in the same collection, Boris Eichenbaum, "Die Illusion des *skaz*", pp. 161–67 and Viktor Vinogradov, "Das Problem des *skaz* in der Stilistik," pp. 168–207.
7. Cf. Bernth Lindfors (Ed.), *Critical Perspectives on Amos Tutuola*, Washington, D.C., Three Continents Press, 1975, p. 7, quoting Dylan Thomas' "Blithe Spirits," in: *The Observer*, 6 July 1952. Ulli Beier, review of Tutuola's *Brave African Huntress*, in: *Black Orpheus*, 4 (October 1958), p. 52.
8. Omolara Ogundipe-Leslie, "The Palm-Wine Drinkard: A Reassessment of Amos Tutuola", in: *Présence Africaine*, 3rd trim. 1969, p. 105.
9. Amos Tutuola, *The Palm-Wine Drinkard and His Dead Palm-Wine Tapster in the Dead's Town*, London, Faber and Faber, 1952, p. 83.
10. Tutuola, *Ajaiyi and His Inherited Poverty*, London, Faber and Faber, 1967, p. 11.
11. Ruth Finnegan, op. cit. ch. 11.
12. Amos Tutuola, *The Brave African Huntress*, New York, Grove Press, 1958, p. 44; Beier, art. cit., p. 52.
13. Ruth Finnegan, op. cit., p. 385.
14. Amos Tutuola, *Simbi and the Satyr of the Dark Jungle*, London, Faber and Faber, 1955, p. 38.
15. William Bascom (Ed.), *African Dilemma Tales*, The Hague/Paris, Mouton Publishers, p. 1.

16. Cf. Obiechina, "Amos Tutuola and the Oral Tradition", p. 101.
17. Amos Tutuola, *My Life in the Bush of Ghosts*, London, Faber and Faber, (1954) 1962.
18. Amos Tutuola, *Feather Woman of the Jungle*, London, Faber and Faber, 1962.
19. Ruth Finnegan, op. cit., p. 387.
20. Gerald Moore, "Amos Tutuola: A Modern Visionary", in: Idem, *Seven African Writers*, London, Oxford University Press, 1962, p. 44.
21. Denise Paulme, *La Mère dévorante. Essais sur la morphologie des contes africains*, Paris, NRF, Gallimard, 1976, p. 23ff.
22. Taban lo Liyong, "Tutuola, Son of Zinjanthropos", in: Idem, *The Last Word. Cultural Synthesism*, Nairobi, East African Publishing House, 1969, p. 167.

Notes to Chapter Six

1. R. Cornevin, *Le théâtre en Afrique noire et à Madagascar*, Paris, 1970, pp. 46–52, p. 68.
2. A. Artaud, *Le théâtre et son double* (1934), Paris, 1977, p. 53 (my translation).
3. A. Graham-White, *The Drama of Black Africa*, New York/London, 1974, p. 14.
4. I have treated the subject more fully in my book *Théâtre et société en Afrique*, Dakar/Abidjan/Lomé, Nouvelles Editions Africaines, 1985.
5. T. Omara, *The Exodus*, in: D. Cook and M. Lee (Eds), *Short East African Plays in English*, London, 1972; C. V. Mutwa, *uNosilimela*, in: R. M. Kavanagh (Ed.), *South African People's Plays* (G. Kente, C. V. Mutwa, M. Shezi and Workshop '71), London, 1981, pp. 6–7.
6. K. Ogunbesan, "A King for All Seasons: Chaka in African Literature", in: *Présence Africaine*, 88 (4), pp. 197–217.
7. C. Dailly, "L'histoire et la politique comme sources d'inspiration", in: *Le théâtre négro-africain, Actes du Colloque d'Abidjan 1970*, Paris 1971, p. 91.

[186]

8. Ngugi wa Thiong'o and Micere Githae Mugo, *The Trial of Dedan Kimathi*, London, 1976.
9. E. Sutherland, *The Marriage of Anansewa*, London, 1975.
10. W. Soyinka, *A Dance of the Forests*, London, 1960, p. 38.
11. Guillaume Oyônô-Mbia, *Trois prétendants . . . un mari*, Yaoundé, CLE, 1969; the subject of the dowry is also central to Guy Menga's *L'Oracle*, which follows *La Marmite de Koka Mbala* in the CLE series, Yaoundé, 1976.
12. See above, note 9.
13. Paul Mushiete and Norbert Mikanza, *Pas de feu pour les antilopes*, Kinshasa, Eds. Congo p. 196. Oyono–Mbia, op. cit., Introduction, p. 7.
14. Cf. M. Etherton, *The Development of African Drama*, London, 1982 and M. Schipper, op. cit.
15. M. Etherton, "The Dilemma of the Popular Playwright", in: *African Literature Today*, 1976 (8), pp. 26–41.
16. Ibid.
17. A. Ricard, "Concours et concert: théâtre scolaire et théâtre populaire au Togo", in: *Revue d'Histoire du Théâtre*, 1975 (1), pp. 44–85. See also his recent book *L'invention du théâtre*, Lausanne, L'Age d'Homme, 1986.
18. IDAF, *Fact Paper on Southern Africa*, "Black Theatre in South Africa", no. 2, June 1976, p. 2.
19. M. Mutloatse (Ed.), *Forced Landing. Africa South: Contemporary Writings*, Johannesburg, 1980, p. 5.
20. Kavanagh, op. cit., pp. xiii–xiv.
21. Ibid., p. xix.
22. Ibid., p. xvii.
23. L. Nkosi, *Tasks and Masks. Themes and Styles of African Literature*, London, 1982, pp. 79, 80.
24. Kavanagh, op. cit., p. xxx. See also David B. Coplan, *In Township Tonight! South Africa's Black City Music and Theatre*, Johannesburg, 1985, and R. Kavanagh, *Theatre and the Cultural Struggles in South Africa*, London, 1985.

Notes to Chapter Seven

1. See e.g. William C. Spengemann, *The Forms of Autobiography. Episodes in the History of a Genre*, New Haven/London, Yale University Press, 1980; Georges May, *L'autobiographie*, Paris, P. U. F., 1979.
2. Bernd Neumann, *Identität und Rollenzwang. Zur Theorie der Autobiographie*, Frankfurt, Athenaeum, 1970, p. 109.
3. Stuart Bates, quoted by May, op. cit., p. 17 (my translation); G. Gusdorf, "De l'autobiographie initiatique à l'autobiographie genre littéraire", in: *Revue de l'histoire littéraire de la France*, 1975, pp. 957–994.
4. Milena Doleželová-Velingerová (Ed.), *The Chinese Novel at the Turn of the Century*, Toronto/Buffalo/London, University of Toronto Press, p. 15.
5. Idem, Ibid., "Narrative Modes in Late Qing Novels", p. 66.
6. Ibid., p. 70.
7. Ibid., p. 72.
8. Ibid., pp. 71–72.
9. Shlomith Rimmon-Kenan, *Narrative Fiction. Contemporary Poetics*, London/New York, Methuen (Series New Accents), 1983, pp. 8–9. See also: Mieke Bal, *Narratology, Introduction to the Theory of Narrative*, Toronto, University of Toronto Press, 1985.
10. More research needs to be done with regard to the comparison of differences in presentation of oral and written texts. Still I agree with Rimmon-Kenan (op. cit. p. 89) that "the empirical process of communication between author and reader is less relevant to the poetics of narrative fiction than its counterpart in the text".
11. Cf. Roland Colin, *Les contes de l'Ouest Africain*, Paris, Présence Africaine, 1957, p. 84; Ruth Finnegan, *Oral Literature in Africa*, Oxford, At the Clarendon Press, 1970, pp. 380–81.
12. D. O. Fagunwa, *The Forest of a Thousand Daemons*, translated by Wole Soyinka, London, Nelson, (1968) 1982, pp. 8–9.
13. Gérard Genette, *Figures III*, Paris, Seuil, 1972. In English

translation: *Narrative Discourse*, Ithaca/New York, Cornell University Press, 1980. Genette combines theory and description in his analysis of possible narrative systems with the application of his theoretical considerations to Proust's *A la recherche du temps perdu*. Rimmon (op. cit.) gives a practical and clear introduction to the new approaches of narrative fiction, in which she also discusses Genette's theories.

14. Chinua Achebe, *Things Fall Apart*, Greenwich, Conn., Fawcett Publications, 1959, p. 72.
15. Wole Soyinka, *Aké. The Years of Childhood*, London, Rex Collings, 1981, p. 2.
16. Cf. Rimmon-Kenan, op. cit., p. 91ff.
17. Mariama Bâ, *Une si longue lettre*, Dakar, Nouvelles Editions Africaines, 1979. The English translation (by Modupé Bodé-Thomas) *So Long a Letter*, London, Heinemann, 1981, has been used here.
18. Amos Tutuola, *The Palm-Wine Drinkard and His Dead Palm-Wine Tapster in the Deads' Town*, London, Faber and Faber, 1952; idem, *Feather Woman of the Jungle*, London, Faber and Faber, 1962. See also my "Perspective narrative et récit africain à la première personne" in the collection of papers I edited for the African Studies Centre in Leiden: *Text and Context. Methodological Explorations in the Field of African Literatures*, 1977, pp. 113–134.
19. Mongo Beti, *Le pauvre Christ de Bomba*, Paris, Laffont, 1956. The English translation (by Gerald Moore): *The Poor Christ of Bomba*, London, Heinemann, 1971, has been used here; Ferdinand Oyono, *Une vie de boy*, Paris, Juilliard, 1956. The English translation (by John Reed), London, Heinemann, 1966, has been used here.
20. Norman Friedman, "Point of View in Fiction: the Development of a Critical Concept", in: PMLA, 70, pp. 1160–84, 1955. Wayne C. Booth, *The Rhetoric of Fiction*, Chicago, The University of Chicago Press, 1961; Bertil Romberg, *Studies in the Narrative Technique of the First-Person Novel*, Stockholm, Almqvist and Wiksell, 1962 among others have not seen the difference between narration and

focalization, as Genette observed in his *Figures III* (cf. note 13) for the first time.

21. Rimmon, op. cit., p. 72.
22. Eleanor Wachtel, "The Mother and the Whore: Image and Stereotype of African Women", in: *Umoja*, 1 (2), p. 42.
23. Cf. Rimmon, op. cit., p. 74 and Mieke Bal, *Narratologie. Essais sur la signification narrative dans quatre romans modernes*, Paris, Klincksieck, 1977, p. 33ff.
24. Cf. Rimmon, op. cit., p. 82.
25. Jean Ikellé-Matiba, *Cette Afrique-là*, Présence Africaine, Paris, 1963, p. 13.
26. Philippe Lejeune, *Le pacte autobiographique*, Paris, Seuil, 1975, pp. 13–46.
27. Béatrice Didier, *Le journal intime*, Paris, P. U. F., 1976.
28. Elechi Amadi, *Sunset in Biafra. A Civil War Diary*, London, Heinemann, 1973; Ngugi wa Thiong'o, *Detained. A Writer's Prison Diary*, London, Heinemann, 1981, p. xi.
29. Cf. Neumann, op. cit.
30. Cf. Emmanuel Obiechina, *Culture, Tradition and Society in the West African Novel*, Cambridge University Press, 1975, pp. 122–139.
31. Zamenga Batukezanga, *Lettres d'Amérique*, Kinshasa, Edition Zabat, 1983.
32. Bernard Dadié, *Un nègre à Paris*, Paris, Présence Africaine 1959; Henri Lopès, *Sans Tam-tam*, Yaoundé, Editions CLE, 1977, p. 5.
33. Ian Watt, *The Rise of the Novel. Studies in Defoe, Richardson and Fielding*, (1957), Harmondsworth, Pelican Books, 1974, p. 217.
34. Oginga Odinga, *Not Yet Uhuru. An Autobiography*, London, Heinemann (1967) 1974, p. xii.
35. Lejeune, op. cit.
36. If the narrator is one of the characters, he/she is not necessarily the main character in letters, epistolary novel, diary or diary novel: one could write about others more than about oneself in these genres. However, this is not possible in the autobiography and the memoir novel, because the writing about oneself is inherent in both.

37. Christopher Lasch, *The Culture of Narcissism. American Life in an Age of Diminishing Expectations*, New York, Warner Books, 1979, p. 53.
38. Doleželová, op. cit., p. 73.

Notes to Chapter Eight

1. Harry Levin, "On the Dissemination of Realism", in: Idem, *Grounds for Comparison*, Cambridge, Mass., Harvard University Press, 1972, p. 248.
2. Emmanuel Obiechina, *Culture, Tradition, and Society in the West African Novel*, Cambridge University Press, 1975, p. 18.
3. See e.g. Michael J. C. Echeruo, *Joyce Cary and the Novel of Africa*, London: Longman, 1973, p. 5.
4. Mineke Schipper, *Le Blanc vu d'Afrique*, Yaoundé, Editions CLE, 1973.
5. Dan Izevbaye, "Issues in the Reassessment of the African Novel", in: *African Literature Today*, 10 (1979), p. 15.
6. Philippe Hamon, "Un discours contraint", in: *Poétique*, 16 (1973), pp. 411–455, a most interesting article on the techniques of realism.
7. Sembène Ousmane, *L'Harmattan*, Paris, Présence Africaine, 1964.
8. Ngugi wa Thiong'o, *A Grain of Wheat*, London, Heinemann, 1967, p. 13.
9. Shatto Arthur Gakwandi, *The Novel and Contemporary Experience in Africa*, London, Heinemann, 1977, pp. 126–127.
10. L. Kesteloot, *Les écrivains noirs de langue française: naissance d'une littérature*, Bruxelles, Université Libre, 1963, p. 283ff.
11. Ibid., p. 432.
12. Sembène Ousmane, *Les bouts de bois de Dieu*, Paris, Le livre contemporain, 1960. English translation (by Francis Price) used here: *God's Bits of Wood*, London, Heinemann, 1969.
13. Philippe Hamon, "Un discours contraint" in: *Poétique*, 16 (1973), p. 427.

14. Ibid., p. 432 and p. 431.
15. See Tzvetan Todorov, *Introduction à la littérature fantastique*, Paris, Seuil, 1970.
16. Cf. Gérard Genette, "Discours du récit", in: Idem, *Figures III*, Paris, Seuil, 1972, pp. 183–267.
17. For the concept of intertextuality, see, for instance, Laurent Jenny, "La stratégie de la forme", in: *Poétique 7*, 1976, pp. 257–281; Jonathan Culler, "Presupposition and intertextuality", in: Idem, *The Pursuit of Signs*, New York, Cornell University Press, 1981, pp. 100–118.

Notes to Chapter Nine

1. See chapter II.
2. René Wellek and Austin Warren, *Theory of Literature*, Harmondsworth, Penguin Books, (1949) 1973, p. 249.
3. In: *Concepts of Criticism*, New Haven/London, Yale University Press, 1963, pp. 17–18.
4. In: Chinua Achebe, *Morning Yet on Creation Day. Essays*, London, Heinemann, 1975, p. 3.
5. E.g. Charles Larson's obvious Eurocentrism in his *The Emergence of African Fiction*, Bloomington, Indiana University Press, 1972, and adequate reactions from an African point of view by Molara Leslie from Nigeria reviewing the book in *The Benin Review*, no. 1, June 1974, pp. 129–135, and by Ayi Kwei Armah from Ghana in: *First World. An International Journal of Black Thought*, Vol. 1, no. 2, March/April, 1977.
6. M. H. Abrams, *The Mirror and the Lamp*, Oxford University Press, 1976, p. 6.
7. These items were described in a Dutch article by H. T. Boonstra, Van waardeoordeel tot literatuuropvatting, in: *De Gids*, 1979, pp. 243–252.
8. I. Even-Zohar, "Polysystem Theory", in: *Poetics Today*, vol. 1, Autumn 1979. See in this book chapters I and IV where the polysystem theory is referred to.

9. Ibid.: pp. 301, 302.
10. This has been overlooked as an essential aspect of the interplay between cultural systems by Douwe Fokkema in his "Cultural Relativism Reconsidered: Comparative Literature and Intercultural Relations," in: *Douze cas d'interaction culturelle dans l'Europe ancienne et l'Orient proche ou lointain*, Paris, UNESCO, 1984, pp. 239–258.
11. Michael Echeruo, *Joyce Cary and the Novel of Africa*, London, Evans, 1973, p. 5.
12. Interview with Chinua Achebe in: D. Duerden and C. Pieterse (Eds) *African Writers Talking*, London, Heinemann, 1972, p. 4.
13. Dan Izevbaye, "Issues in the Reassessment of the African Novel", in: *African Literature Today*, 10, 1979, p. 15.
14. E. D. Hirsch, in a lecture given at the State University of Groningen in 1981.
15. Micere Githae Mugo, *Visions of Africa*, Nairobi, Kenya Literature Bureau, 1978, pp. 187–188.
16. Chinua Achebe, "An Image of Africa" in: *Research in African Literatures*, 9, 1978, p. 9.
17. Peter Nazareth, "Out of Darkness: Conrad and Other Third World Writers", in: *Conradiana*, Vol. XIV (3), 1982, pp. 113–188.
18. Robert D. Hamner, in Idem (Ed.), *Critical Perspectives on V. S. Naipaul*, London, Heinemann, 1979, p. 209.
19. Th. Mpoyi-Buatu, "Naipaul ou les anathèmes d'un brahmane apatride," in: *Peuples noirs, peuples africains*, March/April 1982, pp. 89–106.
20. Idem, "A la courbe du fleuve", in: *Peuples noirs, peuples africains*, May/June, 1983, pp. 146–152.
21. Nazareth, art. cit., p. 182.
22. Cf. theories developed by Peter V. Zima, in his most recent books *Manuel de sociocritique*, Paris, Picard, 1985 and *Roman and Ideologie. Zur Sozialgeschichte des modernen Romans*, München, Wilhelm Fink Verlag, 1986; *Ideologie und Theorie. Eine Diskurskritik*, Tübingen, Francke, 1989.

Notes to Chapter Ten

1. Cf. years '70–'80s of *Index on Censorship* and the half yearly reports of the Writers-in-Prison Committee of International P. E. N. in London.
2. In: Okot p'Bitek, *Africa's Cultural Revolution*, Nairobi, Macmillan, 1973, p. 38.
3. Cf. Mongo Béti, "Human Rights Hypocrisy", in: *Index on Censorship*, vol. 10, no. 6, Dec. 1981, pp. 77–79, and personal information from the author while in Amsterdam, May 1983.
4. "La création littéraire face à la violence néo-coloniale", text presented by Mongo Béti at the International P. E. N. Conference in Stockholm in 1978, pp. 3–4 (my translation).
5. Interviews given to Dutch newspapers (*Haagsche Courant* and *Alkmaarse Courant*, 27 June 1985). See also George Henderson, "How Morocco Treats its Dissidents", in: *Index on Censorship*, June 1984, pp. 30–31.
6. Chinua Achebe, "The Beast of Fanatism"; in: *Index on Censorship* June 1981, p. 61.
7. Ngugi wa Thiong'o, "The Culture of Silence and Fear," in: *South*, May 1984, p. 38.
8. Wole Soyinka, "Climate of Art", in: *Africa Events*, July, 1985, p. 56.

BIBLIOGRAPHY

Abrams, M. H., *The Mirror and the Lamp*, Oxford University Press, (1953) 1976.

Achebe, Chinua, *Things Fall Apart*, Greenwich, Conn., Fawcett Publications, 1959.

Achebe, Chinua (Interviews with-), in: Duerden, D., and Pieterse C. (Eds.), *African Writers Talking*, London, Heinemann, 1972, pp. 3–17.

Achebe, Chinua, *Morning Yet on Creation Day. Essays*, London, Heinemann, 1975.

Achebe, Chinua, "An Image of Africa," in: *Research in African Literatures*, vol. 9 (I), spring 1978, pp. 1–15.

Achebe, Chinua, "The Beast of Fanatism," in: *Index on Censorship*, June 1981, p. 61.

Adotevi, S. S. K., *Négritude et négrologues*, Paris, Union Générale d'Editions 10–18, 1972.

Amadi, Elechi, *Sunset in Biafra. A Civil War Diary*, London, Heinemann, 1973.

Andrade, Mario de, *La poésie africaine d'expression portugaise*, Paris, Jean-Pierre Oswald, 1969.

Anthologie des écrivains congolais, Kinshasa, Ministère de la Culture, 1969.

Artaud, A., *Le théâtre et son double* (1934), Paris, Gallimard 1977.

Bâ, Mariama, *Une si longue lettre*, Dakar, Nouvelles Editions

[195]

Africaines, 1979. English translation (by Modupé Bodé-Thomas), *So Long a Letter*, London, Heinemann, 1981.

Bal, Mieke, *Narratologie, Essays sur la signification narrative dans quatre romans modernes*, Paris, Klincksieck, 1977.

Bascom, William, (Ed.), *African Dilemma Tales*, The Hague/Paris, Mouton Publishers, 1975.

Batukezanga, Zamenga, *Lettres d'Amérique*, Kinshasa, Editions Zabat, 1983.

Beardsley, Monroe C., Aspects of Orality: A Short Commentary, in: *New Literary History*, 8, 1976–77 (3), pp. 521–530.

Benedict, Ruth, *Patterns of Culture*, London, Routledge and Kegan Paul, (1935) 1971.

Beti, Mongo, "Human Rights Hypocrisy," in: *Index on Censorship*, vol. 10, no. 6, Dec. 1981, pp. 77–79.

Beti, Mongo, *Le pauvre Christ de Bomba*, Paris, Laffont, 1956. English translation (by Gerald Moore), *The Poor Christ of Bomba*, London, Heinemann, 1971.

Beti, Mongo, "La création littéraire face à la violence néo-coloniale," text presented at the International P. E. N. Conference in Stockholm in 1978.

Björnson, Richard, "Nationalliteratur und nationale Identität in Afrika": Kamerun als Beispiel, *Komparatistische Hefte* ii, 1985, pp. 69–97.

Block, Haskell, *Nouvelles tendances en litérature comparée*, Paris-Nizet, 1970.

Boas, Franz, *The Mind of Primitive Man*, (1911), New York, Free Press, 1965.

Boas, Franz, *Race, Language, Culture*, (1924), New York, Macmillan, 1948.

Booth, Wayne, C., *The Rhetoric of Fiction*, Chicago, The University of Chicago Press, 1961.

[196]

Carpentier, Alejo, "Problemática de la actual novela latino-americana," in: Idem, *Tientas y diferencias*, La Habana, Cuba, 1974.

Césaire, Aimé, *Et les chiens se taisaient* (1946) Paris, Présence Africaine, 1961.

Césaire, Aimé, *Ferrements. Poèmes*, Paris, Présence Africaine, 1960.

Clark, J. P., *Thèmes de la poésie africaine d'expression anglaise*, in: *Présence Africaine*, 54, 2nd trim. 1965, pp. 96–115.

Colin, Roland, *Les contes de l'Ouest Africain*, Paris, Présence Africaine, 1957.

Cook, David and Lee, M. (Eds.), *Short East African Plays in English*, London, Heinemann, 1972.

Coplan, David B., *In Township Tonight! South Africa's Black City Music and Theatre*, Johannesburg, 1985.

Cornevin, Robert, *Le théâtre en Afrique Noire et à Madagascar*, Paris, Le livre africain, 1970.

Coulthard, G. R., "Parallelisms and Divergencies Between 'Negritude' and 'Indigenismo'," in: *Caribbean Studies*, vol. 8 (1), April 1968, pp. 43–68.

Culler, Jonathan, *The Pursuit of Signs: Semiotics, Literature, Deconstruction*, Ithaca, New York, Cornell University Press, 1981.

Dadié, Bernard, *Un nègre à Paris*, Paris, Présence Africaine, 1959.

Dailly, C., "L'histoire et la politique comme sources d'inspiration," in: *Le théâtre négro-africain, Actes du Colloque d'Abidjan 1970*, Paris, 1971, pp. 87–93.

Damas, L., *Black Label*, Paris, Présence Africaine, 1956.

Depestre, René, *Bonjour et adieu à Négritude*, Paris, Robert Laffont, 1980.

Didier, Béatrice, *Le journal intime*, Paris, P. U. F., 1976.

Diop, David, *Coups de pilon*, Paris, Présence Africaine, (1961) 1973.

Doloželová-Velingerová, Milena (Ed.), *The Chinese Novel at the Turn of the Century*, Toronto/Buffalo/London, University of Toronto Press, 1980.

Echeruo, Michael, *Joyce Cary and the Novel of Africa*, London, Evans, 1973.

Eco, Umberto, *A Theory of Semiotics*, London, Macmillan, 1977.

Etherton, M., *The Development of African Drama*, London, Hutchinson, 1982.

Etherton, M., "The Dilemma of the Popular Playwright," in: *African Literature Today*, 1976 (8), pp. 26–41.

Etiemble, René, *Essais de littérature (vraiment) générale*, Paris, Gallimard, 1974.

Etiemble, René, "Littérature Comparée ou Comparaison n'est pas raison," in: *Hygiène des Lettres*, Tome 3, *Savoir et Goût*, Paris, Gallimard, 1958.

Even-Zohar, Itamar, "Polysystem Theory" in: *Poetics Today*, vol. 1, autumn 1979, pp. 287–305.

Fagunwa, D. O., *The Forest of a Thousand Daemons*, translated by Wole Soyinka, London, Nelson, (1968) 1982.

Fanon, Frantz, *Peau noire, masques blancs*, Paris, 1952.

Fanon, Frantz, *L'An V de la révolution Algérienne*, Paris, 1959.

Fanon, Frantz, *Les damnés de la terre*, (1961), Paris, Maspéro, 1968.

Feinberg, Barry (Ed.), *Poets to the People. South African Freedom Poems*, London, Allen & Unwin, 1974.

Finnegan, Ruth, *Oral Literature in Africa*, Oxford, At the Clarendon Press, 1970.

Finnegan, Ruth, *Oral Poetry. Its Nature, Significance and Social Context*, Cambridge University Press, 1977.

Fokkema, D. W. *Cultureel relativisme en vergelijkende literatuurwetenschap*, Inaugural Lecture, Amsterdam, 1971.

Fokkema, Douwe, "Cultural Relativism Reconsidered: Comparative Literature and Intercultural Relations," in: *Douze cas d'interaction culturelle dans l'Europe ancienne et l'Orient proche ou lointain*, Paris, UNESCO, 1984, pp. 239–258.

Friedman, Norman, "Point of View in Fiction: the Development of a Critical Concept," in: *PMLA*, 70, 1955, pp. 1160–84.

Gakwandi, Shatto Arthur, *The Novel and Contemporary Experience in Africa*, London, Heinemann, 1977.

Gates Jr, Henry Louis, (Ed.), *Black Literature and Literary Theory*, Methuen, New York/London, 1984.

Genette, Gérard, "Discours du récit," in: Idem, *Figures III*, Paris, Seuil, 1972.

Genette, Gérard, *Figures III*, Paris, Seuil, 1972. English translation: *Narrative Discourse*, Ithaca/New York, Cornell University Press, 1980.

Gordimer, N., *The Black Interpreters*, Johannesburg, Ravan Press, 1972.

Graham-White, A., *The Drama of Black Africa*, New York/London, Samuel French, 1974.

Gusdorf, G., "De l'autobiographie initiatique à l'autobiographie genre littéraire," in: *Revue de l'histoire littéraire de la France*, 1975, pp. 957–994.

Hamner, Robert, D. (Ed.), *Critical Perspectives on V. S. Naipaul*, London, Heinemann, 1979.

Hamon, Philippe, "Un discours contraint," in: *Poétique*, 16, 1973, pp. 411–455.

Henderson, George, "How Morocco Treats its Dissidents," in: *Index on Censorship*, June 1984, pp. 30–31.

[199]

Herskovits, Melville (Ed.), *Cultural Relativism, Perspectives in Cultural Pluralism*, New York, Vintage, Random House, 1973.

Hughes, Langston (Ed.), *An African Treasury*, New York, Pyramid Books, 1961.

ICA, *La tradition orale, source de la littérature contemporaine en Afrique*, Dakar, Nouvelles Editions Africaines, 1985.

IDAF, *Fact Paper on Southern Africa*: Black Theatre in South Africa, nr. 2, June 1976.

Ikellé-Matiba, Jean, *Cette Afrique-là*, Présence Africaine, Paris, 1963.

Irele, Abiola, "A Defence of Negritude," in *Transition*, 13, March–April 1964, pp. 9–11.

Izevbaye, Dan, "Issues in the Reassessment of the African Novel," in: *African Literature Today*, 10, 1979, pp. 7–31.

Jahn, J., *A History of Neo-African Literature. Writing in Two Continents*, London, Faber and Faber, 1968.

Jakobson, Roman, "Linguistics and Poetics" in: Thomas A. Sebeok, (Ed.), *Style in Language*, Cambridge, Massachusetts, M. I. T. Press, pp. 350–377.

Jenny, Laurent, "La stratégie de la forme," in: *Poétique* 7, 1976, pp. 257–281.

Kavanagh, Robert, M. (Ed.), *South African People's Plays*, London, Heinemann, 1981.

Kavanagh, Robert Mshengu, *Theatre and the Cultural Struggle in South Africa*, London, Zed Press, 1985.

Kesteloot, L., *Les écrivains noirs de langue française: naissance d'une littérature*, Bruxelles, Université Libre, 1963.

King, Bruce, *The New English Literatures. Cultural Nationalism in a Changing World*, London, Macmillan (New Literary Handbooks), 1980.

Larson, Charles, *The Emergence of African Fiction*, Bloomington, Indiana University Press, 1972.

Lasch, Christopher, *The Culture of Narcissism. American Life in an Age of Diminishing Expectations*, New York, Warner Books, 1979.

Leclerc, Gérard, *Anthropologie et colonialisme*, Paris, Fayard, 1972.

Lejeune, Philippe, *Le pacte autobiographique*, Paris, Seuil, 1975.

Lemaire, Ton, *Over de waarde van culturen. Een inleiding in de cultuurfilosofie. Tussen europacentrisme en relativisme*, Baarn, Ambo, 1976.

Levin, Harry, "On the Dissemination of Realism," in: Idem: *Grounds for Comparison*, Cambridge (Mass.), Harvard University Press, 1972.

Lindfors, Bernth (Ed.), *Critical Perspectives on Amos Tutuola*, Washington, D.C., Three Continents Press, 1975.

Lopès, Henri, *Sans Tam-tam*, Yaoundé, Editions CLE, 1977.

Matthews, James and Gladys Thomas, *Cry Rage*, Johannesburg, Ravan Press, 1972.

May, Georges, *L'autobiographie*, Paris, P. U. F., 1979.

Mbongo, Nsame, "Problèmes théoriques de la question nationale en Afrique," in: *Présence Africaine*, 136, (4), 1985, pp. 31–67.

Menga, Guy, *La Marmite de Koka Mbala*, Paris, ORTF-DAEC, 1969.

Menga, Guy, *L'oracle*, Yaoundé, Editions CLE, 1976.

Moore, Gerald, *Seven African Writers*, London, Oxford University Press, 1966.

Mouralis, Bernard, *Les contre-littératures*, Paris, P. U. F. 1975.

Mphahlele, E., *The African Image*, (Revised Edition), New York, Praeger, 1974.

[201]

Mphahlele, E., Africa in Exile, in: *Daedalus*, 1982.

Mpoyi-Buatu, Th., "Naipaul ou les anathèmes d'un brahmane apatride," in: *Peuples noirs, peuples africaines*, March/April, 1982, pp. 89–106.

Mpoyi-Buatu, "A la courbe de fleuve," in: *Peuples noirs, peuples africains*, May/June, 1983, pp. 146–152.

Mtshali, Oswald M., *Sounds of a Cowhide Drum*, (1971) London, Oxford U. P., 1974.

Mudimbe, V. Y., *Autour de la "Nation". Leçons de Civisme*, Kinshasa/Lubumbashi, Editions du Mont Noir, coll. "Objectif 80," 1972.

Mugo, Micere Githae, *Visions of Africa*, Nairobi, Kenya Literature Bureau, 1978.

Mushiete, Paul, and Norbert Mikanza, *Pas de feu pour les antilopes*, Kinshasa, Editions Congolia, 1964.

Mutloatse, M. (Ed.), *Forced Landing. Africa South: Contemporary Writings*, Johannesburg, Ravan Press, 1980.

Mutwa, Credo V., *uNosilimela*, in: R. M. Kavanagh (Ed.), *South African People's Plays* (G. Kente, C. V. Mutwa, M. Shezi and Workshop '71), London, Heinemann, 1981.

Nazareth, Peter, "Out of Darkness: Conrad and Other Third World Writers," in: *Conradiana*, vol. XIV (3), 1982, pp. 113–188.

Ndu, Pol, "Negritude and the New Breed," in: *Présence Africaine*, 86 (2), 1973, pp. 117–133.

Neumann, Bernd, *Identität und Rollenzwang. Zur Theorie der Autobiographie*, Frankfurt, Athenaeum, 1970.

Ngugi wa Thiong'o, *A Grain of Wheat*, London, Heinemann, 1967.

Ngugi wa Thiong'o and Githae Micere Mugo, *The Trial of Dedan Kimathi*, London, 1976.

Ngugi wa Thiong'o, *Detained: A Writer's Prison Diary*, London, Heinemann, 1981.

Ngugi wa Thiong'o, "The Culture of Silence and Fear," in: *South*, May 1984, pp. 37–38.

Niscov, Viorica, "Bemerkungen über die Dialektik des Begriffes Nationalliteratur", in *Synthesis* X, 1983, pp. 7–18.

Nkosi, L., *Tasks and Masks. Themes and Styles of African Literature*, London, Longman, 1982.

Obiechina, Emmanuel, "Amos Tutuola and the Oral Tradition," in: *Présence Africaine*, 65, (1) pp. 140–161.

Obiechina, Emmanuel, *Culture, Tradition, and Society in the West African Novel*, Cambridge University Press, 1975.

Odinga, Oginga, *Not Yet Uhuru. An Autobiography*, London, Heinemann (1967) 1974.

Ogunbesan, K., "A King for All Seasons: Chaka in African Literature", in: *Présence Africaine*, 88 (4), 1973, pp. 197–217.

Ogundipe-Leslie, Omolara, "The Palm-Wine Drinkard: A reassessment of Amos Tutuola," in: *Présence Africaine*, 71 (3), 1969, pp. 99–108.

Okpewho, Isidore, "Comparatism and Separatism in African Literature", in *World Literature Today*, vol. 55 (1), 1981, pp. 25–32.

Omara, T., *The Exodus*, see: Cook, David, and M. Lee (Eds), London, 1972.

Oyono, Ferdinand, *Une vie de boy*, Paris, Juilliard, 1956. English translation (by John Reed): *Houseboy*, London, Heinemann, 1966.

Oyono-Mbia, Guillaume, *Trois prétendants . . . un mari*, Yaoundé, CLE, 1969.

p'Bitek, Okot, *Africa's Cultural Revolution*, Nairobi, Macmillan, 1973.

Paulme, Denise, *La mère dévorante. Essais sur la morphologie des contes africains*, Paris, Gallimard, 1976.

Pearce, Roy Harvey, *Historicism Once More. Problems and Occasions for the American Scholar*, Princeton University Press, 1969.

Plumpe, G. and K. O. Conrady, "Probleme der Literaturgeschichtschreibung," in: H. Brackert and J. Stückrath (Eds.), *Literaturwissenschaft. Grundkurs 2*, Reinbek/ Hamburg, Rowolt, 1981, pp. 373–392.

Poggioli, R., *The Theory of the Avant-Garde*, Cambridge, Mass., 1968.

Preiswerk, Roy and Dominique Perrot, *Ethnocentrisme et histoire*, Paris, Editions Anthropos, 1975.

Ricard, Alain, *L'invention du théâtre*, Lausanne, L'Age d'Homme, 1986.

Ricard, Alain, "Concours et concert: théâtre scolaire et théâtre populaire au Togo," in: *Revue d'Histoire du Théâtre*, 1975 (1), pp. 44–85.

Rimmon-Kenan, Shlomith, *Narrative Fiction. Contemporary Poetics*, London/ New York, Methuen (Series New Accents), 1983.

Romberg, Bertil, *Studies in the Narrative Technique of the First-Person Novel*, Stockholm, Almqvist and Wiksel, 1962.

Roumain, Jacques, *La montagne ensorcelée*, Paris, 1972.

Royston, Robert (Ed.), *To Whom It May Concern, An Anthology of South African Poetry*, Johannesburg, Ravan Press, 1973.

Sartre, Jean-Paul, *Situations III*, Paris, Gallimard, 1949.

Schipper, Mineke (Ed.), *Text and Context. Methodological Explorations in the field of African Literature*, Leiden, Afrika-Studiecentrum, 1977.

Schipper, Mineke, *Le Blanc vu d'Afrique*, Yaoundé, Editions CLE, 1973.

Schipper, Mineke, "Noirs et Blancs dans l'oeuvre d'Aimé Césaire," in: *Présence Africaine*, 72 (4), 1969, pp. 124–147.

Schipper, Mineke, "Littérature zaïroise et société décolonisée," in: *Kroniek van Afrika*, 1972 (4), pp. 187–194.

Schipper, Mineke, *Théâtre et société en Afrique*, Dakar/Abidjan/ Lomé, Nouvelles Editions Africaines, 1985.

Sembène, Ousmane, *Le Mandat*, Paris, Présence Africaine, 1965.

Sembène, Ousmane, *L'Harmattan*, Paris, Présence Africaine, 1964.

Sembène, Ousmane, *Les bouts de bois de Dieu*, Paris, Le livre contemporain, 1960. English translation (by Francis Price): *God's bits of Wood*, London, Heinemann, 1969.

Senghor, L. S., *La littérature africaine d'expression française*, in: Idem, *Liberté I, Négritude et humanisme*, Paris, Seuil 1964.

Senghor, L. S., "Lusitanité et Africanité," in: *Jeune Afrique*, 21 March, 1975.

Senghor, L. S., *Poèmes*, Paris, Seuil, 1964.

Soyinka, Wole, *A Dance of the Forests*, London, 1960.

Soyinka, Wole, "The Writer in a Modern African State," see: Wästberg, Per, pp. 14–21.

Soyinka, Wole, *Aké. The Years of Childhood*, London, Rex Collings, 1981.

Soyinka, Wole, "Climate of Art," in: *Africa Events*, July, 1985.

Spengemann, William C., *The Forms of Autobiography. Episodes in the History of a Genre*, New Haven/London, Yale University Press, 1980.

Striedter, J. (Ed.), *Russischer Formalismus*, Munich, UTB, Fink Verlag, 1971.

Sutherland, E., *The Marriage of Anansewa*, London, 1975.

Taban lo Liyong, "Tutuola, Son of Zinjanthropos," in: Idem, *The Last Word. Cultural Synthesism*, Nairobi, East African Publishing House, 1969.

Todorov, Tzvetan, *Théorie de la littérature. Textes des Formalistes Russes*, Paris, Seuil, 1966.

Todorov, Tzvetan, *Introduction à littérature fantastique*, Paris, Seuil, 1970.

Towa, Marcien, *Léopold Sédar Senghor: négritude ou servitude*, Yaoundé, 1971.

Towa, Marcien, *Poésie de la négritude. Approche structuraliste*, Sherbrooke, Naaman, 1985.

Toynbee, Arnold, "Widening Our Historical Horizon", in: Martin Ballard (Ed.), *New Movements in the Study and Teaching of History*, London, Temple Smith, 1970.

Tutuola, Amos, *The Palm-Wine Drinkard and His Dead Palm-Wine Tapster in the Dead's Town*, London, Faber and Faber, 1952.

Tutuola, Amos, *My life in the Bush of Ghosts*, London, Faber and Faber, (1954) 1962.

Tutuola, Amos, *Simbi and the Satyr of the Dark Jungle*, London, Faber and Faber, 1955.

Tutuola, Amos, *Ajaiyi and His Inherited Poverty*, London, Faber and Faber, 1967.

Tutuola, Amos, *The Brave African Huntress*, New York, Grove Press, 1958.

Tutuola, Amos, *Feather Woman of the Jungle*, London, Faber and Faber, 1962.

Tylor, E. B., *Primitive Culture* (2 vols.), (London, Murray, 1871), New York, Harper Torch, 1958.

Vodicka, Felix, *Die Struktur der Literarischen Entwicklung*, München, Fink Verlag, 1976.

Wachtel, Eleanor, "The Mother and the Whore: Image and Stereotype of African Women," in: *Umoja*, 1 (2), pp. 31–48.

Wästberg, Per, (Ed.), *The Writer in Modern Africa*, Uppsala, the Scandinavian Institute of African Studies, 1968.

Watt, Ian, *The Rise of the Novel. Studies in Defoe, Richardson and Fielding*, (1957), Harmondsworth, Pelican Books, 1974.

Wellek, René and Austin Warren, *Theory of Literature*, Harmondsworth, Penguin Books, (1949), 1973.

Wellek, R. *Concepts of Criticism*, New Haven/London, Yale University Press, 1963.

Zima, Pierre V., "Les mécanismes discursifs de l'idéologie," in *Revue de l'Institut de sociologie*, 1981 (4) pp. 719–740.

Zima, Peter V., *Manuel de Sociocritique*, Paris, Picard, 1985.

Zima, Peter V. *Roman und Ideologie. Zur Sozialgeschichte des modernen Romans*, München, Wilhelm Verlag, 1986.

Zima, Peter V., *Ideologie und Theorei. Eine Diskurskritik*, Tübingen, Francke, 1989.

INDEX OF AUTHORS AND TITLES OF FICTIONAL AND BIOGRAPHICAL WORKS